YOUNG
AND
Lawless

ALSO BY EMILY IRVING

Novels:
It Takes Two

Anthologies:
Finding You

YOUNG

AND

Lawless

BOOK 1

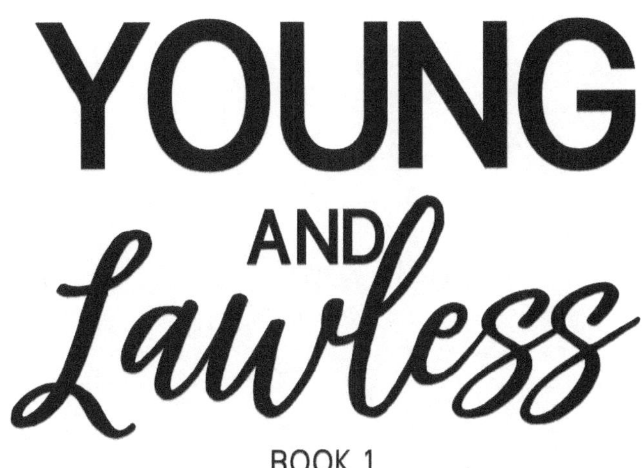

EMILY IRVING

Chapter 1
Addy

I can tell no one else cares for the wind stinging their eyes and tugging their hair as we drive along the backroads. The top of the sleek black convertible is firmly down, letting the harsh glow of the sunset shower into the cab. Already, I can feel the frizz that will settle into my hair as the thin curled locks whip behind me while we cruise twenty miles over the limit. But I can't deny the relief it is to have an excuse not to chat.

Marcus and his friend Deran holler at each other in the front seat, but Ellen and I can't hear a word they say. She's too busy planting her hands firmly on top of her recently done perm to have any conversation with me, her crisp manicure flickering in the golden sunlight.

I lean forward to glance down at Marcus's watch where his hand lies resting on the center console.

We've definitely missed the movie. I was the only one looking forward to seeing *Raiders of the Lost Ark*, even if it already came out a while ago back home. Greydon, California, is probably the smallest and most slow-moving town in the state when it comes to anything. But I was mostly looking forward to, again, having an hour and fifty minutes of not having to talk. Or at least having a valid excuse to not respond to the others at the moment.

"*What?!*" Ellen shrieks over the wind as she squints in my direction, thinking I had leaned forward to say something to her. I just shake my head as exaggeratedly as I can, hoping she can see me through the slits she has crushed her eyes into.

I shake my frizzled hair out of my face as we finally slow to a crawl, the tires bumping over the dip in the road as Deran pulls the car to the outside of the drive-in.

"Shit." He slaps his hand against the wheel as we see shadows from the giant flickering screen dance across the minute gathering of cars in the lot. He looks down at his own watch, just now realizing the time. "Movie's halfway in already."

"I told you not to take so long getting ready," Ellen berates the two boys up front as she finally peels her hands away from her dark curls, petting them carefully back into place.

Deran and Marcus glance at each other, a knowing glint in their eyes, and I gaze down at my peach-colored skirt. We all know Marcus and Deran hadn't merely been taking long to get ready at Marcus's house this evening. More like sharing a bottle of his parents' whiskey before picking us up.

My mother told me not to worry about it when I told her a few days after we arrived this summer about the new drinking habits of my boyfriend, Marcus Tanner, and his friends. She told me boys do it to try to impress girls, that it's harmless. That people like Marcus and Deran will never really do anything that dangerous. They're the golden boys of Greydon, after all. She said the best I can do is ignore it, and let them have their fun for a while before they come back down.

I've tried my best the past couple of weeks, but it's awkward when the boy you've known since you were twelve and see only a few months out of the year is suddenly spending his free time stealing from his parents' liquor cabinet when he used to be a complete square.

"Let's go get something to eat," Ellen suggests, looking around the cab for approval. "I'm starving anyway, I can't sit through a whole movie. Or half a movie."

"Yeah," Marcus agrees, sitting up eagerly in the front seat. "Whose idea was this anyway? Let's bounce."

I say nothing, silently mourning my lost time to throw myself into the daring adventures of Indiana Jones as Deran pulls the car back out onto the road to head a couple blocks down the way to Roller Dollar, the most popular diner in a town that is stuck permanently somewhere around the 1950s.

Deran parks under the faded turquoise-painted overhang, he and Ellen hopping out of the car to order from the window.

"Hey, Addy."

I pause before I can follow them, turning back to see Marcus facing me from the front seat. He cocks his head when he sees my face, his normally passive features turning curious.

He still looks the same after four years. Same crisp blond hair I used to marvel at, since it always flops around his head so perfectly. Same boyish features that are turning more mature, the vague outline of a strong jawline that is fast forming. Same gorgeous eyes that I used to think looked at only me like that. Like they lit up and smiled just at the sight of me. That was before I realized, how would I know how Marcus looks into anyone else's eyes?

"Are you okay?"

He says it jokingly, and I try to match his tone, shaking my head and smiling away my silly bout of daydreaming.

"I'm fine," I confirm. "I'm sorry, I guess I'm a bit tired."

Makes no sense. It's summer vacation and I've been here only two weeks.

Marcus doesn't seem to notice. He alters his expression into a hopeful grin, leaning forward as he reaches for my hand that is still pressed into my lap. I instinctively wrap my fingers around his.

"I hope you're not too tired to be my date to the Lensen summer barbecue next week. I *have* been waiting all year to be able to show off my girlfriend from New York that everyone always thinks I'm lying about."

I can't help but smile as I consider what people at school would say if I told them all about my mysterious rich boyfriend from California who I see only during the summer. A likely story from the boring, strait-laced girl everyone knows me as back home.

"Well, I'd... love to be shown off," I say because it makes Marcus beam even though the words feel awkward coming out of my mouth. "It's not often I get to go to fancy barbecues at home."

Marcus's grin fades as he leans closer, his hand grasping mine more desperately.

"Have you thought more about what we talked about the other night?"

I feel my face turning bright red, inching to turn away from him now, but remaining trapped within the space of the back seat.

"Marcus, it's only been three days since you—"

"I know, but you said you'd think about it."

In truth, I've pointedly spent the past three days *not* thinking about our conversation at his house that night. I thought we'd spend the evening watching old black-and-white monster movies on TV, but he'd been much more interested in trying to convince me to head back to his bedroom before his parents got home.

"Marcus, I told you, I really don't think I'm ready." I reach down for my purse after freeing one of my hands from his. "Come on, we should go get something to—"

"Addy, wait."

I turn back to him reluctantly, my hand still resting on the door handle, after looking longingly at the short line in front of the order window.

Marcus reaches up to brush a few locks of his wispy blond hair out of his eyes. God, I used to be obsessed whenever he did that. "Addy, we've been together three years now, we hardly get to see each other, and I just think we need to prove to one another that—"

"Marcus, please." I shake my head, untangling my other hand. "I don't think your best friend's car is the best place to have this conversation."

"Then when?" he asks insistently, throwing his hands out in frustration. I try to avoid the hurt look in his eyes. "You'll never bring it up otherwise. I don't understand why you're making a big deal about it, everyone our age has done it by now. Half the guys on the team said their girlfriends have let—"

"Oh, so that's it?" I ask before I can stop myself. "You want to catch up with your football buddies?"

"Come on, you know that's not what I—"

"Addy, you getting anything?" Ellen prances back over to the car, a strawberry milkshake clutched in one hand, looking thankfully none the wiser to the conversation.

"Yes," I reply in relief, yanking the door open and extracting myself from the car.

"What was that all about?" Ellen asks slyly as Deran passes by us with a tray of burgers and fries. "Did he ask you to the barbecue?"

"Yeah."

Ellen Kirk, my best friend since before I could talk in full sentences, does not seem to be going through anything close to the existential teenage crisis my brain has been putting me through lately. To her, this trip is like all the rest have been. An exciting time to get to be away from our hometown, be the kinds of girls who hang out with rich boys who play on the school football team and gather at extreme-budget barbecues that feel more like wedding receptions.

"Deran told me he's been inconsolable the past few months. All their friends have girlfriends now, it's not like when they were thirteen anymore and Marcus was the only one. Now he's always just pining away after his true love is whisked all the way to the other side of the country."

Ellen laughs after she says it, like it's some cute little love story.

There was a time I was just as miserable. After Marcus and I got together on my family's summer trip to Greydon three years ago, heading back home to New York every August was unbearable. All I could do in those first few weeks when school began was wallow and pine, making my mother think I was absolutely adorable and my sister want to throw me in a wood chipper. I would spend nights lying awake in bed, worrying Marcus would find some other girl at school in all the long months we were apart. I'd wonder what would happen once we both went off to college, or if his family ever decided to move or my mother stopped taking us to California and we'd never see each other again.

It was never as bad as that first year, but something feels so different this time around. Other things started taking up my time and thoughts, until I hardly noticed when summer began and my mother was preparing us to head off to California once again.

It's not just me. Marcus has changed too. He's louder and dresses in clothes he used to make fun of the older boys for wearing. He's taken a liking to drinking with his friends. And he wants to have sex.

And I have no fear in telling him no. I can't even find myself worrying if he'll break up with me because of it. Thirteen-year-old me would probably faint at the idea.

Neither of us are the same shy, awkward kids we were when we got together.

"What about you and Deran?" I ask Ellen after ordering myself a cheap burger and a large side of fries that sound utterly divine right now, both as yet another distraction from having to talk to Marcus and as something to quell the pit in my stomach.

"Oh, that." Ellen shrugs, taking a long sip of her milkshake before exhaling contentedly. She leans against the wall while the server behind the counter hands me my food. "That was just a summer fling last year. We're friends now. Not everyone can be forever like you and Marcus."

Ugh. Wrong subject.

"What should we do this summer?" I ask as we head back to the car. "We've been doing the same thing every year. Movies, diner, arcade, parties... maybe we should head out of town. We're old enough now."

Ellen chews on her milkshake straw. "Do you think the boys would want to do that?"

"We could go ourselves," I reply, unable to keep the frustration from spilling into my tone. "The boys are getting boring anyway."

I think that Marcus is looking at me as we approach the car. But my eyes follow where his jovial gaze is actually pointed as he leans up against the windshield from the front seat of the convertible. He balances on his knees, his arms resting on the top of the front window as a laugh resounds from his chest, mixing with Deran's, who is standing in front of a gangly, sandy-haired boy whose gaze is turned firmly down.

The boy's blue jeans and plaid shirt are stained and torn, his sneakers barely holding themselves together on his feet. His longish hair is cut at strange angles, as if he had taken a pair of scissors and tried to trim it himself but gave up halfway through. He's lanky, but not frail-looking, the portion of his arms exposed from his rolled-up sleeves lined with lightly toned muscles that look built more from labor than sports.

The only thing with him is a faded brown wallet that Deran has snatched from his hand. The boy looks more subdued than worried as he halfheartedly attempts to grab it back while Deran pulls out two dirtied bills and a few small coins.

"Here you go, Marcus, look!" Deran calls with a loud guffaw that Marcus returns when he sees the small amount of money. "Danny-Boy might have enough to buy himself half a burger this time!"

"Don't wanna save that for your down payment on a brand-new trailer park box, Dan?" Marcus hollers from the car. "Or is one soda going to make your groceries for the week?"

I look over at the boy, who looks around our age, his mouth turned into a small grimace when he glances at Marcus, his bright blue eyes flickering with disdain. Obviously, not only do they all know each other, but this interaction isn't a surprise. Not as much as it is to me.

"Hey."

Marcus turns at my sharp tone that makes even Ellen stiffen awkwardly beside me. I toss my tray of food onto the back seat of the car before marching in front, the horror clear on my face as I glare straight into Marcus's bewildered expression.

"What are you doing?"

"What?" Marcus chuckles, now looking at me like I'm not in on the joke.

"Are you kidding me?" I ask, gazing back at the boy, who is looking at me with uncertainty. "Marcus, please tell me you're joking."

Marcus has been a rich boy all his life. While my family gets by alright, I'm nowhere near the same social standing back home that my mother pretends we are when here in Greydon. While Marcus and his friends have been typically ignorant and a bit out of touch as living in a small town like Greydon will allow, I've never seen them behave like this.

"Hey, c'mon, Marcus," Deran laughs, slinging his arm around the boy's shoulders after shoving the money and wallet back at him, several of the coins clattering to the ground. "The girls haven't met our dear friend Danny here."

Danny is staring at the ground, his face still a resigned grimace as he stuffs the remaining money back in the wallet. "Deran, can I just—"

"Yeah!" Marcus laughs, standing up and jumping out of the car to stroll over to Danny's other side, ruffling his already tousled hair. "He knows we don't mean it, don't ya, bud?"

"Sure," the boy mutters, ducking out of their grasp before backing away toward the center of the diner. "I gotta go—"

"Oh, come on, Danny-Boy!" Marcus calls as Deran runs forward to leap in front of the boy, using his broader stature to bar Danny from walking any farther. "We haven't seen you for a while, why don't you come hang out?"

Danny is forced to inch back toward us as Deran moves forward, a dopey grin on his face while Marcus laughs. I glance back at Ellen, at a loss for what to say. She is intentionally focusing on the crowd of kids at the diner tables as if they are the most fascinating sight she can find. Meanwhile I feel like a lost child, not knowing whether to join her or continue watching my boyfriend bully a poor kid.

"Hey, I'll even let ya sit in the back seat! So long as I make sure you won't dirty it up too bad, of course."

"How's that, Dan?" Marcus snorts at Deran's jest. "Your first time sitting in a car that's not falling apart. Not to mention your first time hangin' around girls!"

The guys laugh and the boy tries edging away again, only for Marcus to stand in his way now, his shoulder roughly bumping into the boy and sending him stumbling back a few paces.

I can't help it now. I stride forward, grab Marcus's upper arm, and pull him toward me.

"C'mon, Marcus, knock it off," I demand, my furious tone and glare surprising him. I'm never angry with him. Annoyed maybe. Especially as of late. But I've never spoken so directly with him. "You're acting like a jerk."

"Now you're offending my buddy's girlfriend," Deran sighs, gripping Danny's shoulders before shoving him lightly. "That's not very nice, is it?"

"Marcus, if you don't stop this, I'm leaving."

Now Ellen's attention is locked firmly on us, her mouth hanging open as she loosely grips her half-finished milkshake in both hands. Marcus still looks dumbfounded, but Deran laughs loudly, his mouth turned into a prominent O.

"Damn, Marc, better get your act together! The wife doesn't like it!"

"Is this what you do with your friends now?" I ask, ignoring Deran. "Drink and mess with people for fun?"

As angry as I am, the relief that rises in me is louder. Because it feels like the easiest out has been offered to me on a silver platter.

Just do it. Right now. No one would question it. People are starting to look.

The words are so close, I open my mouth to say them. *Marcus, I'm breaking up with you. Not because I'm not ready to have sex or I don't feel like I fit in with your friends anymore or I feel like an entirely different person. But because you're a bully.*

All I can do is stand there, my glare softening as my throat opens and closes on the words.

Now everyone is staring.

"What's this, now? Didn't know the circus was in town."

The five of us turn around at the new voice. A figure is strolling up silently to the diner from the sidewalk.

The boy looks around our age as well, and is dressed similarly to Danny. Beat-up faded jeans, Converse with holes lining the sides, and a dark green tank top beneath an open denim vest. But this boy's face looks nothing like Danny's.

His umber-toned eyes are angry and mean, settled firmly on Marcus and Deran. His face is framed by a mane of dark blond hair falling across a black bandana tied around his head.

I can't tell if the others at the diner know who this boy is, or if they are just as stricken by his presence as I am, but the entire area goes quiet, some people eagerly sitting up on the benches as if they are about to watch a fight.

"What are *you* doing here?" Deran asks the boy with a sneer that feels different from the haughty aura he'd had seconds ago. "Couldn't find a dumpster ring to hang out in tonight?"

"Maybe the jails are all filled up this week," Marcus adds, and the same nasty look spreads across his face as he glares at the other boy.

"Maybe," the boy with the angry eyes and denim vest says, his voice a chill of ice reaching toward us, his hands dropping from where they had been casually placed on his hips. I catch the flash of a silver ring on his right hand as he strolls forward. "Or maybe I just got out and am lookin' for some action."

The dangerous look on his face fades ever so slightly as his eyes move between Marcus and Deran. He nods his chin sharply in Danny's direction. "You doin' alright, Danny?"

Danny nods back, his shoulders looking only minimally less tense at the arrival of who I'm guessing is a friend of his. "Yeah, I'm alright, Jackson."

"Uh-huh." The boy, Jackson, nods again, still moving forward until he is standing in front of Deran. Marcus moves past me, his chest puffed out comically as he approaches Jackson from behind. But the boy looks unworried that he's outnumbered. "That's good news. I wouldn't want us to have a little situation here."

He's easily taller than Deran, though Marcus is just his height. I watch the boy's hands curl into fists as he stares down Deran with a look that scares me.

Marcus reaches out and shoves the boy hard. "Let's go, then, huh? You wanna defend your little boyfriend, let's see you fight like a real man!"

Jackson turns toward Marcus now, an amused grin on his face, looking not at all daunted by the threat. I hold my breath, watching helplessly from a few feet away.

"You sure you wanna do that, rich boy? I'd hate to mess up your office attire by knocking your ass in the dirt. What's Daddy gonna say when he finds out you ruined his best clothes?"

Knowing that Marcus did in fact take that light blue button-down and pair of slacks from his dad's closet strangely almost makes me laugh, but it only adds fuel to Marcus's temper.

"You're all talk now, you son of a bitch, but wait 'til you're—"

"*Marcus!*"

He whips around to face me, nearly knocking me over with how close I've marched up to him.

"What?!"

"Get lost."

He blinks, his anger bobbing on the surface as he stares at me incredulously. "What the hell are you—"

"You heard me. Get out of here. You and Deran are drunk and have been acting like morons this entire evening. I'm calling the cops on all of you if you don't leave."

Will I? Probably not. But I'm also not going to wait for a fight to break out here in the middle of the diner.

Marcus laughs, his mouth hanging open in astonishment. "Addy, what is the matter with you tonight? You're—"

"Marcus, I mean it. I'll go up to the staff right now and tell them to call the police." I head toward the diner window to make my point.

"Go ahead." Deran shrugs, his eyes still pinned on Jackson. "The only one they'll arrest is this bum."

When I turn his way, I'm startled to see Jackson's eyes are now on me.

He looks surprised, as if he had indeed noticed me standing here, no more helpful than the paint on the walls, but hadn't expected me capable of human speech. It makes me more angry and I quickly pull my attention back to the others.

"So what? They'll still call your parents. And good luck explaining to them why you smell like your dad's best whiskey, Marcus."

That gets their attention. There may be many things Marcus and his friends are able to get away with that other kids aren't. But messing with anyone's alcohol supply is never a good idea.

"Let's go, Marc. Looks like this place is attracting trash." Deran pointedly bumps his shoulder into Jackson as he rushes to the car, slamming the door as he gets in. "You comin', Ellen?"

Ellen stares between me and Deran, her mouth still hanging open as she shakes her head, a small sound of despair coming from her throat. Deran rolls his eyes. "Whatever."

He starts up the car and Marcus backs away, still staring at me as if I sprouted another head, until he finally throws himself over the door into the passenger seat. I step back as Deran rips the car out of the lot and speeds away.

"Oh my God, Addy," Ellen finally speaks as she runs up to me. I place a hand on my forehead, recalling something my sister said once about dealing with men being akin to wrangling elementary school children. "I've never seen you so angry at him."

"I've never seen him be such an asshole."

We take two steps toward the tables, where everyone has lost interest in the anticlimactic altercation, when my head falls back in despair. "Crap. I left my food in the back seat."

"Oh," Ellen says mournfully as she twists the straw in her milkshake. "Um..."

"I can get you some food."

We both turn to see Danny standing behind us, his wallet still twisted in his hands. Up close, his kind eyes are an even more striking shade of crystal blue, and his face is actually quite handsome. He glances back at the money he has, frowning.

"Uh... I could get you something we could share, if that's alright."

"Don't worry about it." I offer him a smile.

"No, really," he insists with a depleted sigh, running a hand through his uneven hair. "It's my fault you don't have any food—"

"It is *not* your fault," I assure him.

"—and I feel really bad. Please, let me get you something."

I glance over at the diner window, grinning, before turning back to Danny. "No, it's okay. Why don't I get something for all of us?"

"I could chip in!" Ellen nods eagerly. "All I got was this milkshake."

Before Danny can protest, a sarcastic grunt sounds from behind him.

"Bet you feel like a real hero, don't ya, princess?"

Danny turns around to reveal where the other boy, Jackson, is still standing. He's leaned himself up against one of the metal support beams that used to be the same turquoise color as the roof of the diner, but has faded to a sickly yellowish tan. He crosses his arms over his chest, clearly imagining how unbothered yet intimidating he must look, his dark eyes narrowed straight at me accusingly.

A prickle of irritation scrapes at me as I return his glare.

"What's your problem?" I ask him, crossing my arms to match his stance. I would have thought he might be grateful that I de-escalated the situation for him before the cops could become involved. Because yes, in this town, they would have arrested him without a thought before laying a hand on Marcus or Deran.

"Oh, there's no problem, hun." He kicks the ground lightly with his toe. "Except you little rich snobs messin' with anyone who's below you."

"Come on, Jackson," Danny pleads. "You saw, she's not like that."

"Yeah," Jackson chuckles humorlessly, still aiming his suspicious gaze at me. "They'll try anything once."

Ellen sticks her chin up at the boy before turning briskly to the ordering window. But I remain where I am, unable to turn away as my anger continues to surge. The boy smugly pushes himself off the support beam and reaches into his back pocket for something.

"Oh, you're right," I reply coldly. "The proper thing to do would be to stand back and watch you three fight it out like animals. Exactly how I want to spend my evening."

"No one's dyin' for your presence, sweetheart," Jackson says as he lights a cigarette. "If you don't like it, get lost."

"C'mon, Jackson," Danny repeats, his voice lower and more serious than before. "Chill out, man."

"No, let him talk," I argue, keeping my glare on the infuriating boy, no doubt envisioning himself looking as cool as a movie star as he takes a drag off his cigarette. "He didn't get the chance to show off his grandiose fighting skills, maybe he can impress us all with his powers of limited speech."

I turn away before I can see his reaction, following Ellen to the order window.

"Addy, ignore him," she whispers to me as soon as I'm standing next to her, as if she's afraid Jackson has super-hearing. "You don't know what he could do."

"Oh, please." I roll my eyes as I help her gather up the food. "He looks like he hardly knows how to light a cigarette."

"No, I'm serious," Ellen insists as we head over to an empty table, where Danny is standing awkwardly. "Jeremy told me once that there are some real psychos in this town."

"Jeremy can't dress himself without his mother's help."

Danny still hovers beside the table after Ellen and I have sat with the food. I turn to look up at him, offering an encouraging smile before moving over and sliding my tray in front of him.

"You really didn't have to—"

"Please. Sit down."

He returns a small smile before sitting beside me, eventually reaching for a couple of fries. "Thanks."

"Don't mention it," I assure him, reaching for the chocolate milkshake in front of me. "I'm sorry about Marcus and Deran. I've never seen them act like that."

An exaggerated chuckle from behind me makes me jump. Jackson rounds the side of the table as I wave the smoke from his cigarette out of my face.

Asshole.

"You gonna adopt him too, princess? How many points does feeding a poor kid get you on your private college applications?"

Ellen is frantically shaking her head at me in what she probably thinks is a subtle gesture. My fingers curl around the condensated milkshake cup.

Jackson leans up against the table across from us, ignoring the server at the window who calls over to tell him to take his smoking someplace else.

"Have you never seen civilized interaction?" I ask pointedly without deigning to turn in his direction. "Is that why you're so intimidated?"

"No." His voice is lower now. Almost scary, if I cared to admit it. I can see him lean forward out of the corner of my eye, his hands resting on his knees, the smoke shriveling from the cigarette held between his fingers. I still don't face him even as I can feel his eyes burning into me. "I don't take too kindly to people like you screwin' with my friends, in case you haven't noticed."

"It's fine, Jackson, seriously," Danny repeats, sounding as exasperated as I'm feeling and as anxious as Ellen looks. "They didn't do anything."

"Oh, don't say that," Jackson drawls as I crush my fist tighter against the cup. "Our new little friend here will be upset if her charitable efforts aren't properly appreciated."

I finally turn to look at him, my eyes burning fire into his smug little face as leans back casually on the table, taking a puff from his cigarette.

"You're right. And keep acting scared, Ellen. We wouldn't want him to think he's anything less than absolutely terrifying, even though he smokes like he learned from watching late-night TV."

"*Addy!*" Ellen hisses, but I rise to my feet, keeping my gaze level with the boy I approach. I don't know why I don't heed her warning. Though I've always silently chafed at people telling me what to do, I like to think that I am usually smart when it comes to keeping my temper in check at the right times. Keeping any unsavory thoughts within my own head while maintaining a pleasant and polite smile on the outside. But now, I can't describe how outraged I am at the audacity of this complete stranger who I had the courtesy to side with against my own boyfriend.

Jackson is slumped against the table so that he's down to my height. He looks unaffected by my comment, tilting his head in amusement as I approach, the milkshake cup still gripped in my hand.

"And if you want someone to call 'princess' or 'sweetheart,' I suggest you get a dog."

My hand moves of its own volition, though I have no desire to stop it. And soon my cup is empty, and Jackson's entire face and front is covered in chocolate milkshake.

He rises to his full height at the shock of the sticky cold drenching him, his ruined cigarette dropping to the ground. His minute choke of surprise is drowned by the chorus of gasps from the onlookers at the surrounding tables.

I turn away and head back to the table as Jackson whips some of the gooey liquid out of his eyes. I return to my food as if I don't feel the stares from Ellen and Danny and as if I don't care what Jackson's next reaction will be. I half expect him to throw something at me, which I can't bring myself to be entirely fearful of.

But instead, I hear him laugh. A breathy laugh that sounds like he's reemerged from beneath the thick wave of milkshake.

"Well," he sighs, stepping away from the table and looking down at the chocolate splattered all over himself, "I guess this cuts my night short." And with that, he heads out toward the sidewalk, acting like he's not completely covered in milkshake. "See ya around, Danny."

The silence at our table lingers long after Jackson has walked away, and only when he's out of sight of the diner, striding off into the sunset, does Ellen nearly leap across the table at me.

"*Are you crazy?!*"

Chapter 2
Addy

"I have never seen anyone do that," Danny says. "Not a girl, any-way."

"I find that hard to believe," I answer, easily imagining that Jackson's oh-so-eloquent charm would make a girl or ten throw their drink on him.

"Smart way to get yourself *killed*, Addy," Ellen berates me, outraged as she manically sips on the remainder of her milkshake.

"Jackson's not like that," Danny quickly defends through a mouthful of the small burger he'd started devouring. "He can be rude sometimes, and I'm sorry he was being such a moron just now, but he's not danger-ous or anything. He just likes people to think he is."

"That's obvious." I shake my head. "Whatever, we don't need to talk about him anymore." I turn fully toward Danny as he finishes off the tiny burger and wipes his hands on the cheap paper napkin in front of him. "I'm Addy. It's nice to meet you."

He smiles shyly and shakes my hand.

"Hey, Addy. I'm Danny."

"This is Ellen." I nod toward my friend who is still frantically chewing on her milkshake straw as she stares in horror at the plastic table. "She'll recover in a minute."

"God," Ellen mutters into her straw.

"Are you new to town?" Danny asks me. "I know I would recognize you if you went to our school."

I smile to myself as he blushes furiously.

"No, we're here for the summer. Our mothers used to live here when they were young, and they started bringing us a few years ago. Now it's a staple."

"Wow." Danny gives a glum look. "Lousy summer vacation."

"It's not so bad," Ellen finally speaks up just as I reply "I'll say." Danny shoots me a quiet grin.

"It's nice to get out of our hometown," Ellen continues.

"Where do you live?"

"New York," I answer.

Danny's jaw drops slightly as he looks between us.

"*New York?*"

"Not as glamorous as the movies make it look," I inform him.

"Where we live is a lot bigger than Greydon," Ellen says with a nod, glancing about the sparse shops that line the sidewalks giving way to nothing but empty fields that reach toward the mountains. "But Greydon's nice. Where we live is so *big*, it can be overwhelming. I like a small town."

"It's alright." Danny shrugs, looking as if he doesn't believe those words at all. "But coming from New York..."

"It isn't all that interesting," I assure him. "A regular suburban neighborhood in White Plains. It's like people imagining Greydon being LA because it's in California."

Danny takes a quick moment to consider that, nodding as he pops a french fry into his mouth. "Fair point."

"I don't know about this, Addy..."

"Oh, come on, Ellen," I sigh heavily as I follow alongside Danny across the street from the diner. "I don't think Danny's a serial killer luring us to his farmhouse."

"Trailer is more like it," Danny calls back to her, his hands in his pockets as he leads the way. "Farmhouse would be a mansion compared to my place."

"I didn't mean that," Ellen mutters, her face red as she catches up to us.

The sun has nearly set all the way by now, casting the streets with a low purplish glow, bringing a refreshing breeze that cools the summertime air.

I don't know why walking with Danny feels like such a good idea. Maybe it's because I still don't know what to do about Marcus and want an excuse not to think about him. Maybe it's that I have no idea what else to do since I already explored everything there is to do in this town by our second trip here. Maybe it was the way Danny had asked, his head dipped low and his voice unsure, but with that kind hopefulness in his bright blue eyes as he offered to walk us wherever we needed to go since Ellen and I didn't have a ride anymore. And it sounded like something different to do for once.

"How old are you?" I ask. We cross to the other side of the street once we reach the gas station, and walk along a road I always thought led to nothing but the more run-down homes in town my mother always made sure we stayed away from.

"Sixteen," Danny answers.

"Same. I'll be seventeen in September."

"How has it been for you?" he asks, his lanky legs kicking against the broken sidewalk as we walk down the path lined by a chain-link gate, drawing closer to what I assume is a dead end. "Everyone always puts being sixteen on this pedestal. Like that's the moment everything's gonna change and you'll feel different. But I feel the same as I did when I was thirteen."

"Actually, I do kinda get that," I answer.

I gnaw on my fingernail as I debate whether or not to get into my full-on crisis about Marcus, especially with Ellen here listening. But I'm too relieved that someone brought it up to not talk about the odd feeling I've had the past couple of months.

"It wasn't until recently, but... I do feel different. Definitely different than when I was fifteen. Not in the way everyone talks about, but the person I was when I was younger seems super far away."

Instead of looking confused or disappointed by my answer, Danny gives an understanding nod. "That's normal, I think. Probably just happens gradually. I'm not the same as I was at thirteen, even if I don't feel any different."

"I don't think different's bad though," I say, wondering if that sounded as desperate and pathetic as it felt. "Do you?"

"No." He shoots me an amused expression. "I think it's called maturing."

Something crashes against the chain-link fence beside us, a booming yell accompanying the sharp clank. Ellen screams, I leap back into the road, and Danny looks prepared to bolt across the street and into the trees.

A raspy laugh echoes in the near darkness coming from the figure that is now crawling up the side of the fence and swinging over the top to drop down on the sidewalk.

"*Christ*, Benji," Danny sighs, the smile back in his eyes as he moves toward the curb, me following behind him. Ellen is still frozen, her eyes wide as she stares at the boy who runs up to Danny and gives him a noogie.

"Hey, you and your bodyguard disappeared on me. What happened to Cropsy Park at seven?"

"We were gonna head to the movie tonight instead, remember?" Danny tells him, trying to shake the other boy off. "And I was starving, I stopped at the diner."

The boy playfully clinging on to Danny's side turns his head in our direction, his eyes widening as he takes us in. He has a round face lit up by his orb-like green eyes and framed by a tangle of spiky hair that sticks out in all directions. He's a few inches shorter than Danny, but looks around the same age. He wears a worn-out leather jacket with at least twenty different symbols patched onto it. The only one I can make out is a bright orange circle on his left shoulder that reads *FUCK 'ROUND, FIND OUT* with an image of a spiral beneath it.

"Well well well." The boy shakes his head, clicking his tongue. "Dan, you really are a ladies' man."

Danny flushes and turns away. "Shut up."

"What's Cropsy Park?" I ask, looking between the two boys.

"The park across from the library with the metal playground," Danny answers.

"The one where everyone in this town has gotten third-degree burns going down the slide in the summer," the other boy adds, flashing a grin that shows off crooked teeth. "An hour of playing around on that thing and you'll be a spittin' image of Cropsy himself."

"*The Burning*," I affirm. "You mean Cropsy from *The Burning*."

"Oh, shit," the boy gasps in mock astonishment as he turns to look at Danny. "The secret code has been broken! You know the slasher movie deep cuts, huh?"

"This is Benji." Danny nods to the now-cackling boy hanging off him. "Benji, this is Addy and Ellen."

"Pleased to meet ya, ladies." Benji bows dramatically, tipping an invisible hat above his brow. "Don't know what the hell you're thinking hangin' around with us losers, but welcome anyhow."

"Maybe we're looking for a little change," I quip back. I expect Ellen to look scandalized, but she is watching Benji with wide eyes, curiously awaiting his response.

Benji sweeps his gaze over us once more, clicking his tongue again as he seems to decide on something. "You came to the right place."

Danny ends up leading us off the empty street, into the unkempt grass, past a hole at the end of the chain-link fence, and toward a line of trees. It's darker here with the dusk shaded by the branches and the absence of streetlights, and Ellen gives me an unsure look. But I only shrug, following the boys into the trees, feeling leaves and sticks scraping against my feet through my sandals. Danny and Benji chat casually with each other ahead of us, Danny glancing back occasionally to make sure we're keeping up.

"You're still sure we aren't about to be killed?" Ellen whispers as she stumbles beside me, her shoes no better than mine for tramping through the foliage.

"You shouldn't hide your face any time we watch a horror movie," I can't help but tease. "I'm very confident in my ability to fight my way out if we get into trouble."

What I think is a loud hissing sound begins to echo through the trees the farther we go along, a sound I realize to be a stream I can't see until Danny and Benji hop through a break in the trees that leads to a clearing where a long creek runs beneath the clear summer sky. On the other side of the water, an array of small trailer homes sprawl across the tiny field enclosed by the trees. The lights coming from the windows and the string lights lining the front porches ignite the area in a warm yellow glow.

Benji throws his shoes and socks off before splashing into the cool water, soaking his jeans up to his knees as he wades into the middle of the stream.

"You live here?" I ask Danny, turning to him in amazement, imagining what it's like to have all of this as your backyard. I can't see as well in the dark, but I'm sure Danny is blushing again.

"Yeah. Nice to have in the summer."

"How is there so much water?" I ask in amazement, watching the thick water rushing through the large creek, off into the distance down short piles of rocks that make the water arc in fountain-like patterns.

"We got lucky with a lot of rain throughout the spring. This stream hardly ever runs dry, even in the middle of summer."

The sound of Benji splashing and whooping is the only noise louder than the stream tumbling along the rocks. He whips his head up, his spiked hair splashing flecks of water from when he dunked his head right into the creek, his eyes focused on Ellen.

"Come on in, get your hair wet, girl!"

I glance over to Ellen, seeing a smile fighting its way onto her lips as she views the inviting water, likely imagining the refreshing coolness against her skin that would wipe away the lingering heat still sticking to us both.

I kick the sandals off my feet, wincing at the tiny rocks digging into my soles until I wade down into the stream, gasping at the shock of icy cold. Danny follows behind me, rolling up the legs of his jeans before tramping into the water. Ellen looks as if she is preparing to walk the balance beam after she has removed her shoes, rising onto her toes and sticking her arms out beside her as she treks slowly into the water.

To my surprise, Benji skips over, taking both her hands in his and helping her deeper into the creek, despite her short cries of horror as the cold water splashes up toward her skirt.

It's nice. To be weird and loud and kicking around in the water under the clear summer night sky. I'm glad I don't know these boys. I'm glad it's dark out and I can feel like no one is watching, like today is some strange dream that won't have any consequences in the morning.

Danny and I sit on a pile of rocks on the edge of the stream, our feet and most of our legs still submerged in the water, watching Benji chasing Ellen around, her shrieks echoing through the trees along with his boisterous laughs as he threatens to splash her with handfuls of water.

"Does Benji go to school with you?"

"The days he shows up. He's only a year older, same year as Jackson."

My easy expression freezes as I stare out across the creek, watching shadows of people moving back and forth within the windows of the small trailer homes.

"How did you all become friends?"

"I met Benji in elementary school when he moved here from Colorado. You can imagine I was never the most popular among the kids, but that's all it took for Benji to want to hang out with me. With my clothes that were always too small and him always speaking every single thing that crossed his mind, we became a nice unpopular duo."

Danny speaks of the memory with an obvious air of fondness.

"Jackson moved here when we started middle school. We stayed away from him at first. Seemed like he wanted nothing to do with anyone, he got suspended the first week for fighting." He leans back on his hands, an exasperated sigh quietly escaping him that I imagine is a common feeling associated with his pigheaded friend. "It wasn't long before Jackson Lowell got a reputation for being the school criminal."

I can't say that surprises me. And if I saw someone like Jackson Lowell at my school, I'd stay several feet away from him at all times too.

Danny's expression shifts, outlined by the gentle light from across the stream, his eyes sad or scared, his mouth softer.

"Then one day, there were some guys from gym class that were..."

His face changes again, as if he's backing away from something.

"These guys were teasing me in the locker room after class one day. It's not like it was a big deal or anything, I was used to it by then, but... I guess it looked pretty intense to someone on the outside."

I feel my own face heat as I move my gaze back down to the water, watching the blurred outline of my toes curling against the jagged pebbles. Maybe Danny's embarrassed about getting teased. It doesn't necessarily mean he doesn't want to tell me it was Marcus. It probably wasn't. If I know anything from my own school, almost anyone will jump at the chance to bully the poorest kid in their grade with the dirtiest clothes and the barest amount of lunch money.

"But Jackson happened to come back in," Danny goes on as the awkward moment between us passes. "And he... flipped out. He threw me out of there and started this huge brawl, right there in the middle of the locker rooms. They all ended up getting suspended."

Danny's face shifts again, this time into a more pleasant expression, similar to the one he had when talking about Benji. But maybe something deeper.

"He found me after school that day. He wanted to know if I was alright. I was super confused and I told him I didn't know why he cared. He'd never spoken to me before. I don't think he even knew my name." Danny shrugs, the fond look still in his eyes. "He didn't care. He told me he hated bullies. That he didn't plan on making any friends in this town, but he might as well now. So he started hangin' out with me and Benji, and I guess he liked us. We're all best friends now."

Loath as I am to admit it, it is a sweet story. And it makes me more confused and therefore irritated that someone like Jackson Lowell comes out looking better than the bullies who I'm still not a hundred percent sure aren't the boys I've been hanging around here with for the past four years.

"Jackson isn't a bad guy," Danny tells me earnestly as he turns to face me. "He's had a weird go of it in life. His parents..." He trails off, shaking his head. "He isn't all he seems, is all. He likes his reputation and everything, but you'll hear a lot about him that isn't true. It's like you said back at the diner: he hardly knows how to smoke a cigarette properly. He hates the things, but he smokes 'em so people will think he's Clint Eastwood or something."

I laugh and close my eyes in disbelief. "And how does poorly smoking a cigarette make one a Clint Eastwood type?"

Danny grins, looking down at the water. "You'd have to ask him."

Ellen is finally getting into the spirit of whatever game Benji is trying to play, seeing as she is now aggressively flinging water at him with what looks like every bit of strength she has, his laughter still roaring as he's forced to shield himself with both arms.

"It's nice to see there's something else to do for fun around here."

"Oh, yeah," Danny says, leaning back on his hands again. "Besides the movies, the diner, or getting burned alive at Cropsy Park, you have to get creative. We don't even have a decent music shop around."

"I've noticed," I agree, any music-related activity being the first thing I made Ellen try to seek out with me on our initial trip here. "I was hoping for a couple more jukeboxes, at least."

Danny laughs, throwing his head in a way that makes his hair fall back, the glowing lights illuminating the handsome lines of his face. "There's one at Johnny-Jay's, but it's busted half the time."

"What kind of music do you like?" I ask him, my voice lowering, wanting to hide our conversation from the world.

"Anything," he says, turning to blink his bright blue eyes at me. "Rock mostly. And don't tell anyone, but I like a lot of pop too."

"Yeah?" I ask with a small laugh of surprise.

He nods. "Olivia Newton-John would be playing on every nonexistent jukebox I came across if I were in charge."

I laugh again, feeling that pleasant bubble of late-night giddiness wash over me as I wave my feet through the water. "That is not something to be ashamed of. Rock and pop are the best genres of music. I'm keeping the radio on as much as I can so I don't miss a single time any station plays 'Eye of the Tiger' before I can buy the record when I get home."

"You're a music guru as well as a slasher movie connoisseur, huh?"

"What can I say?" I shrug, leaning back beside him. "There's much to enjoy in life."

I tell Danny about pooling money with my two cousins back home to buy a Fleetwood Mac album when I was younger. He tells me about his first record, the *Bohemian Rhapsody* single, that his parents bought for him when he was ten and that is still his most prized possession.

It turns out talking with Danny about music is as cathartic as it is to listen to it. There aren't many people, aside from the cousins I grew up with back home, who could talk so long about music. Not just what artists we like or how the perfect guitar chord can make or break the final chorus of a song (a debate my youngest cousin and I get in regularly) but about that special thing that happens. That feeling we get when we're alone in our rooms listening to the radio with the lyrics and beat of a song flowing through every inch of us, picturing ourselves onstage with the energy of thousands of screaming fans buzzing through our veins.

It's a specific feeling that I had not expected to have in relation with this random boy I met today. But we find we have a lot in common. And for tonight, lazing about with my feet in the water, my best friend now being chased around by Benji with a frog he found in the creek, a nice boy chatting beside me about whether *Rocky II* and *III* are better than the first, and no difficult conversations or thoughts pressuring me, it feels more how an actual summer vacation is supposed to be.

Chapter 3

Jackson

I guess even in Greydon, you gotta be prepared for anything. Because there is no universe in which I thought I would begin tonight covered in chocolate milkshake.

Ward, the owner of the liquor shop on the corner across from Cropsy Park, whom I wisely decided to befriend the day I arrived in town, is thankfully here to let me upstairs. Ward is the image of what I'm sure I'll be by age fifty, which is probably why the guy begrudgingly allows me to sleep in the spare bedroom above the shop and feigns temporary blindness whenever I swipe one of the bottles from the store.

The man raises his bushy white brows in mild interest after unlocking the back door to let me up the skinny stairwell leading to the apartment.

"Must be gal trouble," he deduces as I clomp my way up the stairs, feeling my shirt already stuck to me from the gooey mess.

"Not exactly," I answer. Not any gal I've seen around here before, anyway.

Granted, given who she was hanging around with, I normally wouldn't want to know her. Whoever Marcus Tanner's girlfriend is must be someone braindead enough to think he's a great guy, which should say everything I need to know about her.

I throw the door shut behind me and peel the sticky clothes from my body that have grown warm from the late evening heat on my walk here. A walk of shame, as I'm sure it was intended to be, but what was spent fuming in confusion.

The chick has to be from out of town. Not only is she way too cute for me to have not recalled her round face and sharp eyes framed by those bouncy, shiny bronze locks that flew every which way when she talked, but a girl with a temper like that would have stuck out immediately among the flock of girls that usually hang around people like Marcus and his collection of dopes.

I toss the stained clothes on the ground before heading to the tiny porcelain sink installed in the corner of the bedroom almost as an after-thought and run the pathetic stream of water to throw over my face.

The new girl has an attitude. So what? It's easy to act like a hero when you've got a captive audience.

I dig a black shirt out of the top drawer most of my clothes are shoved into and grab a jacket in case the breeze kicks up later tonight. I rarely spend summer nights indoors, not until two or three in the morning kicks around. Being free from any responsibility of getting to school on time for almost three whole months is too valuable to sleep through. Not that my attendance record is ever superb.

I tromp back down the stairs after I've cleaned up, skipping out the back door and onto the street to head to... I don't know. It looks like the night Danny and I had planned of sneaking into the late-night showing of *Death Race 2000* is a bust, I've got no clue what Benji's up to, and I don't feel up to risking trouble with the cops tonight after the debacle in the arcade lot last week that got me a full night in the slammer.

And no, that does not mean I'm grateful to Little Rich Girl for getting me out of that fight tonight.

I wander about the streets for a while, the sun gradually dipping farther from view until the heat from the day turns into a humid warmth leftover from the ninety degrees it reached in the late afternoon. Most people are inside by now to get out of the muggy heat, leaving the streets mostly empty aside from the occasional car rolling by or the group of kids heading from one location to the next.

Johnny-Jay's Bar and Grill comes into view as I turn the next corner, and I jog across the street to dive into the dimly lit bar. Half of the shades over the windows are closed to block out the harsh sunlight from earlier in the day, and a cool blast of AC hits my face and makes me thankful for the jacket I decided to bring.

The Rolling Stones playing softly from the shitty jukebox at the back of the bar mixes in with the low chatter from the handful of patrons drinking or munching down on baskets of fries and onion rings and the sound of soft yipping and skittering paws against the sticky wooden floor.

The owner's beagle puppy, an insatiable monster named Skerritt, is now a Johnny-Jay's staple. He's probably not allowed to be in here, but you gotta be willing to put up with him if you wanna hang around.

My feet carry me up to the bar, next to the tall man with a sweat-stained sleeveless plaid and a pile of matted ginger hair on his head sipping what looks like his third beer of the evening based on the lineup in front of him.

"How's it goin', Teddy?" I ask as I slide onto the stool beside him. Ted flicks his gaze toward me, giving a small dip of his head as he raises his beer to his mouth.

"Not bad, Jackson, how've you been?"

"Danny ditched me for a couple of rich girls and I got a face full of milkshake chucked at me. It's not eight p.m. yet and I'm the town fiend."

Ted chuckles as he swallows his beer. "What else is new?"

"You know you aren't allowed up here, you little turd."

I turn to face the brawny man with pointy jet-black facial hair that makes him look like Satan.

"Can I get a beer, Jay? Forgot to nab one from Ward's place."

Jay points a familiar stern finger at me as he moves forward to wipe down behind the bar. "You're lucky I don't throw ya outta here. Don't push it."

I laugh and Ted sets down his now-empty third bottle of beer. "Cut him some slack, Jay, a girl threw a milkshake in his face and he's got no one who wants to hang out with him tonight."

I'm about to comment on his annoyingly condescending parental tone he uses way too often, but I turn to him with a furrowed brow instead.

"I never said it was a girl."

Ted and Jay both scoff.

I roll my eyes as Jay slides a Coke my way. "Shut the hell up, you two."

"Goddamn it, Jay!" a rickety voice hollers from the corner of the bar, loud enough to rise over the music and the light chatter of the other patrons. We turn to see an old guy with gigantic glasses that look like magnifying lenses angrily waving a cane in our direction as Skerritt darts out from under his table. "Get this goddamn dog outta here or I'll kick it out the door myself!"

"You lay a toe on him, Gerald, and I'll cut ya off from your free Wednesday night Screwdrivers for a month!" Jay hollers back without missing a beat, aiming his stern finger in the old man's direction now.

"Well, he better stop gnawin' at my track pants or you're buyin' me a new set," the old man grumbles, though with noticeably less gusto.

Jay goes back to cleaning down the bar while Skerritt scampers away to start trying to climb up the blinds over one of the windows. I crack open the bottle of Coke, letting the icy condensation drip down my arm as I take a gulp that indeed already has me covered in chills and aching to get back outside in the warmth.

"You talk to Brenda yet?"

Ted's voice is different, the brief levity gone from his face, replaced with pity that he commendably tries to hide.

I feel my own expression drop as the Coke bottle hits the wood of the bar with a loud clunk. "Not yet."

Not in two weeks. Not since I had to spend the night in jail after smart-mouthing the sheriff in the lot. Not since Ted informed me he happened to see her with some schmuck at the Hare last weekend having a tongue-war with each other in front of the whole bar.

Whatever. She can do what she wants.

I can see the shift in Ted's face. The settle of his dusted jaw, his chest puffing out slightly, his shoulders set sternly. I'm about to get Ted-dad-advice.

"Jackson, I know how difficult it is for you when you get into these relationships and they're not what you're—"

"Alright, Teddy," I sigh heavily before throwing my head back to take a heavy gulp of the ice-cold soda. "Good talk."

"Come on, you need to hear it, you little Casanova," Jay chides from across the bar. "He was a bit of a Romeo himself back in the day, right, Teddy?"

"Look, I don't see how my love life is any business of you nimrods, alright?" I exclaim, looking between the two.

"Hey, this whole town has to witness the drama of all the fallouts."

"Jay, kindly tend to your other customers and leave me in peace."

"I'm just saying, it's okay to wait a little bit to get what you're after," Ted continues as I finish up my Coke. "Jumping into these things with girls you've known only a day is how—"

"Look, Teddy, I'd love to chat, but... actually, I'd rather do anything else. See ya." I hop off the stool, slapping him lightly on the shoulder as I head toward the door, longing for the humid air outside.

Ted, unsurprised as always, shakes his head to himself, resigned as he has to be at my determination to not sit and listen to advice from a twenty-seven-year-old bachelor.

"Stay outta trouble."

"Not on your life."

Unfortunately, I can't keep my promise to Ted when there's jack shit to get into trouble with. I don't know how long I wander around, waiting outside the arcade, sitting on the sad-looking swings at Cropsy Park, and generally looking pitiful as I wait to see if Benji might pop up somewhere like he often does. It's pretty dead on a Thursday night, even though it's summer. Maybe that's a good thing. I can at least be sure I'll avoid running into Brenda tonight.

God. Ted and his holier-than-thou preaching. What a load of crap. What was he gonna tell me, wait 'til I'm thirty and my true love will come? Shit.

Maybe I don't care what Brenda does when I'm not looking, I think to myself as the worn rubber of my shoes kicks along the loose gravel of the off-road I've wandered toward, away from the main hub of town. Closer toward the wide, empty fields and small ponds that litter the enclosure of Greydon. *Maybe I won't even say anything to her. Maybe I want her to stick around.*

It sounds pathetic even saying it to myself. More so when I remember that Brenda, despite telling me how she couldn't go a minute without thinking about me the last time we made out behind the video store, probably spends exactly none of her free time with my name anywhere near the vicinity of her mind.

The sound of shuffling feet and gruff voices near the empty sidewalk makes me turn back toward the street from where I'm sinking farther into the brush. And when I see the two figures glancing around hastily before emerging from their hiding spot at the edge of the chain-link fence, my fists curl eagerly at my sides.

Spoke too soon. Trouble is always afoot.

I don't know the two goons by name, but I can easily pick them out as members of Shelly Criston's gang. More like "group of twenty-year-olds desperately clinging to their teenage youth," but "gang" is typically the term thrown around when it comes to Shelly.

Shelly Criston fancies himself the Michael Corleone of Greydon, but as far as I know, the craziest thing he and his band of mice have done is rob a liquor store or two and bully the local ten-year-olds. The rest of us are old enough to see through his bullshit.

And who the hell *hasn't* swiped something from a liquor store?

The two goons look to be sharing a stash they jacked from a shop right now as they slink out of the bushes and down the street, their skinny necks outstretched to jut out their chins and look tough for whoever might be watching as they clutch crinkled paper bags at their sides, just obvious enough.

Clearly they don't see me, or else a brawl would have started by now. It's tempting to follow them and goad them into something right there on the street. Maybe because I'm bored, or to stick it to Ted's advice, or because it's too much fun to knock these assholes in the dirt every now and then.

Unfortunately, Ted did have a point. Sheriff Numb-Nuts did mention something about "hard time" in juvie if I get caught up in anything else this summer. It's been only about a couple of weeks since the incident in the lot, so I'd better lie low, unless I want to spend my summer in a correctional facility upstate surrounded by fifty other Shelly Cristons.

Reluctantly, I hang back and watch them leave, reaching for the pack of Marlboros in my back pocket. I brace myself for the bitter, charred taste as I place the white tube between my teeth, pulling the lighter from my jacket pocket. I swear I'll get used to it one of these days. Ever since I first tried a cigarette at ten years old I've been unable to comprehend why so many people spend hours with these things in their mouths. Not that I'd ever admit that out loud even with a gun to my head.

There must be something great about it. Everyone in movies does it.

Before I can move on with my solo trek through the brush, the sound of voices across the street draws my attention now to two girls who've turned the corner beside the ice cream parlor, walking across the empty street. One of them is holding her shoes in her hand, prancing across the asphalt on tiptoe.

As they reach the other side of the street, I can see it's the two girls from the diner earlier. I nearly give myself away as a laugh almost crashes through me.

"You sure, Addy?" the girl with the big curly black hair and high voice asks, stepping back into the sandals that had been dangling from her hand. "My dad won't tell your mom anything when he drops you off. He doesn't tell *my* mom stuff if I ask him not to."

"No, it's alright," the girl with the bouncy bronze locks that shine under the streetlights answers.

Her voice is instantly familiar, even though I've heard it only once for about five minutes today. But a little rich girl relentlessly giving you shit without flinching before tossing a milkshake in your face is memorable.

"I could use the walk."

"Addy, it's a thirty-minute walk to the cottages—"

"Ellen, I'll be fine. Trust me, I want to walk."

She sounds like she means it too. If she's going where I think she's going, it's indeed a half-hour walk to the rental cottages at the edge of town.

Her friend bites her lip nervously (nervous seems to be her default) before sighing. "Alright. I'm going to the payphone by the coffee café. My dad will be here in about fifteen minutes, I'm gonna get an iced mocha. Do you want something?"

"No, that's okay. I'm gonna head back."

The girl stays to watch her friend walk back across the street before turning to begin a casual stroll down the sidewalk.

I take another drag of the cigarette, the smoke puffing up toward the chain-link fence. The girl pauses, her head tilting up, smelling the cigarette smoke. I remain where I am, waiting for her to turn around, but before she can, her attention and mine is pulled across the street again where a familiar black Chevy Camaro rolls around the corner, pulling up along the sidewalk as the girl turns fully to face the two guys who stagger out of the front seats. I stay where I am, not making a move to come out, but not bothering to hide myself away. A fight tonight might not be lost after all.

Marcus approaches the girl, his arms crossed as he nearly stumbles on the curb of the sidewalk. "I see you've managed to keep yourself busy tonight."

The girl doesn't flinch as she meets his gaze with a steely glare of her own, only hers is more intimidating given the fact she's actually sober. And Marcus Tanner is too much of an idiot to be taken seriously at any time.

"Marcus, why don't you go home? You shouldn't be out like this."

"You ditch us 'cause you think we're immature, and then you go gallivanting around town with a bunch of deadbeat losers?" Deran asks from where he's hanging from the door of the Chevy.

She leans over to meet the guy's dopey gaze without blinking. "What I do and who I hang out with isn't any of your business, Deran. And this conversation doesn't involve you, so can you get back in the car? Last I checked I only have one insecure boyfriend."

My chuckle is covered up by Deran's pathetic shriek of "Screw you, Addy!"

"Addy, I'm not going anywhere until we talk," Marcus protests, his arms still crossed, looking like the pouty little boy he is. "There's no excuse for how crazy you acted tonight."

"For how *I* acted?" the girl laughs in astonishment.

"Yes, how *you* acted! Who are you criticizing me when you won't even have sex with your own boyfriend, but you're quick to go runnin' off with a bunch of low-life—"

I don't have time to raise my eyebrows at the accusation before the girl shoves Marcus so hard, it knocks him backward a few steps.

Despite the violent tendencies I've personally witnessed from this girl this evening, this isn't a regular occurrence from her based on the wide-eyed reactions from both Marcus and Deran, and the way she freezes for a moment after.

"Don't you ever speak to me like that again, Marcus," she hisses, her voice steady despite her brief shock. "And if you think I'm getting in that car with you two, you're insane. Now get the hell out of here, unless you want me to tell your parents you've been driving their car around drunk, Deran."

I roll my eyes to myself as I take another puff of my cigarette, watching curiously as the two boys stumble back into their car. A pathetic threat if you ask me. But still, the girl's bite from back in the diner wasn't just a show. Impressive.

"You're gonna regret this, Addy," Marcus growls in what is surely supposed to be a warning tone but sounds more slurred and unsteady than he realizes.

The girl stands where she is on the sidewalk, watching them go. I continue to watch her quietly from my spot back near the tree line until she turns, gazing through the chain-link fence at me. Her expression isn't surprised or angry. I can't tell what her reaction is.

"Not bad, princess." I nod, the cigarette clasped between my fingers. "Or did you know I was watching?"

She stays where she is, the distant lights from the Chevy flashing across her, casting her shadow along the sidewalk before disappearing, leaving us both in darkness only broken by the silvery light of the almost full moon.

Her voice isn't angry or annoyed like I expected. It's softer in a way that surprises me more than anything else I've seen her do tonight.

"You ever feel like everyone around you has lost their minds?"

I nod, shrugging as I try not to show my surprise at her casual tone. As if she and I always have conversations like this when we run into each other. Wondering why the people around us are so unbelievably stupid.

"That's my life, sweetheart. I'm always surrounded by idiots."

She doesn't seem to hear me, lost in her own thoughts. "Hm."

"So what, is your boyfriend into you emasculating him in front of his friends, or somethin'? That was pretty hot."

Now she rolls her eyes, shaking her head in disgust as she turns to head down the sidewalk.

"Creep."

"That's me," I sigh, crushing the unsatisfying cigarette under my boot until it's out before turning to continue my direction out into the empty fields as she heads the other way, down the street leading out of town. "Have a nice night. *Addy.*"

I hear her footsteps slow. I don't turn back.

Chapter 4

Addy

My mother thankfully wasn't up by the time I got home last night, so she wasn't there to interrogate me about why I had walked all the way from town to the rental cottage we stay in every year. She also wasn't there to encourage me to make things right with Marcus or to warn me that hanging around the town riffraff is dangerous, which would be the exact scenario if I disclose to her everything that happened last night, and why I would love to put it off for as long as possible.

Not unlike the conversation I've been pushing myself to have with Marcus.

I come out into the kitchen this morning to see Lorry sitting where she was last night when I got home, on the tiny couch between the kitchen and the dining room, only today she has a bowl of Cap'n Crunch in her lap instead of a bowl of popcorn.

My younger sister got the full scoop the second I got home last night. Mostly because Lorry is like a bloodhound when it comes to me keeping secrets and would be able to sniff out if something was wrong from one look on my face.

"Mom wants to know why you got home so late last night," she warns as I go to grab an apple from the bowl on the table. She keeps her eyes on the small television propped up on the kitchen counter playing a rerun episode of *Welcome Back, Kotter*. "Plus her friends are all gonna know you fought with Marcus last night, so she's gonna find out. You know how much Marcus probably whines to his mommy and daddy about his mean girlfriend."

I stare at the green apple in my hand, my stomach turning at the thought of eating.

"I'm going to have to talk to him. Today."

I say it like I'm hoping someone will excuse me from it. *No, Addy, you don't have to ever speak to your boyfriend again. You don't even have to break up with him. You can fade him out of your life and pretend he never existed. No one will even notice!*

Lorry lets out a pointed, Lorry-typical sigh as she rises from the couch and crosses into the kitchen to put her bowl in the sink. "You should leave him."

"You've never liked Marcus," I remind her as I put the apple back into the bowl. "You thought I should have left him the second we got together."

"Yeah," Lorry says, eyes wide as she turns back toward me. Her long, couch-frizzled hair swings over her shoulders as she places her hands against the counter, leaning over to look me in the eye. "My intuition is a thousand times better than yours. And we both know it's better than Mom's."

Lorry has been like this since she could speak. Never afraid to act older than me and tell everyone what she thinks about everything at any time. Part of why Mom hates bringing her along to any social events. Me, on the other hand, I was trained from birth to be the perfect polite girl my mother and everyone else thinks I am.

"You hate him too."

"I don't hate him," I say, my chest seizing at the idea. I could never hate Marcus. I don't. I hate how he's become an asshole as of late. That's all.

Lorry widens her eyes pointedly once more, walking around the kitchen counter and back toward the couch. "Whatever you say…"

Before I can defend myself further, the sound of shuffling footsteps brings my mother sweeping into the room from the short hallway leading back toward her bedroom.

As always, she looks as if she's been up since five a.m., her close-cropped brown hair perfectly styled, her light-toned makeup applied, her low pearl-white heels complementing her floral-patterned, puff-sleeved dress.

She brushes merrily past us into the kitchen to begin making the coffee she obviously doesn't need, greeting me with a chipper good-morning I'd never hear back home.

"You're ready to go nice and early," she observes, nodding toward my own state. "Meeting someone?"

"Just Ellen." I nod toward her. "Brunch again?"

"Giselle's hosting," my mother confirms, leaning down to glance at her reflection in the metal teapot and fluff up her hair as she waits for the coffee. "Marianne and Arabelle are coming along, hopefully Grace."

"Mm," Lorry hums loudly at the mention of Marcus's mother's name. I bite my lip.

"And you?" my mother asks, turning back to face me. "How was your night last night?"

She can guess something's amiss by my expression, because her cheerful demeanor begins to wane. "What's the matter? Did something happen?"

I guess we're doing this now.

I can practically hear Lorry straining at every second of my silence, aching to retell the story I relayed to her last night.

"Marcus and I..."

"What?" Now true alarm is beginning to descend on my mother's expression. "Did you two have an argument?"

Guilt claws at me as I look up to meet my mother's anxious gaze. Despite how refreshed her spirits become when we stay in Greydon for the summer, the tiredness that has been present in her eyes for as long as I can remember still lingers.

There's never much I can do to cheer her up about our mundane life back home. Being a single parent working full-time to support an average house and two daughters who are well below the social class than she'd hoped was never the life she envisioned for herself. The least I've been able to do is encourage her that my time here in Greydon is just as exciting and wondrous as she pretends it is.

"It's not anything to worry about," I assure her, stepping over to the cabinets to grab one of the white porcelain mugs and handing it to her before going to get the cream and sugar for her coffee. "I'll handle it."

Too late. I've worried her.

"I know how you tend to overreact sometimes, Adrienne. Not everyone is going to be perfect all the time."

"Yes, I know, Mother."

"That doesn't mean he gets to be a douche."

"*Lauren!*" my mother gasps, whipping around.

Lorry shrugs from her spot on the couch, her gaze still fixed on the TV, unfazed by the admonishment. "It's the truth."

My mother turns her exasperated gaze back to me. "Do you think you said something that made him upset, or—"

"Oh my God, Mom, she didn't do anything," Lorry huffs.

"Lauren, that's enough of your input."

Lorry shakes her head disapprovingly. I bite back a grin. My mother turns back to me with another heavy sigh, not looking any lighter thanks to Lorry's sarcastic taunts.

"Adrienne, you and Marcus should go somewhere private and talk it out. Whatever happened, I'm sure he didn't mean to hurt your feelings."

Much as I know she's trying to help, I feel irked at her phrasing. Maybe he didn't "hurt my feelings." Maybe he just pissed me off.

"I know," I answer, forcing an amicable smile. "I'm going to. Just wanted to talk to Ellen about it first."

My mother's eyes lift in relief, her hand going briefly to my shoulder before she turns back anxiously to her coffee. "And Lauren?" she calls over her shoulder. "What do *you* plan on doing today?"

"I'll be at the library, ma'am," Lorry calls back from her slumped position on the couch. "As I always am. There's supposed to be this great book on the predicted deterioration of capitalism in the US. You think the commies are taking over, Mom?"

I give my mom a somewhat sympathetic glance before turning to head to the door. Part of the reason I feel the need to be the perfect daughter my mother has always dreamed of is because we all know Lorry has no desire to even pretend to try.

***

Ellen tells me she's talked to Steven Nulty already when I meet her at the coffee shop. Steven Nulty is another one of the guys in Marcus's friend group and also the sheriff's son, which has made him the most somewhat level-headed of the group. He's also had a crush on Ellen since she was twelve.

I'm unsurprised to hear that Marcus has regaled the tale of last night to all of his buddies, and that he wants to talk to me.

"He knows where to find me" is my only response after taking in the information as I mindlessly stir my mocha.

"Are you gonna break up with him?" Ellen asks, leaning over the small circular table, as if the two elderly ladies sitting in the corner, the only other customers in the shop, might be listening intently to our conversation. I shrug. "God," Ellen huffs, sitting back in her chair and nervously picking at her napkin. "The summer just started and there's already so much *drama*."

Greydon's the only place she and I get involved in drama. Sure, there's plenty back home at our school, but we are casual bystanders, given that we aren't a part of any group large enough for drama to be created. Here, when we pretend to be rich kids for a couple months, there's always something that happens.

Though nothing like this. Nothing between Marcus and me.

Ellen invites me to the shopping center with her after we've finished our drinks to look for something to wear to the Lensen barbecue, but I tell her I'm going to try to find Marcus so we can hash all of this out.

And that's what I should do. That's what I mean to do, I think. But I don't bother looking hard as I wander about town, blending in with the rush of kids running around in flip flops, eager to soak in the warm summer day, and adults rushing to work or to get some early shopping done. The small town is alive in a way it never is past sundown, a happy hum in the air that matches the bright flow of the early morning sun.

My pace slows as I find myself in front of the video rental store.

I don't get to come here much while I'm in Greydon. Every now and then when I stay in with Lorry for the evening, but whenever I'm with Marcus and the others, movie nights aren't exactly their style. If I'm spending the night out, it's usually driving around or going to someone's house party at their impressive, but ultimately boring mansion. I'm lucky if they agree to go to the movies once or twice, but even then, the boys eventually convince us all to leave early.

The rickety glass door swings open before I step inside, chilled by a welcome wind of air-conditioning and a gentle silence disturbed only by some shuffling up near the checkout stand and the singular customer I can see: an older man in the back who looks to be seriously perusing the X-rated section.

Stepping around an intimidating life-size *Death Wish II* cutout of Charles Bronson, I make my way toward the horror section stationed at the far right side of the store. My eyes sweep over rows of familiar slipcovers and titles, a number of which I've already checked out a couple times at the video store back home to watch with my cousins on our weekly scary movie night. There's something that will never get old about looking through the outlandish cover art and enticing titles, suggesting bizarre murder and mayhem within every tape.

"Here's the one!" I hear a familiar voice call. "*Nighthawks*. Came out last year. We've got Stallone, Hauer, and Lando Calrissian himself." The sound of a tape slapping down onto the counter echoes from up front. "Discount, baby."

"Nope."

"Come on!" I hear Benji protest. "I'm your best bud, your treasured confidant."

"Sorry. Not allowed."

"Cully's let you work here for five months now and still doesn't trust you?" Benji calls over the counter as I grab one of the tapes from the shelf and head toward the front.

"He doesn't trust *you*," Danny answers, lugging a pile of tapes from one of the bins below the counter. He places them on the surface and begins to sort through them, pausing when his eyes meet mine over Benji's shoulder.

I smile. "Hey."

Benji turns around, his brows raised almost all the way to his spiked hair. "Hey! Addy, right?"

I nod. "Benji." My eyes rise back up toward Danny. "And Danny."

Danny offers a shy grin, his blue eyes blinking down as he shuffles through the piles of tapes, looking to be stacking them into a second pile rather than organizing them.

"What've we got here?" Benji asks eagerly, snatching the tape hanging from my hand. His eyes sweep over the cover art showing an extreme close-up of a woman's face, her eyes wide, a thick trickle of bright, paint-like blood spilling from her mouth. "Aha! I recognize this. You know they play these at the drive-in once a year every summer."

"I try to catch them every time."

"You hear that, Danny?" Benji asks as I walk up, grabbing the VHS of *Two Thousand Maniacs!* back from him and setting it down on the counter. "I finally have someone to go with me at the end of the summer."

Danny scans the tape and clicks something into the computer. "So you're a *big* horror movie fan, then."

"The biggest." I grin, leaning up against the counter. "Maybe not as big as my cousin, Jenny. She's had a subscription to *Fangoria* magazine since it first came out. I don't think she watches anything that isn't horror."

"Hold up, Danny," Benji calls as he waltzes across the store to the side of the room I had come from. "Can I get a discount if I rent three tapes?"

Danny shakes his head, though he's grinning as he rolls his eyes. "He's never gonna watch any of them," he tells me quietly. "He can't sit still for more than half an hour of anything."

I laugh, preparing to tell him how my boyfriend and his friends are the same way, but I catch myself before the words can slip out. Instead, a sudden guilt floods me as I pass Danny three dollar bills across the counter.

"I'm sorry about last night."

Danny looks confused as the cash register clatters open with a sharp ding. But he quickly seems to realize what I'm talking about.

"It's fine," he says, busying himself with the register. "Don't worry about it."

"They didn't used to be like that. When we were younger... Lately Marcus and his friends have started to..."

I don't know what I'm saying. Danny seems to be only politely listening, but is wishing I would stop talking about it. I wish I could stop talking about it too. But I feel anxious to both apologize for how awful Marcus and Deran were yesterday, but also to defend them. And maybe defend myself.

"They're just different people now."

Danny hands me a yellow paper receipt and slides the tape across the counter toward me. "It's okay."

"Addy, don't you dare say another word," Benji says as he strides back up to the counter, placing a stack of five different tapes down in front of Danny. "S'not your fault your friends decided to be dickheads for the umpteenth time." He bounces on the balls of his feet as he reaches into his pocket, pulls out a small bundle of dollar bills, and begins sorting through them while Danny scans the pile of tapes. "Won't be the last time those morons get away with no consequences."

Danny casts me a quick, apologetic look before moving his gaze back down to the tapes.

"What about you?" I ask, eager to change the subject I stupidly brought up. "Have you got a horror movie of choice?"

"I can't ever watch them," Danny admits. "They scare me too much."

Benji lets out a sharp laugh, as if that's an understatement.

"That's alright." I shrug. "Most guys would never admit that."

"I read somewhere that women make up the majority of horror fans anyway," Benji says.

"Twelve bucks," Danny informs him after ringing up the tapes.

"*What?* Not a single deal on any of these?"

"You got one. There's a two-for-one deal on *Don't Answer the Phone!* and *Don't Go in the House.*"

"Alright, take off *Nighthawks* and *Maniac.*"

"Don't take off *Nighthawks*," I recommend, placing my tape under my arm and turning toward the door. "Take off *Motel Hell*. It's not that great."

Benji looks curiously back down at his selection of tapes and I head for the exit.

"Hey!"

I turn back to where Danny looks surprised at himself for speaking.

"Are you doing anything today?"

Chapter 5
Addy

I hang around the video store for the rest of the morning through Danny's shift. I don't mind, seeing as not only am I desperately trying to avoid Marcus and anyone I know in this town today, but I could easily spend twenty-four hours in a video store without getting bored.

There's an eventual steady flow of customers later on, mostly families with their children looking for movies to rent for the night, a few teens who try to rent X-rated films that Danny has to refuse when they can't show legal ID, and the occasional single adult or couple perusing.

Danny and I spend most of the time moving around the store, talking about all our favorite movies as he restocks the returns onto the shelves or puts out the fresh stock of new releases. I can now see where he's gotten the definition in his arms with all the gigantic boxes and stacks of tapes he constantly hauls all around the store and unpacks.

On his break, he gets us some ice cream pops from the mini freezer up front that his boss allows him to swipe from every now and then and we sit out on the curb outside where the conversation turns to music after we've had a long debate on whether *Rock 'n' Roll High School* was actually a good movie or not.

"I've always wanted to be a rock star," Danny sighs happily as we munch on the cookies 'n' cream ice cream pops in the warm early afternoon sun, sending steady drips of stickiness down the bright blue wrappers and onto our hands. Much like last night, talking with him for a while has mostly broken down his wall of initial shyness. "Ever since I saw *Phantom of the Paradise.*"

"I thought you couldn't watch horror movies."

"Is that a horror movie?"

I grimace. "Hm. No, I guess not."

"I was gonna learn to play guitar. Never got around to it, I guess."

"Do you have a guitar?"

He laughs to himself. "Nope."

"I have one. I could teach you."

He turns to look at me, his brows raised, the hint of a smile on his lips, as if he thinks I'm making a joke.

"I took lessons for about ten years," I explain. "My mom wanted piano, but it was always guitar for me. My cousin Jenny plays too, and my other cousin, Heather, learned drums. We used to play in their garage and annoy the whole block."

He laughs with me, going back to his ice cream and not saying anything else.

"I'm serious. I can come by your place and teach you. It'll give me something to do this summer."

This time when he looks at me, he seems to believe me.

"Well... sure, if you want to. We can meet at Ted's place. His is cleaner than mine anyway, and he lives across from me."

"Ted?"

Danny nods, polishing off another chomp of the slowly melting ice cream pop. "Ted's our unofficial dad. Benji, Jackson, and me."

"Why's that?" I ask, ignoring the jolt that Jackson's name brings me. I still can't fathom how an arrogant jackass like that could be friends with people like Danny and Benji, despite Danny's explanation last night.

His face turns into a painful grimace, and I realize I might be prying. But he answers before I can retract the question.

"It's complicated. Benji's parents hardly remember they have a kid, they're so busy fighting each other all the time. My parents try, but they've been busy working and trying not to lose our place the last couple of years. I don't think they know who I am anymore. It's kinda awkward between us now. And Jackson..."

He pauses here, and I find myself holding my breath, my fingers becoming drenched in melted ice cream as the pop is held forgotten in my hand.

"Our home lives can be pretty crappy sometimes," Danny laughs, the noise sounding more like an automatic reaction than a forced one. "Ted moved in across from me a while ago after leaving his folks' place. He's lived here his whole life. He went through similar stuff when he was young, so he's always opened up his house to me and Benji and Jackson whenever we need it."

Something inside me feels heavy as Danny goes back to finishing off his ice cream. I can't bring mine to my lips.

I remember my mother telling me about the few people around this town who were dressed in the beat-up clothes Danny and Benji have, who lived in areas like the one Danny took Ellen and me to last night. How they were people very different from us, who were involved in things she didn't want Lorry or me anywhere near.

What she meant were things like gangs, drugs, crime, everything good polite girls like me should stay far away from. But now I think it's something much different than that. Something I'll never be able to understand.

I haven't had a father since I was four, and though my mother can't be described as the most understanding and motherly of parents, she's still always there. She still loves Lorry and me. She knows what we like and what we don't like. She knows we're there. She cares, just in her own somewhat outdated way.

I can't imagine not having any parent at all. And I really can't imagine having them there, but not. Around, somewhere, but not aware or interested in anything about my life.

"It's good you have that," I say. "Your friends. And Ted."

Danny nods. "It's the closest thing to family I've ever had before. I never had siblings or cousins or anything other than my parents. Meeting Benji and Ted, and then Jackson, was like finally getting that... *thing* I was missing my whole life."

I know what he means. Life without my cousins or my sister would be a million times harder. Having something like that, people who know you better than anyone, who you can always count on to get what you're going through... In a world where being young can feel completely confusing, it's invaluable.

"Are your cousins here too?" Danny asks, finishing off his melted ice cream.

"No, just me, my mom, and my sister. My aunt Connie hates it here. Once my grandparents moved her and my mom to New York when they were younger, she never wanted to look back."

"Hm. Too bad."

I sigh wistfully. "I know. After I teach you guitar, we could have all formed a band and let a different block be annoyed by the noise for once."

"Guitar, huh? You're full of surprises, aren't ya, princess?"

I freeze at the voice coming from behind us before rolling my eyes harder than I think I've ever rolled them before.

"Hey, Jackson," Danny greets him as we both stand up, me keeping my gaze anywhere but on Jackson Lowell as I barge toward the trashcan.

"Whoa, easy," Jackson laughs, throwing his hands up as he leaps out of my way. "I've had it with the dairy product attacks from you, woman."

I'm upset I didn't hold on to my melted ice cream pop to chuck it at his face, something I'm sure I'll want to do by the end of this interaction.

"Hey, Benji said Shelly Criston's been looking for trouble with you," Danny says seriously. I can feel Jackson watching me as I stand like an idiot for several seconds with my ice cream–caked hand before spotting a water fountain down the other side of the rental store. "He heard you were the one who ratted him out last week."

"I wasn't about to go down for his shit," I hear Jackson answer as I rinse my hand at the fountain. "I may have backtalked a few cops that night, but I sure as hell wasn't stupid enough to try shoplifting from the gun store."

Water splashes onto my skirt, making me jump back as I shake my hand dry.

"Doesn't matter," I listen to him continue as I turn from the fountain, hovering behind the wall out of sight. "Sheriff Numb-Nuts has it out for me, he'll stick a gun store shoplifting charge on me when he can. Anyway, I heard he only swiped a couple holsters. Too chicken shit to get anywhere near a bullet cartridge."

I'm guessing he means Sheriff Nulty, Steven's dad. Steven, I've always been friends with. His dad, on the other hand, has always had the air of a righteous church pastor with a gun and a badge that's always creeped me out, to be honest.

"Please be careful," Danny pleads as I hover at my place against the wall, unsure why I want to listen in on their conversation without them knowing. Without *Jackson* knowing, specifically. "If you get into a brawl with Shelly right now and get caught, you'll go to juvie for sure."

"Eh. Big deal."

"It is a big deal, Jackson. Juvie isn't a weekend or night in jail. You don't want to *be* like Shelly Criston, do you? With a real criminal record and everything?"

"Ha! Criminal record? What, for chasing eight-year-olds down the block? For charging the elementary school kids their lunch money so he can buy a pack of cigs? Shit, Danny. I'd like Shelly Criston to see a real criminal someday."

"Well, it isn't gonna be *you*. Not if I have anything to do with it."

"And what're you gonna do to stop me, tough guy?"

It's quiet on the other side of the store for a moment as Danny tries to come up with an answer.

"I'll... tell Ted."

"*Shit.*"

"Addy?"

I jump as I spin around to face the figure standing a couple feet behind me that I didn't hear as I was listening to Jackson and Danny's conversation, trying to figure out who this Shelly Criston person is.

Marcus is staring at me through his tufts of white-blond hair pulling delicately in the light breeze, one hand gripping what looks like a raspberry slushie, the other holding his car keys.

A group of three of his friends are standing behind him, of course.

"Hey" is the only thing I can think of to say.

I don't realize it's gone quiet on the other side of the wall until Marcus's eyes rise up somewhere over my shoulder and immediately narrow into a glare.

I turn around to see Jackson now standing behind me, a smirk on his face as he casually leans up against the wall of the video store, his arms crossed. I get a full look at him now in his dark denim jeans and black tank top. The bandana's gone from his head, but the weird silver ring is still on his thumb. The sun casts a direct glow on his hair, making it look a much lighter shade than it had been last night, though his eyes remain a black hue.

"You lookin' for round two? I see you brought your frat brothers this time."

"You better watch your mouth, pal," Eddie, one of Marcus's friends typically known for throwing the biggest house parties and for running away from any threat of conflict, speaks in his nasal voice from behind Marcus. I notice he stays firmly stationed at the back of the group.

"Oh, yeah," Jackson replies, heaving away from the wall with his hands out as he moves casually forward, making me tense. "I wouldn't wanna mess up your fancy clothes. Goin' to a wedding today, boys? Whose dad's gettin' remarried for the third time, huh?"

"Marcus, let's go," I say, turning back and gently grabbing his wrist. "We need to talk."

"That's for damn sure." His furious glare turns to me now as the guys chortle obnoxiously behind him, nudging each other as they watch us. "What the hell are you doing here?"

"Nothing," I answer, eager to defuse this situation. "I was looking for you."

"My, my. How things quickly change."

I turn to glare back at Jackson, whose eyes are startlingly focused on me now, his lips turning up into a teasing sneer.

"Ready to run back to your boyfriend already?"

Before my anger can continue to rise, my eyes land on Danny's figure behind Jackson, hugging close to the wall, looking halfway between joining him and trying to stay out of Marcus's line of sight.

"Why don't you stay out of it?" I bite back at Jackson as I step toward the street, anxious to pull Marcus away before any of them can come close to getting into a fight again. "I know my love life is of great interest to you, but I don't care to deal with your commentary today."

I tug Marcus's wrist harder to lead him across the street.

He thankfully follows as I drag him in the direction of his car, which I now see is parked along the side of the street across the way. The boys eventually follow behind us, throwing some last petty insults at Jackson, who meanwhile is focused only on Marcus and me.

"Maybe take a hint this time, buddy."

Marcus turns at Jackson's parting words, but I drag him farther, not stopping until we've reached his pale green Buick. I grab the keys from his hand, unlock the door, and climb into the passenger seat.

Marcus and I don't speak until he's driven us back to his house, where the guys jump out of the back and head around the side of the large white stone Colonial, probably toward the pool, whistling and oohing back at us as they go. I gnash my teeth together and fight the urge to roll my eyes.

I remain quiet, still fuming over the audacity of Jackson Lowell to assume he knows anything about me and my relationship. What right does he have to butt into my business? It's not "running back to my boyfriend" if Marcus is... well, *my boyfriend*. How can he paint me as some stuck-up snob when all I've done is try to prevent a pointless fight from breaking out? He should be thanking me for getting him out of trouble again, given what I just heard about his recent trouble with the sheriff. Standing there like he knows everything, like he's some saint when—

"Addy?"

I startle as I look over at Marcus, who is staring at me with widened eyes, waiting for me to talk.

"Oh. Sorry, yes, I'm... Marcus, we need to talk about what happened last night."

"Christ, Addy, what's gotten into you? You've been a complete rag this summer and now you're off running all around town with a bunch of nobodies?"

My gaze stays focused on the raspberry slushie in the cup holder beside me, watching the water pooling down the sides of the plastic cup.

"Is this what you're like all the time?"

"What?"

I look up at him now, into his confused squint, willing my voice to be firm.

"Do you treat Danny like that when you're at school too?"

Marcus's face sinks as he leans back in his seat, rolling his eyes. "Seriously? That's what this is all about?"

"Yes."

"God, Addy, you know none of those lowlifes would ever concern themselves with you, right?"

"I'm not talking about them, Marcus. I'm talking about *you*. *You're* my boyfriend, and I'm a little thrown off that you're acting like a completely different person."

He is the one keeping his eyes off me now, his brow furrowed as he stares down at his knees, his thumbs tapping against the steering wheel.

"Or is this how you've always been and I'm seeing it for the first time?"

I turn away when he looks up at me. The silence hangs heavy, and I hear that voice in my head again.

Now's the time. Say it. Get it over with already. It will be bad for only a second...

"I'm sorry, alright? Is that what you want me to say?"

Marcus's arm is around my shoulders as he leans in close enough for me to smell the light hint of the same cologne he's worn since he was thirteen. A scent of damp wood after a rainy day and a hint of something minty. It startles me almost as much as his arm around me does as I realize we've hardly touched each other since my last visit here.

"I would never want to hurt you or make you feel uncomfortable. And I... I know I got out of hand last night. I was totally wasted and I acted like a jerk. I'm sorry."

I stare at the sleeve of his crisp blue button-down shirt where his arm comes to rest over my shoulder and down toward the rim of the passenger window.

"Addy?"

Like a puppy. That's what I thought when we first got together. When he made my heart flutter and blood rush to my face, a giggle always on my lips. Marcus was like a puppy with wide eyes, a million-dollar smile, and he was completely obsessed with me, of all people.

I don't feel anything now. None of the giddiness that swept me off my feet when I was thirteen.

I turn to look at him, a soft smile on my lips that does the job of convincing him based on the way his shoulders relax.

"Thank you."

It's easier to say those words. To pretend. To tell myself none of this will matter, that I'll go home again in a couple months anyway. That Marcus and I will have to break up at some point before our parents push us to settle down and get married right after high school or something.

But that all can happen later. When I've figured out why I feel this way, why I'm chafing so much more than I ever have before at the idea of a possible future I wanted so badly just a couple years ago.

Ellen and my mother are right. Why cause all this drama now, why destroy something so special to me just because I have my own problems I need to reconcile with?

Marcus leans away before reaching down to clasp my hand where it lies curled up against my leg. "So we're good now?"

I interlock my fingers with his.

Later.

"Yes. We're good."

Chapter 6
Jackson

"What're your plans this summer?"

"Who're you, the school counselor?"

"Just askin' a fellow boy what he's up to with all the newfound free time."

"More like bothering a fellow boy with dumb questions," I point out as Benji and I hike up across the empty fields, the dead grass and brush glowing with the heat of the late afternoon. "A boy bothering a *man*."

"Ha!" Benji nudges me on the shoulder roughly. "Man my ass. My three and a half months' headstart makes me more of a man than you any day."

"And don't you always make sure I remember," I mutter as we reach the chain-link fence, the both of us heaving ourselves over and onto the concrete before heading back into town.

"I know what my plans are," Benji declares as we walk across the street, me flipping off the Toyota that honks at us, Benji giving them an enthusiastic wave. "Get drunk off my ass, run down Cherub Road naked at least once, learn all the lyrics of 'Johnny B. Goode,' and find the love of my life."

I chuckle humorlessly as we make our way down through the enclosed shopping center, passing wafting scents of fried food and the distant music from within clothing shops as the early evening begins. "Finding the love of your life in one summer at seventeen, huh?"

"Hey, why not? Summer romance is in. And I didn't say it had to be a woman. It could be I find a new passion, a new hobby, a new favorite special at Crazy Cups 'n' Cones."

He jolts me again on the shoulder before running past me to the open doors of the arcade. "Or a new game I can kick your ass at!"

The dim lighting of the arcade blinds me after spending all day today in the glaring sun, but the cool air is nice, and the pleasant buzzing and trilling of multiple machines creates the perfect hum of noise in my head.

Danny waves us over to where he's standing at the *Donkey Kong* machine, stepping away as we approach.

"You take over, Benji, I'm shit."

"Gladly!" Benji doesn't waste a second sliding into place behind the controls, easily rescuing Danny's poor attempts at guiding the Jumpman up and over the obstacles to rescue his damsel from the ravenous gorilla. Danny and I go get some sodas as Benji proceeds to beat his own high score for the third time.

"How'd the rest of your sentence go?" I ask him.

"Alright. I snatched a copy of *The Sword and the Sorcerer*. Maybe we could all have a movie night at Ted's."

"As much as I don't envy you being a slave to the system, I do admire your ability to pay for all our shit."

Danny rolls his eyes as he plunks down a few dollars for our sodas, grabbing his Coke while I carry mine and Benji's back to the *Donkey Kong* machine.

"So what's up with that chick from last night?" Benji asks, his eyes still focused on the screen, his hands maneuvering the controls without any rhyme or reason, still translating to flawless jumps as he racks up a bundle of points. "You get her number?"

I don't know who he's talking to until Danny shakes his head as he leans against the side of the machine. "Nope."

"No? Shit, me either. I think if I asked that curly-haired one, she would have kneed me in the nuts."

I look between the two of them, the straw of my Coke frozen halfway to my lips. "You talkin' about those rich girls Marcus and Deran were runnin' with last night?"

Danny nods. "They're nice people, Jackson."

Now my soda drops completely away from my mouth as I lean my head back in disbelief, a laugh choking from my throat. "Danny, tell me you're not that stupid. Please, do me the biggest favor and tell me that."

"Addy stood up for me to her own boyfriend, and in front of all those people at the diner."

Addy.

See, this is why Danny needs someone like me. Without Benji and me, the poor guy'd probably be dead by now with how laughably naive he is.

"Let me tell ya something, Danny." I wait until he looks up at me, his face alight with the glow of the game screen as Benji continues his campaign without a flinch. "Girls like that enjoy an occasional tumble around town with the 'bad boys.' The guys from the wrong side of the track. The poor bums, like you, me, and Benji."

"Hey!"

"Shut up, Benji. Now listen, I'm serious." I step around Benji until I'm standing in front of Danny, my free hand grasping his shoulder. "Those girls want trouble, and nothing more. You saw how big of a scene she made last night 'defending' you? And now she's hangin' around you all day today, waitin' for her boyfriend to show up and catch you bein' all friendly so she can play the tragic heroine again?"

Danny rolls his eyes. "Jackson, it wasn't like that, if you'd just talk to her without accusing her—"

"I've talked to her all I need to. I *know* everything I need to. She's nothing but a bored little rich girl who wants to be a damsel caught between a bunch of fighting boys. And you don't need that crap."

Instead of agreeing with me, stubborn bastard that he is, Danny raises his brows, unimpressed.

"And why are you saying that?"

I squint at him. "What?"

"Are you saying that because she's 'one of them'? A rich girl? A girl from the right side of the tracks? If so, then that makes you just as bad as them."

I know he doesn't mean it like that, so I don't get too angry. But I still can't help but want to rip at my hair in frustration at this boy's stupidity.

"Ah, leave him alone, Jackson," Benji chimes in, still clanging away at the game. "The gals were alright."

"Am I the only one in this group who sees reason anymore?" I ask helplessly.

"No. And watch it before you spill that soda I just paid for." Danny nudges at my arms that had swung open in exasperation, chuckling with Benji.

"Fine, don't listen to me." I shrug, irritated with the whole topic, finally taking a large swig of my Coke. "Enjoy your time sucked into a torrid love affair."

"It's not like that, Jackson," Danny tries to assure me. "We're friends."

"Uh-huh, we'll see how long that lasts."

"Whoo!" Benji jumps as he bumps his fist into the air, the screen flashing with a new high score. "BeejzNutz kicks the ass of every other schmuck in town once again."

"You've gotta change that name." I shake my head as the name Benji chose for himself four years ago blinks tauntingly on the screen before our eyes.

"Hell no. I've built up a reputation here, Jackson. Those letters strike fear into the hearts of my would-be usurpers. This is a name of intimidation."

"It's a nut joke that wasn't even funny when we were kids."

"You laughed," Danny reminds me as he stands behind me, sipping innocently at his soda.

Maybe this kid does need to get his ass kicked.

"Both you pansies get the hell outta my way." I slam my soda into Benji's hand as I shove him away from the machine. "I'm about to blow both your nuts off, *Beejz*."

"You still use the same name too," Danny points out. "*theJackSon3*. Brings back memories."

"Memories of this dumbass trying to get us to call ourselves that," Benji says as he butts his shoulder against mine.

"I did *not*."

"You definitely did," Danny laughs.

"Will the both of you shut up? You always say I never win 'cause I suck, when we all know you two intentionally sabotage me."

I don't beat Benji's high score. I use up most of my spare change to try, but I swear he has cheat codes he's not telling us, even though I've watched him without blinking several times. If he does have a cheat, he's sneaky about it. I also might have arthritis in my hands or something, because there is no way a human can maneuver their fingers over the controls like that so quickly and still execute perfect moves every time.

It's one thing Danny and I can agree on.

Danny gets us some fries and chicken tenders and we head over to the Skee-Ball station next. The one game Danny is good at, and I'm still shit.

"The boy has talent, charm, and a half-decent haircut in the year of our God, 1982," Benji narrates in a dramatic announcer's voice as he and I stand off to the side munching on the chicken and fries while Danny shoots score after score, ignoring us. "Will he make it to the Olympic finals? Time will only tell."

"One thing's for sure," I add in my equally dramatic commentator's voice, "the small town of Greydon, California, isn't ready to discover the secret weapon that is their very own Danny Macklin, a superstar living right under their noses for sixteen years..."

We go on like that, even though it doesn't break Danny's concentration. And we're close to finishing all of the food he bought for us without him before Benji nudges me pointedly.

"*Wha?*" I growl in annoyance, looking over at him as I chow down on the second-to-last chicken piece. But his eyes are directed somewhere across the room without an ounce of humor. He nods.

I turn my head to follow his gesture. And I briefly regret shoveling down all that food.

It's not that the sight itself makes me sick to my stomach. It probably should. That's how you should react when you're watching your girlfriend curling herself around another guy while he's shooting baskets at the Pop-a-Shot stand in the corner.

Because Brenda's not my girlfriend. Who even talks about that stuff anymore? We met outside the drive-in theater. I thought she was cute, she thought I was cute. We started hooking up. Not meeting over a cup of coffee or an overpriced dinner and waxing poetic about what we *mean* to each other.

It's seeing her that makes me feel sick. I didn't want to have to deal with this shit again. Plenty of girls have moved on from me to something else, and I have no problem with it. I really don't. I don't even need them to tell me. Never seeing a girl again is a million times less embarrassing than being told to your face that you've reached your expiration date.

Never running into each other again is preferable. Unfortunately, in a town like Greydon, far from likely.

I know she's already seen me by now, given the usual loudness that accompanies Danny, Benji, and me whenever we're together. But I still reel inside when Brenda leans her head over, her dark brown hair tumbling over her bare shoulders as her hazel-tinted eyes gaze across the Skee-Ball machines at me.

I don't look away though. No way am I that cowardly. No, I look right back at her. Let her know that I know. That I don't care. That it didn't mean anything to me either, so she doesn't have to gloat or feel guilty or whatever she might have been feeling. Or maybe she doesn't care either.

I hope she doesn't care either.

Everyone's quiet. I hate when things are quiet. Quiet makes me feel like I should be sleeping. And I know Danny and Benji aren't speaking because they feel awkward, or they're waiting for me to say something about Brenda.

"Fuck, I'm *bored*!" I exclaim into the quiet as we walk through the dark, along the road toward Benji's house. "There's nothing to do in this damn town."

Part of why I ran away from New York to California is I thought I'd find something different. Turns out I stumbled into an even smaller town than the one I grew up in, and this time with the absence of the city nearby which could offer something of interest every now and then.

And still I stayed here. Maybe I'm insane.

"I'm gonna head home," Danny says quietly, sounding tired. "Got work early tomorrow."

"I'm hittin' the hay too," Benji sighs, picking up his pace as the darkened house comes into view, the front porch still nearly rotted through and tilting to the side. "My folks are out tonight, maybe I'll get some sleep for once."

Danny and I wave him off before continuing on toward the tree line to the trailer park by the creek.

"I'm gonna crash at Ted's tonight," I decide, still uncomfortable with the silence hanging over us. "Don't wanna walk all the way back to Ward's." Danny nods, keeping his gaze down. The silence returns, aside from the gentle crunch of grass beneath our feet.

"Are you..."

Danny trails off, and now I decide the talking is worse than the silence. I really don't want him to finish that sentence.

"I'm goin' to the movies tomorrow to see that new John Carpenter alien thing they're playing. Wanna go?"

"I have work."

"You don't have to make up the excuses." I nudge him jokingly. "I know you're too scared to see it."

Danny at least smiles at that. And he doesn't say anything until we reach the creek, stepping across the rocks to get to the large patch of grass dotted with trailer homes strewn throughout the open space beneath the trees.

We wave good-night and I jog over toward Ted's trailer tucked under a couple of larger trees, their branches hanging so low that the leaves drape over the roof, yellow lights glowing through the cracks in the blinds covering the windows.

I rap on the door and wait about five seconds before Ted is pulling open the rickety thing, a beer in his hand as he looks down at me with unsurprised eyes.

"Can I crash?" I ask, bouncing on the balls of my feet, eager to get inside so I don't have to keep standing out here on the grass, looking up at him like a lost dog begging for food. He nods and steps aside.

Ted's house is a lot bigger on the inside than it looks on the outside. That's because he's one of the most organized people I know. If I lived in this place, or Ward, or Benji, we'd never keep it as clean as Ted does.

I swipe a beer off the counter as I pass through the small kitchen, and Ted takes it back out of my hands before I can make my way to the couch.

It's pointless to argue with him about it. Ted may let anyone who needs it crash at his place, but he's never once let anyone underage drink under his roof. "You don't need to become a drunk like me when you're still a kid" is his response every time. Never mind that I've been drinking beers since I was nine.

But I'm too tired to bite back tonight, so I kick my shoes off and splay myself out on the couch, closing my eyes under the dim glow of the lamp bulbs.

"Rough day?" Ted calls out from somewhere, shuffling around in the back bedroom. It's not in a sarcastic or condescending way, though it probably should sound like it coming from a guy who just spent over eight hours in the ninety-degree weather today cutting grass, pulling weeds, and clearing away tree foliage all over town.

He says it like someone who knows being seventeen can be just as exhausting as all that.

"No," I grumble back, already feeling sleep weighing over me as I sink into the stiff couch. "Just... a lot."

I hear Ted's laugh echoing distantly as I slip into unconsciousness. "Sometimes summers are tougher than being in school."

Chapter 7
Addy

"Two for *E.T.*, please."

I take the two tickets the girl sitting behind the booth hands to me, giving one to Lorry before we head into the lobby. Lorry stops us at the snack counter to get herself an extra-large tub of popcorn that's bigger than her, making me carry her large Coke and extra-large Nestle Crunch bar. We casually stroll to the back hallway, looking around to make sure no one is watching before we quickly slide into the theater about to start *The Thing*.

"For someone so smart, you're gonna give yourself a heart attack before you turn thirty," I tell Lorry as she jumps down into her seat, several pieces of popcorn trickling from her enormous bucket that she can't even see the screen over.

"We could all die at any moment, Addy," she informs me, setting the bucket on the floor between our seats as she heaves up her gigantic Coke and takes a gratifying sip. "I'm not gonna go through life not partaking in the biggest popcorn and soda I can get just because I'm afraid of death."

I don't have an argument for her, so I plop down beside her, giving a quick scan of the mostly empty theater. There's an older guy sitting a few rows ahead of us, and someone toward the back I saw when we came in, otherwise we're alone.

"People really are choosing *E.T.* over this," Lorry drones in disapproval as we watch an ad for Laffy Taffy glowing on the screen.

"You haven't seen it yet," I laugh as I take a few pieces of popcorn from the mammoth pile. "It could suck."

"Doubtful. People will always choose something safe over the unknown."

"Some people get nightmares. Like some people watching *Invasion of the Body Snatchers* when they were eight years old."

Lorry turns to give me a look. "That was unrelated. You know Mom cooked that terrible fish fry that night. It's a wonder I got one hour of sleep."

"Mm-hm."

The theater gets darker and the movie begins. And, as usual, Lorry is right. It most certainly is not for the *E.T.* crowd. It's filled with the gore and the animatronics and all of that, but also paranoia and deception and human fear and panic at its finest. Fear of the unknown, just as Lorry had said.

She's burned through all her Coke, the entire chocolate bar, and her share of the popcorn bucket by the time the credits roll and the lights go up.

"Told ya," she says without having to know my reaction.

"You don't even like movies," I point out as I stand up to gather my things. "How are you always more intuitive than me about this stuff?"

"I appreciate *art*. Just because I don't spend every waking moment watching ridiculous sex comedies, or muscle-man action flicks, or people getting dismembered on screen doesn't mean I can't appreciate a well-made..."

I don't hear the rest of what she says. Instead, I'm caught half crouched over my seat, my mouth slightly open as I stare into the face of the person who had been sitting toward the back row.

Jackson Lowell doesn't look surprised to see me looking at him. He must have recognized me when I came in.

I look away before Lorry can notice me staring at some random stranger, sitting back in my seat and pretending to look for something in my purse. Lorry stays seated; she likes to watch all the way through to the end of the credits, and it gives me time to get myself together again.

But why should I? Who cares that Jackson Lowell caught me sneaking into an R-rated movie? Everyone does that. Why should I care that he had a perfect view of me this entire time? It's not like he spent the last two hours staring at the back of my head. He may be a creep, but I'm sure he's not *that* level of ridiculous.

When the screen goes blank, Lorry hops up with the big empty popcorn bucket filled with the candy wrapper and soda cup and we head toward the back exit. My eyes go straight to where Jackson had been sitting, even though I spent the past several minutes telling myself I would keep my eyes straight down and march toward the door.

He's not there.

"I'm getting something from Roller Dollar, then I'm meeting Berry and Tina at the arcade," Lorry tells me as we pause outside the movie house, putting her long, frizzy brown hair up into a ponytail as we're baked in the afternoon heat.

"I thought you hated them," I say, recalling Lorry's tale from a week ago about her Greydon crowd of acquaintances. "You said Tina thinks she's in an intense romantic relationship with Jesus, and that Berry's political beliefs are a result of 'the small mind of a small-towner.'"

How twelve-year-olds get into conversations with each other about religion and politics over summer break is beyond me.

Lorry rolls her eyes in resignation as she heads toward the sidewalk. "Sometimes stupidity is the most interesting interaction available. Plus Mom kicked me out of the house for the day and the renovations at the town library are annoying me. See ya later."

"Bye."

I didn't particularly have any plans for the rest of today myself. But Mom is having one of her friends over at the house, so she won't love to see me back there so early. And it will no doubt lead to more questions about Marcus that I am not prepared to discuss.

I normally would be with Marcus right now. It's what I would do with most of my free time here, but especially when I didn't have anything to do. Going over to his house was second nature. Hanging out in the huge game room, or out in his yard by the pool, or in his dad's study, which was the exact picture of what a *study* in a fancy mansion looked like in movies.

I'm not going there now. Because I might break up with Marcus if we're alone again. Or because I might not.

I glance across the street before I can decide on a way to go, spotting the figure standing there before I can pretend I didn't.

Jackson Lowell is leaning against the gate to the small water park across the street from the movie theater. *Water park* is a generous term for a cement circle with only two water spouts, but it's attracted a good group of kids all crowding around to get some relief from the heat.

He's staring at me again. And I look back as I shift uncomfortably on my feet, unable to find an excuse to stop.

There's a bandana around his head again, pulling the hair back from his face so that I can see that his expression isn't angry or annoyed or smug or anything I've come to expect whenever he looks at me. Instead, he appears to be waiting patiently at the gate, looking unbothered. Waiting for me to do something. To go to him. To acknowledge him. Maybe to make a decision.

I tear my eyes away, trying and failing to look as casual as him as I glance around the street, acting as if I hadn't noticed him, before walking away from the theater, down in the opposite direction.

I don't look back for a few long seconds, then glance uncertainly over my shoulder to see Jackson walking away from the gate the opposite way. I don't know why the sight makes me feel disappointed. And I don't know why I wish I had said something to him.

***

"What is your favorite movie, Danny?"

"*It Happened One Night.*"

My eyes scan the shelf of old black-and-white movies in front of me, searching and searching until the yellow-printed title jumps out at me.

"Clark Gable. I remember this. They play it on TV sometimes."

"I never understood why people don't like black-and-white movies anymore," Danny sighs as he heaves up a box of returns onto the counter while I continue to peruse the classics section. "Do people really find different color shades to be the most entertaining thing about films?"

"*Target Earth* has always been one of my favorites."

"Huh?"

"Nothing." I shake my head, walking up to the shelf beside the counter where Danny is sorting through the small pile of this morning's returns. "You still interested in learning guitar?"

His eyes go wide as he lifts the small stack of teen sex comedies and walks them to the back wall. "Oh... you don't have to—"

"I want to," I assure him, resting my chin on my hands as I lean against the noir shelf. "I told you, I've got nothing to do this summer. And I don't want to waste all this valuable free time."

"You will waste it cooped up in a beat-up trailer home for hours every day trying to teach me how to hold a tune."

"I promise you it will be more interesting than anything I can come up with right now."

It really is something I want to do. Not just because I'm avoiding my problems. It's because I like Danny. I like that he feels the same way about music as I do. And I can't imagine not knowing how to play it, so I'll be damned if I leave here at the end of the summer without having passed at least a bit of knowledge to him.

Danny turns to me slowly, unable to hide the eager expression on his face as he bites back a grin, leaning an arm up on the opposite side of the noir shelf in front of me.

"If we're gonna do it, we should sit outside. By the creek. I'm sure I'll make all my neighbors' ears bleed, but maybe the sound of the water will cover it up."

I grin back in triumph. "You're on."

I move back around the shelf toward the counter, fishing through the rack of sour candy snacks for something to get Lorry as an apology for making her sit through *Two Thousand Maniacs!* last night.

"I wanted to ask you something." Danny turns to me again as I examine a large box of Pop Rocks.

"Yeah?"

"So... there's this bar, Johnny-Jay's, that Ted's buddy from high school owns. There's gonna be a big party this weekend, live music and all that. I thought you and your friend might wanna come?"

I know Johnny-Jay's only from the familiar sight of the hanging sign that looks like it's from an 1800s saloon and the bulky, old-fashioned brick building that takes up a chunk of the block at the end of its street. It's not a spot Marcus and his friends frequent, so I've never been inside. But I've noticed the upbeat music and the decent crowds pouring in and out of the constantly swinging front doors some nights when a band is playing and a party is swinging.

In other words, exactly the sort of scene that sounds enticing right now.

"I'd love to."

The sun is going down as I head toward the road leading to the edge of town. A breeze picks up, kicking around the brush along the sides of the road that slowly turn from the old-style buildings of the center of town to the sprawling, dead-looking fields that reach toward the hills miles away.

Laughter rings out from somewhere near a closed-down garage, laughter that sounds like it's coming from a group of boys. For a moment, I worry it's Marcus and the others, until rationalizing that they would never be caught dead hanging around a run-down garage on the outskirts of town.

I stay on the other side of the street as I approach, seeing a group of three boys who look a couple years older than me circling someone almost too short for me to see standing beside a fallen bicycle on the ground.

The little boy, who can't be more than ten years old, looks resigned as he attempts to push through the taller boys around him who easily push him back into the center of their little circle, knocking the red baseball cap from his head.

A boy with stringy hair and a leering grin that shows off a flash of a silver tooth, shoves the little boy from the back of his shoulders hard enough for him to fall to the ground.

"C'mon, ya little nerd." The taller one of the group with a tattered biker jacket and a widow's peak leans down over the young boy. "I know you've got more money on ya than that."

"I gave you everything!" the boy insists, choosing to stay on the ground when the two other boys loom over him. "My parents only gave me five bucks for the arcade!"

"Bullshit, freak. How'd you get this new ride?" The sneering boy with the silver tooth kicks the bike on the ground so roughly, one of the handles clanks loose.

"It's not mine!" the boy shouts, diving toward the bike until one of the boys leaps in front of his path, kicking him back. "It's my brother's!"

At first, I think it must be a joke. Three older boys all teaming up on a ten-year-old to steal his arcade money? How could anyone over the age of thirteen be that pathetic? But as I watch the three fully grown boys surround the small boy who is not getting out of this without either his bike destroyed, the rest of his money stolen, or a black eye, I realize this is actually happening before my eyes.

I stand like a complete fool, frantically trying to work out how I could do anything to help without either getting myself in trouble with the questionable-looking group of miscreants or making it worse for the boy.

"Still lookin' for lunch money to swipe, Criston?"

The group across the street and I turn at the voice that comes from the brush surrounding the garage.

Jackson Lowell emerges from the trees, as if he'd risen from the field itself, his boots thunking against the dead grass, a cigarette in his mouth that he throws to the ground and crushes under his foot. He walks up to the group at a purposeful stride, anger glinting in his deep brown eyes as he approaches the silver-toothed boy who he easily has a foot in height over.

"Beat it, Lowell," the other boy growls as his two cronies back him up. "Your little friends aren't here this time. I'll knock your teeth out."

"Remember last time I heard that threat?" Jackson asks as the little boy shuffles up quietly from the ground, shoving his cap back on and scooping up his bike to ride away as the group aims their focus on Jackson, who looks unbothered by the troublesome three-to-one odds. "I think it was when I threw your gangly buddy into the river and you tripped over your own feet trying to sock me across the face and ended up almost knockin' your own teeth out. I'm ready to take my chances."

"You think you're real funny, don't ya?" one of the boys standing in the back huffs, straightening out his fists, flipping his cargo jacket dramatically.

Jackson shrugs. "I've been told."

The silver-toothed boy lunges forward, and my hands fly to my face as Jackson catches him easily, the both of them tumbling to the ground. The two other boys stand there, noticeably steering back from the brawl, but cheering their leader on... even as Jackson rolls over on top of him, swinging his fist to crack into the other boy's face before leaping to his feet, prancing backward a few paces with a grin on his face as he watches the boy roll around on the grass, disoriented as he tries to stand up.

"Alright there, Shelly?" Jackson asks, light on his feet as he circles the stringy-haired boy, looking nothing but delighted while I stand watching like a scandalized 1940s housewife across the street, wondering why I don't keep walking. "Looks like I caught ya a little fast there. Should I slow down a bit?"

"You bastard!"

The taller boy with the biker jacket lunges at him next, but he isn't well coordinated. Jackson easily swipes his foot out from under him and sends him sprawling to the ground with a kick to his chest.

"The reason you never beat me, Shelly, is because you guys never go for it all at once," Jackson comments, making me want to strangle him. I'd been thinking the same thing, but why would he be so stupid as to give up such an obvious advantage?

The last guy finally runs forward, aiming a clumsy, but ultimately successful punch across Jackson's jaw. Jackson is thrown off for only a quick moment, his focus realigning despite the purple bloom already rising on his face as the boy tackles him against the side of the garage.

The leader, Shelly as Jackson had called him, finally crawls up from the ground, joining his friend in trying to pin Jackson against the wall, throwing his arm out to a painful-looking strike against his ribs.

I gasp, turning sharply to prepare to run back toward town and find somewhere to call the police as Jackson drops to the ground against the barrage of strikes and kicks being pummeled into his body. But he's even fooled me this time as he rolls out from under the attack, jumping back onto his feet, grinning against the small trickle of blood coming from his nose as he reaches into his back pocket. Something shiny glints in his hand as he backs toward the tree line. Something that clicks, revealing a tiny orange flame that springs from the lighter he had grabbed from his pocket.

"I have a way more fun idea," he says as the three boys clamber toward him, eyeing the lighter with confusion. "Why don't I set this whole place on fire? Shit, it'd go up in less than a minute, don't ya think?"

"What the hell are you playin' at, Lowell?" Shelly spits.

"I'm just thinkin', who do ya think Sheriff Nulty will blame for the old Harrison garage burnin' down? Can you afford another round in juvie? Or wait... you might get thrown down to the real prison, huh? I know it's hard for you to notice, but you ain't no kid anymore, Criston."

Shelly's eyes flick toward Jackson's face and the lighter in his hands. "You wouldn't do it. He'd know you were down here too."

"Probably." Jackson shrugs, hovering the lighter over the pile of discarded car parts and dry brush lingering along the side of the run-down garage. "What d'ya think, Criston? Shall we go down together?"

As much as this Shelly Criston person wants to appear to be tough, it looks like the thought of real prison trouble has him and his friends suddenly apprehensive.

"You're fuckin' crazy, Lowell," he growls before he and the other two back away, heading toward the street before turning and running off across to the other side of the road. I go to step out of the way, but they don't notice me as they hop the chain-link fence on the other side and disappear.

I turn back to Jackson, who watches them go, the grin still plastered on his face as he clicks the lighter off and shoves it back into his pocket. "And you're a dipshit for thinkin' I'd ever go to jail for you."

I don't know if he sees me. I'm not exactly hidden. I feel like a moron, standing here on the street watching a group of absolute idiots kill each other and possibly start a wildfire. But Jackson's eyes now move toward the interior of the garage. The boy with the red baseball cap has been hiding himself there this entire time, his eyes wide as he looks at Jackson, his arms and legs still poised on the bike as if he's ready to dash away any second.

"What're you doin'? Get the hell outta here, little man." Jackson nods at him. "And stop givin' that dickwad all your money. You see what a pussy he is."

The boy nods, his mouth hanging open and his eyes still wide as saucers as he hops firmly back onto the bike and turns away from the garage, riding back onto the street and toward town.

As the sound of the wheels crunching against the gravelly street fills the growing silence, I turn away and walk briskly in the other direction, not turning to see if Jackson notices me or not.

Chapter 8
Jackson

I'm never up this early. Technically I'm usually awake at three a.m., but never prepared to be out in an area inhabited by other living beings.

My ribs and my face were aching like a bitch all night so I couldn't sleep anyway, and for whatever reason, an ice-cold chocolate shake at Roller Dollar sounded like just what I needed.

Therefore, here I am sitting in the old 1950s-aesthetic diner in a sickeningly turquoise-colored sticky booth at an equally sticky table, with a bruised face and a medium-sized glass of sugar and further headaches before me.

Worth it to see Shelly Criston cower thinking I'd be stupid enough to burn down an abandoned garage... I think. Ask me when I don't feel like my skull is outgrowing my skin and my eyeballs are about to eject from my head like some messed-up *Scanners* display.

The boys aren't up yet, or anyone remotely in my age range, since most kids are sane and sleep in on summer mornings when finally nothing is expected of us. But to be honest, it's nice to have a breath of fresh air when I don't have to talk to anybody, explain why I look like I rammed my face into a brick wall, and why I'm sucking down a chocolate milkshake like a dying man at 8:45 in the morning.

As it turns out, my trip to the diner this morning was a stroke of fate. As I exit the gaudy joint, the thumping hum of Buddy Holly thankfully fading from my ears as I let the glass door swing shut behind me, I see none other than Miss Uppity herself strolling across the street, looking determined.

I hadn't got the chance to talk to her last night when she ran off after enjoying the show of my brawl with Shelly because I was too damn tired. I'm too tired now, but what the hell?

I jog across the street from the diner, shoving my shades on my face and ignoring the car horns blaring at me until I'm at the sidewalk and keeping along with her stride.

She gives no indication that she sees me, her eyes pointed straight ahead as she walks faster.

"Where are we goin?"

"Why do you care?"

I swing around in front of her as we turn a corner at the edge of the sidewalk, leaning against the chain-link fence. She reels to a stop before she can run into me, crossing her arms and swallowing back what I hope would have been a pointed swear.

"Maybe I just wanna know."

She finally looks at me, unimpressed. "Maybe you should just go away."

I don't move. I can't help but grin at her disgustingly annoyed expression. She looks like she wants to smack me.

"Will you please just—"

"How come I've never seen you around here before?"

She cocks her head, a smirk beginning to play on her lips. Now we're getting somewhere.

"Why are you talking to me? I thought I was some spoiled little brat you don't want hanging around you and your precious gang of misunderstood castaways."

I bite my tongue, considering her. "I'm still tryin' to figure that out."

"Oh, by all means, I'm at your mercy, then," she huffs humorlessly. "Do take your time to figure out exactly what you think about me, someone you met a couple days ago, and let me know what your conclusion is. I'll be on the edge of my seat waiting to hear it."

"Ah, come on, don't get offended. If you wanna hang around the people in Danny's crowd, you've gotta get some thicker skin."

She glares at me. Opens her mouth to say something, then decides against it. She walks around me, stepping out into the street before resuming her trek.

"Alright," I groan, turning and following behind her. "I was a dick. I can be like that. Don't take it personally, I'm not nice to anyone."

"Charming."

"Look, maybe I was wrong about you, alright?" I relent, jogging up alongside her again. She walks *fast*, even in these ridiculous heeled sandal things she's got on. "Danny's been tellin' me you've been cool, and... look, it was pretty bitchin' to see you put your dumbass boyfriend in his place that night, alright? There, you got it outta me."

"Oh, I'm so pleased!" she exclaims sarcastically. "I did it just for you. God forbid Jackson Lowell doesn't think I'm the coolest chick on the block."

Despite her gibe, I can't help but laugh. Something strange goes through my chest when I hear her say my full name, as if she's known me for years while I had no idea of this girl's existence until a few nights ago. Normally I'd be annoyed, even paranoid that someone might know more about me while they're a complete stranger to me. Instead, with her... with Addy... it's exciting.

Like a game. Something between her and me.

"So... *The Thing*."

"What about it?" she asks, her tone distracted as she glances around the street before we cross toward the small bridge that leads across one of the many empty chasms around here that used to be a creek at some point.

"Pretty good, right?"

"Yeah."

"I never met a chick who was into horror. I don't think I ever saw you jump once."

She gives a quick, exasperated sigh, looking as if she's heard that one before. "Oh, please. I've seen stuff that would give you night terrors."

"Are you kiddin'? I'm the horror king around this town. Who do you think came up with the name for Cropsy Park?"

I can barely catch the smile she tries to hide.

"Why *are* you talking to me anyway?" she asks as we step off the other side of the bridge. I adjust my sunglasses, which are doing their dutiful job of blocking out the sun from worsening my migraine. "Trying to figure out my motives for corrupting your poor innocent friend?"

"I think you're interesting," I tell her, recalling the shock I'd felt at seeing her waltz into an R-rated movie yesterday that she had obviously snuck into, at seeing her stand up to her dipshit boyfriend even when she was all alone and surrounded by his friends. "And unexpected."

"How flattering." Her smirk vanishes into a somber frown as we walk at a somewhat normal pace along the road, down toward one of the nice neighborhoods. Not Mansion Row, but not a place you'd ever catch me hanging around. "You're kind of unexpected too." She turns to look at me and it startles me, making me grateful for the shades mostly covering my face as her piercing eyes dig into me. "That was nice of you. What you did for that boy last night."

I let out a careless chuckle. "Shit. By all means, sweetheart, put me on a pedestal for something, but anything other than that. Shelly Criston and his merry band of morons could get taken down by a horde of squirrels."

"You didn't have to do it," she continues. "But you did."

This conversation's turning way too corny for me.

"So you got a little sister?"

She's quiet at the change of subject, and I wonder if she's not going to answer.

"Yes."

"She's into gory movies too, huh?"

"She'd probably rat me out if I didn't take her along to sneak into R-rated movies. My friend Ellen usually doesn't want to go, so she's my best bet while I'm here."

While she's here. So she is visiting. Makes sense, if she's staying in the rental cottages outside of town. Why anyone would want to spend their summer visiting Greydon, California, is forever beyond my comprehension. It doesn't bode well for Addy's competence, which is already questionable if she's hanging around Marcus Tanner. But she's probably at the mercy of delusional rich parents, which isn't her fault.

"You get along?"

"Sure." Addy shrugs, her eyes staying on the sidewalk, which has become a lot smoother as we enter the realm of white picket fences and perfectly polished vehicles lined up alongside finely manicured lawns. "She likes to act like she's the older sibling most of the time... but sometimes I need that."

I nod, not realizing the quiet that takes over when she's done talking. When I've begun to disappear into my own head. When her words inexplicably turn my thoughts toward a memory, a memory from so long ago, I was certain I'd finally forgotten about it.

A memory of the girl I used to sit with in a cluttered backyard. A girl I used to hold hands with. A girl I used to talk with about everything.

"I used to always want a kid brother when I was younger," I say, keeping my tone the same as before as I chase the memory away with words before it can fully form again. "Mostly because I wanted an excuse to be able to push someone around."

Addy rolls her eyes again. "A stereotypical sibling concept."

"It wasn't like that when I got older though. After a while, I thought it might be nice to have someone like that. Someone always on your side that you can team up against your parents with."

I turn to see her looking at me as we walk. Like she's waiting for me to say more.

I pull my jacket closer to my neck, despite the rising heat as we walk beneath the hot sun. "But I don't really have any of those anyway, and now I've got Danny and Benji. And between the three of us, we give poor Ted a hell of a time. That's enough for me."

Addy stays quiet and I hate it. It makes me feel like I said something wrong, that she's thinking something about me that I'm dying not knowing. Silence makes me anxious enough, but her silence is driving me insane.

"So where are you takin' me, princess?" I huff, looking out over the rows of quiet, picture-perfect houses straight out of a suburban magazine we're strolling past. "Am I about to be jumped by a band of your khaki-wearing boy toys?"

"I'm meeting my friend at the courtyard," she answers, nodding toward a clearing up ahead between all the neatly trimmed homes.

"Oh, right." I nod. "Of course. The *courtyard*."

"Why are you still following me?" she shoots back. "Afraid Ellen and I are meeting up to plan your demise?"

"Hey, it sounds kinda hot when you say it like that," I tease, getting the immediate satisfaction of watching her blush angrily. "Maybe I want to make sure you're not luring any more unsuspecting young boys."

She halts in her tracks, whipping around to stare at me as I slow to a stop beside her.

"What is your problem? Is it because I actually like Danny and think he's a decent person and not a lazy degenerate like you?"

The insult doesn't land. She'll have to try a lot harder than that when I've been called every name under the sun by everyone I've ever met.

"Maybe you don't think you're doing anything wrong, but he'll never tell you when you treat him like an injured puppy with a terminal disease and think of yourself as the saint of the town by giving the poor kid some of your oh-so-envied attention. It makes him feel more like shit."

She blinks at me, her expression lowering as she considers my words. It's not like she can deny them. I know how she works.

"You may not be as nasty or as outright stupid as your boyfriend, but you're just as delusional," I continue, not caring to spare her feelings. "Sorry to tell you that your generosity comes off a bit condescending when you have to make a big deal out of taking a guy you see as a tragic lost cause under your wing like you know anything about the world."

She stiffens slightly, her arms crossing over her chest again.

"Condescending, huh?"

"You heard me."

"Hm. Like calling people 'sweetheart' and 'princess' like you're their father?"

My mouth hangs open for a few seconds and I lean back on my heels. I allow a laugh to grunt from my chest as I look out into the field of silent houses surrounding us like sharks.

"I actually don't have a defense for that one. Touché."

She doesn't exactly look triumphant, but she does give me a pointed nod before she continues walking.

I keep following.

"So you were in jail?"

It's not a payback question. Not the way she asks it. More like she's making casual discussion. I guess I'd be curious about the same thing.

"In and out."

She gives me a look.

"What, it's true! Holding cells count as jail."

"You've never been sent away."

"Sheriff Nutsack sent me off to a weekend at some correctional facility or whatever the hell it's called. Wasn't anything much. Kinda like school, but more boring."

"What do you do to get sent there?"

"Why? You interested?"

This time, I'm waiting for her to slap me.

"I don't know, it could be anything," I sigh. "Swiped some things from the store a few times, graffitied the park once, broke into the school to try to sneak porno tapes into the classroom VCRs."

Addy, to my shock, doesn't look surprised at any of this. "My, my. What a track record. You must be so proud."

"Jeez, you sound like the goddamn adults in this town. I'm not doin' it as a career or anything. I like to have some fun sometimes, sue me."

She doesn't look convinced. Whatever.

"You know what I think, Jackson Lowell?"

"That I'm a dangerous misfit who needs to be taught a lesson."

"You care a lot."

My beat-up boots look comical against the perfectly kept bright green grass that has to be fake as we enter the courtyard.

"What?"

She doesn't look sympathetic or pleading when I look at her. She seems as if she's just pieced together the strangest and ultimately pointless puzzle ever.

"You care a lot about people. Danny, Benji, kids getting bullied who don't deserve it. But you want everyone to think you're some scary troublemaker who's gonna burn down the town one day. You like your reputation. But it's like what happened last night."

She turns toward me, leaning up against one of the picnic benches in the center of the picturesque little park.

"You're willing to hold the lighter out knowing you'd never in a million years drop it. Because deep down, astonishingly, you're not an idiot."

I nod exaggeratedly. "Wow. Great. And how much do you want for that analysis, Doctor? I'm a modern teenage cliché."

She shrugs. "No. You're just a typical teenage boy with a slowly developed prefrontal cortex. There, did you like that fancy diagnosis?"

She looks at me like a parent waiting for their toddler to flip out and throw a tantrum in the middle of the park. But instead, I give a slight shake of my head.

"See? Interesting and unexpected."

I move closer to her. Now she begins to frown.

"You know it's not safe to hang around rowdy teenage boys with poor decision-making skills," I say, reaching to grip the sides of the wooden picnic table as I lean close to her. "Particularly *alone*."

"God, you're a pig," she sighs, using one hand to shove me backward.

"You wanna hang out tonight?"

She laughs. "And why would I do that?"

"So we could get to know each other better. Prove that you're a punk rock, horror movie–watching rebel who doesn't give a shit, rather than the picture-perfect daddy's girl you pretend to be."

Something shifts in her now. The glare she aims at me is filled with as much if not more venom than it had been in all our other interactions.

"And what makes you think I'd want to know *you*? In case you weren't paying attention, I've learned everything worth knowing."

She turns from me, shoving away from the picnic bench and marching across the court field, or whatever this *Stepford Wives*–looking place is called.

I watch her go, feeling pissed, wanting to laugh, I don't know what the hell. I refuse to focus on the lingering nudging that wants me to feel bad. To feel guilty that I struck a nerve to upset her so much. Who cares? She's cute, she may actually be my type despite all of the previous pointers I had been fixated on beforehand, but so what? She's a rich brat going through a rebellious phase.

Just as I turn to stomp back toward the shitty side of town that feels a hell of a lot less creepy than this plastic dollhouse venue, a car that had been sitting across the street pulls away violently, screeching on its wheels as it veers down the road Addy and I had come from.

The stupid green Buick I have to look at in the school parking lot every day trundles away into the distance, but not quick enough for me to not see.

I don't know what Marcus Tanner was doing down here at this hour, but he definitely saw me and Addy just now. And looks like he didn't like it.

Chapter 9
Addy

"He's such an *asshole*! God, you can tell how highly he thinks of himself, standing there in his stupid leather jacket with that stupid ring on his thumb, his sunglasses on his face, like he's some James Dean, misunderstood head case. Trying to smoke a cigarette even though he looks like he's about to accidentally swallow the damn thing. He really thinks he's something, and he says *we* walk around here thinking we're better than everybody..."

I finally trail off only because I need to take in a large inhale. Ellen sits on the bench, twirling a finger through her curly hair, watching me pace on the grass in front of her for the past ten minutes.

"That's why you needed to meet me all the way across town instead of the courtyard?" she asks calmly.

"I wasn't about to stay there with *him*!"

I walk back over to the bench, heaving myself up beside her. I lay myself back across the warm wood of the picnic table, blinking up at the violet sky dipping between the trees overhead. It's evening now. Ellen and I had spent most of the day shopping for last-minute accessories she wants to wear to the barbecue tomorrow, talking about whatever party Deran or Eddie or whoever is throwing next, interspersed with me venting about Jackson Lowell's insistence on putting a definitive black mark on my summer.

Ellen slumps down beside me. "Imagine if your mom found out you had a whole conversation with someone like Jackson Lowell."

I hum a tired laugh. "She'd never let me out of the house again." I'm already hesitant to mention someone like Danny to her.

Jackson's words come back to me again, and I can't help the sting of guilt. Does Danny feel I treat him like that? Like a sad charity case?

"He's kind of... scary, isn't he?" Ellen asks. "That could have been dangerous, you being alone with someone like that. You don't know what he could do, he could pull a knife on you or something."

I can't help the laugh that jerks through me. "Trust me, there's nothing dangerous about Jackson Lowell. Just particularly annoying teenage boy stupidity."

"How do you know?" She turns to look at me and I meet her gaze, our noses comically inches apart, as if we're ten years old again staying up late at a sleepover, gossiping under the sheet of the bed. "How do you, Addy Moreno, know anything about people like Jackson Lowell? I know Danny's okay, and that Benji guy. But Jackson doesn't seem like them."

I turn away, looking back up through the trees at the darkening sky.

Maybe I should be afraid of Jackson Lowell. He's the kind of unpredictable, unstable boy my mother and the universe itself are always warning about.

I can't tell exactly how I know he's a complete fake. Maybe because he can't hold a cigarette right. Maybe something else.

"Imagine what Marcus would say."

Ellen says it overly casual, her voice smaller.

"Ugh." I close my eyes.

"You're still mad at him? Gosh, Addy, you can't let this ruin your whole summer."

"I'm not. Just don't bring it up to him, or anyone, okay? I'm trusting you to keep this on the down-low so we can prevent any more ridiculous macho fighting."

"Oh, I won't tell another living soul, I swear."

"Hi, Ellen!"

Ellen shoots up, giving Steven Nulty the biggest smile as he saunters across the park toward us. I sit up, pulling my oversized jacket over my shoulders as a gentle breeze whispers through the trees. I don't bother to muster up a fake smile.

I also try not to roll my eyes as Steven approaches with his perfectly slicked-back hair and crisp white khaki shorts and forest green polo shirt.

I really hate Jackson Lowell.

"Hi, Steven." Ellen grins as she hops down from the picnic table, and Steven blushes as he twists his shoe awkwardly against the ground. Are they a thing? I should probably know. Or ask. But I feel suddenly exhausted by the whole thing. "Are we still all going to Deran's tonight?"

"Eddie and the guys are heading down now." Steven nods his head back toward the street where I'm guessing the car is waiting. I don't bother to look.

I catch Steven's gaze as I slip unwillingly down from the bench. We've never been awfully close. He's always preferred to get to know Ellen better. But now when he looks at me he seems uncertain about something.

"Hey, Steven," I greet him to break the awkward tension as Ellen looks between us.

"Hi. Um... Marcus was looking for you earlier. How come we haven't seen you around as much this summer?"

I shrug, trying my best not to show my annoyance. "Just busy, I guess."

My response makes no sense. What unemployed sixteen-year-old is busy during summer vacation?

He nods. "Uh... yeah. Cool. You guys ready to go?"

Ellen follows behind Steven, casting a backward glance my way when I don't immediately catch up alongside her.

I stand still. Consider staying here in the empty park alone. Until it gets all the way dark. Until I would have to walk back to the rental cottage by myself in pitch blackness. Probably a stupid idea.

So I follow.

***

My mother spends all morning fussing over me in my ridiculous outfit for the Lensen barbecue. I look like a dolled-up daughter from the prairie days off to get married in a cowshed. But it makes my mother happy that I made somewhat of an effort to dress in the stylish preppy clothes the kids wear around here. Lorry's going in jean cutoffs and a cardigan she's had since she was eight. My mother hasn't spoken to her all morning.

It's a relief when my mother has a sudden fit of panic about not having enough lemon biscuits and I'm sent out to pick up some more from the supermarket bakery. It gives me a moment to myself, a task to focus my mind on as I walk into town and purchase a container of the golden-shaded biscuits my mother will take out of the plastic container and place into a wooden cloth-lined basket after heating them up in the microwave. None of us can cook or bake well, and she's not about to try and fail in front of the biggest summer get-together in town. I don't have the heart to remind her that everyone in this town will probably know what the lemon biscuits from the Greydon Market look and taste like.

I for one am not looking forward to the rest of today one bit. Lorry and Ellen being there is the only highlight, but other than that, my mother will expect me to socialize with every one of her friends, all of them the parents of the boys I hang out with. Not to mention Marcus himself, whom I will have to continue to smile and laugh and be content with so my mother and her friends don't start suspecting that perfect little

Miss Addy Moreno isn't happy anymore with the boy she thought she'd marry when she was thirteen.

With my luck as of late, it should be no surprise to me that I run into Jackson Lowell yet again. Or see him from across the street, rather, as I step out of the supermarket.

He's standing inside the alleyway between the comic book shop and a closed-down antiques store that's up for rent. From here I can see his eyes are tired, the bruises on his face from the fight the other night only slightly lighter on his tan skin. His dark blond hair falls in messy streaks all around his head and his gray Poison T-shirt looks like it's on backward, like he blindly rolled out of bed this morning and stumbled down here after only a couple hours of sleep.

But what catches my attention the most, makes me pause and stare like a ridiculous old bitty trying to snoop, is the girl standing across from him.

She's tall, almost taller than him, with long legs, golden skin that complements her billowing silky hair, ripped-up denim shorts, and an electric blue crop top I'm instantly jealous of in this summer heat while I stand here in my ridiculous, stuffy getup.

I think that they're arguing at first. I assume she's his girlfriend. Or just a girl. I don't think Jackson Lowell has girlfriends.

But when I look closer, it looks more like a parent trying to reasonably but firmly let down her child. The girl has her arms crossed, a stern look on her sharp features, her head nodding sharply along with whatever she is saying. Something that makes Jackson look strangely stoic. He keeps his expression blank as she talks. But something's different in him. I thought he was just tired, but it's more than that. He looks... defeated.

He says something to her. Something that makes him lean forward as he speaks. Something like a desperate plea that even he looks to feel pathetic about. The girl shakes her head, appearing unfazed by it. And then she turns and walks away.

Jackson stays there, standing in the alley. From whatever just happened, I expect him to be angry. Or to shrug it off before bounding away to irritate whoever is unfortunate enough to cross his path today.

Instead, he stares at the ground, his foot kicking mindlessly at some debris on the cement before walking back through the alleyway.

And before I can ask myself if this is really the best idea I can come up with, I cross the street and follow him.

The alley comes out into a back lot lining the brick shops, where only a handful of cars are parked. I find Jackson leaning up against the wall of the back of the empty antiques store, a cigarette in his hand that he doesn't light, but instead just stares at.

He doesn't look up or react as I enter the back lot, my Mary Jane shoes crunching against the gravel. So I call out to him.

"Finally giving up pretending like you know how to smoke those?"

I expect to have one up on him, but he doesn't even flinch at my voice. Just keeps his slightly drooping eyes on the short white stick in his hand, twirling it over and over as he slumps against the wall.

"I should get you to teach me. You givin' out smoking lessons to us downtrodden too?"

I wait for regret to start flooding in for following him down here. But it doesn't. For whatever bizarre reason, it makes me feel more at ease to hear him meet my banter.

He still looks off. And I still don't know why I care.

I move closer, waiting for him to lift his head. He stays where he is.

"You seem distraught," he states, somehow gauging my complicated mood without looking at me.

My resolve sinking away, I walk the rest of the way toward him. He finally turns to look at me, and I see his brow rise in the slightest reaction of surprise as I lean against the wall beside him, staring blankly out at the grimy parking lot that reeks of cigarettes, oil, and probably urine.

"I thought I'd try to clear my head this morning."

"From what? Your boyfriend's lack of functioning brain cells?"

"From... things."

I continue staring straight ahead while he looks between me and the box of lemon biscuits in my hands. "Eatin' your feelings away?"

"I wish."

We're quiet for a moment. It's the most normal conversation we've ever had. It's the most easy I've ever felt around him.

And funny enough, it's the first time I've felt I've been able to take a breath this summer without anyone watching, anxious to read my mind and find out why I'm acting so differently.

"I thought—"

"You thought you'd come on down and teach me to puff on a cigarette like a real cowboy?" He turns against the wall to face me, tossing the unlit cigarette away into the gravel.

To my surprise, I can't help but grin as I lower my eyes to the ground. "Everything you say sounds incredibly double entendre-d."

"That says a lot more about what's on your mind than mine."

When I turn toward him, I'm surprised at how close we are. His arm rests against the wall, a small appreciative grin on his lips. His eyes flick up and down as I face him. Something about it makes me press harder into the wall.

"What are you doin' back here in this dirty lot with this getup on?"

Now I can't help but laugh humorlessly as I glance down at myself. My dark floral-patterned skirt reaches nearly to my ankles to meet the shiny black Mary Jane shoes and frilly white lace socks, and my button-down periwinkle shirt goes to my elbows, the shoulders puffed like I'm a 1930s schoolteacher, the color matching the ribbon tied in my half-pulled-up hairdo.

"We've cracked the case." I sigh, looking back up at him. "I'm subconsciously hoping I fall in a trash heap and destroy this grandma outfit. Then I won't have to wear it again and could get out of going to the Lensen barbecue."

Jackson laughs silently, his eyes staying on me as I shake my head in disbelief. "Sounds like a blowout I won't be sad to miss."

"No, you won't," I tell him. "God, it's bad enough having to walk around here pretending everything's all fine and perfect with Marcus and the rest of the guys, now I have to do the whole performance in front of my mother and all their parents and pretend everything is going so well and I'm doing great and I'm so happy, and I—"

I cut myself off when I realize Jackson is staring at me, a subtle grin still on his face while I unwittingly release all of my inner monologue on him.

"It's horrible, so I needed a moment before heading back to—"

"Don't go, then."

My head snaps up to him. Has he moved closer?

I have to laugh again. "What?"

"Don't go."

I wait for him to laugh too. For him to finish the joke. But he doesn't. He stares at me, his dark brown eyes, always either teasing or trying to be intimidating, looking strange now. Serious. Pleading?

"Oh, right. I'm sure that would go over well." I try to keep the levity in my voice, but it's fading fast.

"Just say I kidnapped you." Jackson shrugs. "Dragged you along on a crazy adventure of death, danger, and sabotage worthy of a James Bond flick. None of your uppity folks will question it."

"That bad of a reputation, huh?"

"Sure. That's what you like about me, isn't it?"

His voice is still strange. Softer. Not teasing even when it should be.

I shake my head, pushing myself away from the wall. "I'd better go..."

"I'm serious."

I freeze when his hand wraps gently but insistently around my arm, pulling me back to face him again. My palms begin to sweat against the plastic box I grip on to like a lifeline from the heat shooting down my arm. I easily turn back toward him as he moves closer, his body an inch from me. The faint scent of cigarettes and something fresh and rich, like jasmine, fills my awareness.

"Why don't you and me just... get outta here?"

His hand trails down from my arm, his fingers grazing across my waist, my stomach, his other hand moving up toward my hip, his forehead nearly touching mine as he leans closer...

I jerk away before he can move any farther. The loss of his touch is like a shock wave of ice cold, zapping me back to my senses. Allowing the anger to seep back in.

I take a deep breath, shaking as I try to compose myself and cling on to the box of lemon biscuits before they can scatter across the gravel of the lot. My face is bright red as my skin continues to shiver with a god-awful tingling.

"You... you're... you can't just..."

My enraged stuttering is apparently hilarious to him as he now leans his arm against the dark red Toyota closest to him. "Jeez, did I misread something?"

I try to find the absolute worst insult I can muster, but nothing comes to my mind. Nothing but the lingering feeling of his touch, his smell, the odd way the entire lot seemed to warp when he leaned in close enough that all I could think about was deep brown eyes, his touch, how close his mouth was to mine.

What an absolute *asshole*.

"Go to *hell*."

It's all I can think to say before turning from him and walking back toward the alleyway.

"Have fun at your little party!"

I hate him. I actually *hate* him.

Chapter 10

Jackson

Do I know what my deal is? No. Am I the absolute biggest hypocrite and possible idiot in this town? I'm closer than usual with this behavior that's come over me.

It could be the fact that Brenda officially broke it off with me this morning. Nothing surprising, including my pathetic plea for us to carry on as we were. That I didn't care if she saw other people. That I wouldn't mind keeping those nights, even every now and then, between us.

I went into town yet again bright and early on a summer morning to try to catch her alone when I knew she'd be on her way to her shift at Halo's Comics. I'd made up my mind about it at two a.m. last night, lying awake in the dead quiet of the mangy room above Ward's store, hating the silence, needing someone to talk, to listen to me talk, or at least another body close in the room.

But it had been the wrong choice. Definitely the wrong choice. Because now it's over for good.

And then I ran into Addy again. Or, she came to me. And now I can't get her out of my head.

Danny's working all day today, and Benji's passed out with a massive hangover from last night's bender when he threw back ten beers and half a bottle of tequila. Even I couldn't keep up with him.

That's why, I reason. That's why I feel this need to hang around this chick. Addy. I'm bored. And she's been just... showing up. Everywhere.

Probably why she keeps showing up in my mind, when I'm alone, when I'm with the guys, when I'm trying to sleep.

And since I'm such a dumbass, I decide that I'm bored enough to crash this moronic preppy barbecue.

It's not difficult to find where all of the rich people on Mansion Row are congregating this afternoon. I feel notably more criminal than I usually would as I make my way to the outer circle of the east side of town, where the glamorous homes are dotted along the road, a road that is a lot smoother and spotless than anything else in Greydon. It feels like I'm in some *Invasion of the Body Snatchers*–type apocalypse as I walk down the streets devoid of anyone in the entire neighborhood, the towering homes looking creepy in their obvious emptiness. A smattering of Mustangs and Porsches and Cadillacs are all parked in one of the gigantic circular driveways at the very end of the street, and a decoration of crisp white tent tops peeking up from the backyard gives away where the smarmy get-together is happening.

There's at least a small thrill now when I approach the ugly pink-shaded concrete wall shielding the backyard, stepping onto one of the gaudy decorative rocks lining the bottom of the fence to haul myself up and over the barrier.

After a quick peek to make sure I'm not about to land right in the middle of the main serving table (as hilarious as that would be), I confirm that none of the adults in grandmotherly sundresses or polos and sweater vests are looking before dropping myself down into yet another fake rock bed. I make sure to knock over as many of the mini garden gnomes as I can that look like they've been regularly *polished*.

It's easy to hide within the giant backyard that reaches to the tree line and extends into who knows how far back. This "backyard" doesn't deserve the word, looking to be more the size of a soccer field.

I refuse to admit the smell of sausages, grilled steak, fresh salmon, citrusy fruits, and pasta salad makes my mouth water as I sneak off into the tree line to keep myself out of sight for now. As many people as there are milling about that I could technically disappear in, something tells me I'd stick out like a sore thumb in my ripped-up Poison T-shirt, blue jeans smudged with ten years' worth of dirt and grime, and brown Chucks with laces so thin, they're practically threads dangling from the tops of the shoes.

As I pause to watch the train wreck before me, I find myself surprisingly entertained, enough that I make a mental note to round up Danny, Benji, and maybe even Ted and Jay to sneak in with a couple beers and kick back hidden in the bushes to watch the Greydon comedy hour next time one of these comes around.

In the span of fifteen minutes, I watch a woman smack her husband in the face with her glove for allegedly ogling their young newlywed neighbor, two men in their sixties arguing seriously over whether or not the world will officially come to an end on the last day of 1999 because of punk rock music, Deran Burth throwing up in the bushes and trying to convince his hovering mother that his friends must have slipped him some booze without him knowing, and a toddler throwing an ear-piercing tantrum when the little friend he's hanging out with won't give him all of her toys to watch him play with.

I can't get TV this good sometimes.

But the real reason I'm here thankfully appears soon after the toddler conundrum.

Addy looks like she really does wish she were anywhere else. She's surrounded by a group of adults when I see her, all of them with sickly fake smiles that she returns with an obvious grimace that the others might not see but I know quite well from the irritated looks she's given me over the past couple of days.

"Adrienne, *please*," a woman with short brown hair, who I assume is her mother, berates her after the group has departed and Addy has tried to step away into the sidelines. "What is the matter with you?"

"Nothing."

"I told you about your attitude. It's showing again. This isn't like you."

"Mom..."

"The least you could do is be grateful to Helen and Gerry, they put on this whole event and are kind enough to invite us every year..."

"Helen basically told me I'm not smart enough for college and Gerry said I looked 'much perkier' now that I'm getting older. I think I held myself together well."

I snort, but Addy's mom just closes her eyes with a heavy sigh.

Addy can't be alone for two seconds once her mom sweeps back off into the thick of the party before Marcus Tanner glides in from the sidelines, mustard-yellow sweater tied over his shoulders like a superhero cape and all.

"Addy, I've been trying to talk to you all day. Where've you been?"

"My mother's been forcing me to talk to every adult here and inform them of what's in store for the next ten years of my life," Addy mutters, still staring off after her mom.

Marcus slings an arm around her shoulders that she doesn't reciprocate, leading her away from the crowds and toward one of the picnic benches set up in the yard. I follow along, stepping through the bushes in my hiding spot, my thread string shoelaces suddenly catching on the roots and almost yanking my shoe off.

I nearly blow my cover when I land crashing onto my side, crushing some of the branches beneath me. Marcus doesn't notice the noise, but Addy glances over, her eyes narrowing momentarily where I'm thankfully still hidden.

Addy sits across from Marcus on the bench as I brush myself off and rise back to my crouching position. Marcus runs a hand through his wispy hair, and I can practically see the fake coy little grin he's giving her even if his dopey face is turned away from me.

"Addy, I have so many things to say to you."

I cannot wait.

Addy looks like she's preparing for deep-sea diving before answering. "Marcus, I know that..."

Her eyes widen in stunned horror as I emerge from the bushes behind the bench. I merely cross my arms over my chest, staring at the back of Marcus's head.

"You said you forgave me for what happened, but to be honest, you haven't been showing you care much about us at all."

Marcus hasn't picked up on Addy's expression. When she sees I'm not moving, she hastily attempts to refocus her gaze on her boyfriend, her eyes riddled with slight panic and confusion.

"Don't you see how hard I'm trying here?" Marcus continues, leaning over the table and gesturing to himself. "I want this to work. Everyone wants this to work. I don't understand what has you acting so different this summer, you've barely spoken to any of us." He leans back, giving a pointed huff. "Except your new lowlife friends, of course."

I make an exaggerated shocked face, my hand clasping my chest in mock offense. Addy pointedly keeps her gaze away from me. But I swear her eyes crinkle, just a bit.

"I am different, Marcus. I just... I don't know how to..."

"People are gonna start noticing. All my friends are already asking why I'm the only one not bringing a date with me everywhere we go, like I'm some... some..."

I wave my hands, eager for him to get on with it. Now I know Addy's trying not to smile.

"Can I ask you something, Marcus?" she asks, her hands clasping on the table in front of her.

Marcus stares at her, as if he's surprised she would interrupt such an eloquent speech. "What?"

Addy hesitates for only a moment before staring at him with an un-blinking gaze. "Do you actually care about me?"

I make sure Addy sees my silent reaction, acting like I've gotten a juicy reveal from a soap opera. She ignores it.

It takes a moment for Marcus to react, and when he does, it's an obnoxious laugh that sounds relieved more than anything. "God, Addy, you're my girlfriend, aren't you?"

"That wasn't my question."

He laughs again, this time sounding rightfully more uncomfortable. "Do I... Of course I care about you, Addy."

My eye roll reaches the heavens. Addy leans back, glancing up at me for only a brief second.

"I know what this is about," Marcus continues, eagerly leaning for-ward, anxious to educate her on whatever grand revelation he's had. "But look, it's not just 'cuz you're obviously a babe, alright?"

Now it's Addy's turn to let out an incredulous laugh. I wait with bated breath for the rest of Marcus's spiel, my eyes widening in amazed curiosity. Addy glances at me knowingly.

"Really, it's more than that. I swear."

Addy nods, looking down to regain her composure. "Alright, I'm curious. What is it you like about me, Marcus?"

"It's... it's... well, it's how shy you are."

I straighten up. My curious facade drops. I stare at the back of this guy's head like he just said the most ridiculous thing I've ever heard. Because he did.

Addy? *Shy?*

Marcus continues, his voice sounding encouraged, meaning he is entirely misreading the way Addy is trying her best not to laugh in his face again. "I know girls like you want to feel confident. You want to find that *inner voice*. You already have the looks, you just need to feel good standing next to a man you know will take care of you."

I need a fucking minute. I lied, *this* is the most entertaining thing I could ever hope to watch. I take a step back, nearly keeling over as I try to gather my sanity, Addy watching me and laughing silently along with me.

"Trust me, I know you can feel intimidated, about me and my friends, and all of this." Marcus gestures grandly around him. At the goddamn trees. "Especially since you don't usually live like this when you're not here with me. But you don't have to worry. I'm more than capable of being the man for you, Addy. It's normal, it happens to all girls. That's probably why you say you don't want to have sex with me."

Addy's face goes pale and stricken now. I straighten up, my brows rising as I look between her and Mr. Smooth over here. *I think it's a bit more than that, bud.*

"You're afraid someone like me only wants you for your looks. But that's not true, Addy." He leans forward again, his hand sliding across the table to thump down on top of hers. "I see you."

I cock my head, looking straight at Addy. Her eyes are on me. She obviously doesn't need me to signal the absolute bullshit this nimrod is spewing. And I like to think we share one last moment of united dumbfoundedness in our silent stare.

"Well... thank you." Addy gives him an incredibly condescending smile when she looks back at him. "This conversation has been very enlightening."

"Oh, I agree. If you'd told me this was the problem from the start, I could have saved you a lot of worrying."

"I'm sure." Addy nods, her laughter hardly stifled as she begins to stand up. "I just need to find Ellen. I'll be back."

Marcus seems satisfied with that. I hop back into my hiding spot in the bushes once he stands up to run off back to his buddies, probably to tell them all about how his girlfriend is definitely ready to jump into bed with him now after his articulate wooing.

Addy watches me, walking alongside me until she is far out to the edge of the gigantic yard, where the finely kept lawn begins to turn into the fields that crawl toward the hills. There's only the occasional tent and bench set up that are abandoned for now this far away from the main hub of the gathering.

Now feels like an okay time to emerge again.

"You can't be here."

Addy is facing away from me, looking back out at the party, but not moving toward it.

"No," I protest, "I definitely had to be here for that."

She turns, her arms crossed over herself. She seems more relaxed and yet more dejected than she was when I saw her this morning.

"So your mom kinda sucks, huh?"

She jerks her head up to look at me, startled, until she begins to work out that I may have been spying on her for longer than she thought.

"She means well. But... she's kind of oblivious."

Her hands fall to her sides now as she walks along the edge of the grass, the toe of her shiny black shoe scraping at the rigid line where the healthy green lawn turns into faded, dead shrubbery. I follow behind her.

"She's happy here. Happier than she is at home."

"So what, your family only stays here during the summer?"

"Since I was twelve."

"Sounds like a shitty summer vacation."

Addy scoffs to herself, about to say something before seeming to change her mind. I wait silently.

"I liked it when I was younger. Getting to go to a new place. We've never been anywhere else."

I'm about to ask how the hell her rich parents haven't loaded the family up to five European vacations by now. All I hear from Marcus and his kind are all the different states and countries they hop around to every few months. Though I wouldn't be surprised if they were lying.

"I don't mind the small town thing, I just... This year, it's different." She shrugs, looking down at her feet as her walk slows to a stop underneath the overhang of one of the white tents, this one empty aside from a few extra chairs stacked together. "I don't know if I'm bored with it, or I'm just not the same person."

"From when you were twelve? Jesus, I hope not."

She grunts an unwilling laugh. I lean one hand against the skinny metal pole of the tent, the other resting on my hip as I look at this odd rich girl who is Marcus Tanner's girlfriend, who hangs out with his friends, but who also stood up for my best friend, who sneaks into horror movies, and who is just as unamused with life at the moment as I feel like I am all the time.

"Why don't we get outta here?"

Even I'm surprised at how desperate the plea sounds, but I am desperate. Desperate to try to have a fun night, desperate to ditch this Silicon Valley cult gathering, or desperate to see this girl in any other setting than one surrounded by guys wearing sweater capes. Maybe desperate to try to figure out why this girl I couldn't stand a few days ago refuses to get out of my head.

"Yeah," she laughs, moving across from me, leaning her hip against the opposite tent pole. "Just disappear into the night."

I shrug. "Why not?"

"My little sister already took off, my mom will have a heart attack if I'm missing too."

"So what? Live a little."

She gives me a playfully amused look until she realizes I'm not joking. "Jackson, I can't just leave."

"How come? And are you planning on puttin' up with another couple hours of Marcus Tanner's romantic soliloquies? Because if so, I'm gonna have to check in tomorrow morning to make sure you haven't suffocated on violent unenthusiasm."

She begins shaking her head incredulously. "You don't know—"

"I don't know him? I'm the one who has to go to the same school as the dimwit for months on end, and let me tell ya, he's not givin' off signals to other chicks that he already has a girlfriend, if you know what I mean."

Addy doesn't look surprised or concerned at this statement. Which makes me more irritated for some reason.

"You really wanna waste another summer on him? He ain't worth it. Trust me."

"Oh, and who is, then?" she asks, raising her brows. "You?"

I cock my head, not hesitant to take the bait. "Maybe." All it earns me is another eye roll. But I notice she still doesn't turn away or look interested in returning to the party.

"You drive me up a wall, Jackson Lowell."

"I like that you call me by my full government name."

"You're a big enough idiot to require the full first and last every time."

I smile. "Sure."

She looks away. But the anger in her stance is quickly melting away.

And I'm a dumbstruck idiot after all, so focused on gauging this girl's immediate thoughts, that I don't notice the footsteps that have approached behind us until a stern and aggravatingly familiar voice bellows out.

"And just what the hell are you doin' here, boy?"

Luckily, I'm still facing away from Sheriff Nulty where he's entered the back of the tent, enough that I can school my face into a sly grin when I turn to look at him, as opposed to Addy's horrified and slightly sick expression. She has shot away from the tent pole and straightened into an unmoving column.

"My apologies, Sheriff," I greet him. "I musta gotten lost on the way home. My street looks just like this one."

Sheriff Nulty isn't in uniform, but from his broad Superman-imposter stance, he sure is imagining that he is. Though he's missing his own sweater cape, he's got on a blindingly lime green button-down and a pair of suspenders that will be a ridiculous image I can laugh about in my head the next few times I see him in his actual uniform. And without his sheriff's hat, the side burns and bald patch are glaringly prominent.

He steps forward, that self-satisfied smirk plastered across his shiny red face as he narrows his beady eyes in my direction, hands looped on his gaudy silver belt buckle. "You heard me, boy. Unless you want another stint in juvie, you're gonna get the hell off this property this instant."

"Damn, Sheriff, where's that gentlemanly hospitality I was promised?" I ask, standing my ground casually. "From what I'm told, I'm supposed to get treated better here with your kindly civilized folk than any other spot in this shit stain of a town."

He steps forward now, his mouth turned into a sharp frown that looks more like an exaggerated pout to me.

"I'm warning you, Lowell. I'll cuff ya and drag you down to the station right now if I have to."

I see Addy from the corner of my eye look as if she's about to protest. I don't give her the chance to even pretend. She's already backed almost all the way out of the tent and into the bushes. Because a crowd has begun to form. A crowd of snickering kids from school and their parents who either glare at me like Nulty is right now, or look horrified that someone untoward has infiltrated their nest of refinement.

"Oh, that's alright, Sheriff," I say, my hands held up as I step backward out from the overhang of the tent, beginning to turn back toward the party. "I'd be an asshole too if genetics weren't kind to me either. I'll just find Mr. or Mrs. Benson, or Jensen, or whatever the hell, and have them show me to the door. Good ol' walk of shame never hurt anybody."

"I don't think so."

I pause, turning back to where Nulty stands with his chest puffed high, the smirk back on his face as he jerks his head out toward the field. "You run off like the little rat you are. Find your way back into town that way. Maybe that'll teach ya not to sneak around into good folks' homes, messin' their property with your filth."

Deran Burth's obnoxious snort choruses over the tiny crowd of on-lookers.

I guess it's meant to be a shameful thing, being hustled out into the bushes rather than even being given the courtesy to leave through the front door. But the sheriff doesn't know me well enough. For me, running around the fields on the edges of town is like second nature.

"Now, Sheriff," I gasp mockingly, my hand clutched to my chest as I walk around him toward the field, still keeping myself turned to face him, not entirely trusting he's not gonna pull a Taser on me. "What happens if I get dragged off by a wild coyote?"

"Then I'd be damn glad to never hear from ya again."

That gets another chortle from the kids and a few satisfied huffs from the adults watching.

I want to be amused by Addy's horrified, uncomfortable expression as she remains standing beyond the tent, strategically just out of view of anyone looking. But now when I look at her, I can't help but feel rage shaking beneath my skin again. At the way she stands there. At the way she clearly wants to move, say something, do anything. But she doesn't. She doesn't know what to do. She never does.

Doing something would be helping out the scruffy, dangerous troublemaker. Right in front of the sheriff, her friends. Possibly her parents.

And it's just as I thought, I realize now as I slowly strut away, turning toward the ragged fields once my shoes crunch against the dry brush instead of soft grass and I'm sure Nulty isn't going to try to tackle me or shoot me or anything.

She's nothing but a typical bored rich girl. Who likes the excitement of playing with the "bad boys" only when the adults' backs are turned.

Whatever, I think to myself as I stomp through the scraggly bushes and dried-up tree roots in the fields, the sounds from the party growing distant until the only noise is the thump of my footsteps, the chirping of a few crows, and the skittering of the occasional squirrel or rabbit.

Why should I care that she wouldn't lift a finger to stand up for me? It's not like she likes me or anything. Which is fine, because I don't give one damn about her either. I never did. We aren't even friends. She has her friends, I have mine. We need nothing from each other.

It's sunset by the time I get back into town, throwing open the door to Ward's shop and marching inside, invigorated from my brief jaunt through the empty fields.

I'll have to thank the good ol' sheriff one day for the lovely time of clarity.

"Girl trouble again," Ward mutters to himself as he casually peruses a cigar magazine behind the counter while I swipe a beer bottle from one of the shelves just out of his line of sight. He doesn't pose it as a question. Just says it like he knows. Like he knows by now what all my different moods mean without me having to say a thing.

I march upstairs with my beer, slamming the upstairs bedroom door closed firmly behind me.

Idiot. *Girl trouble.* As if.

Chapter 11
Addy

I call Marcus first thing in the morning. I get his mother on the line, since Marcus is still passed out at noon. Mrs. Tanner tells me he might be coming down with something, and I pretend to buy it, even though it's certainly another hangover from the multiple flasks he and Eddie and Deran were passing around at the barbecue yesterday. I ask her to tell him to meet me at the gas station this evening at six, if he's conscious by then.

I arrive almost an hour earlier than that, thinking I'll get a hot dog and a soda from the food stand alongside Brixie Gas & Go. But I'm too focused to eat. Not nervous. Not upset. It feels more like determination. Something that manifested in me over the course of last night, when I lay in bed awake for hours after the barbecue, recounting every last second of the entire ridiculous event. Angry at myself above anyone else, despite how many people got on my nerves that night (everyone).

Now there is a steadiness. Something that feels different, but maybe good this time.

It helps to know I'm meeting Ellen after this to head to the party at Johnny-Jay's. So no matter how this goes, I at least have a distraction where I won't have to think about the repercussions tonight.

Marcus doesn't show up in his car. When he does make his appearance at 6:22, he's strolling up to the station from across the street, looking incredibly confused and a bit disgusted at the choice of location. The gas station isn't a scenic venue, but it's always pretty empty and enough out of the way that I thought it would work best for the conversation I'm trying to have. We don't need an audience.

It's quiet when he sits down. I can see from the look on his face he suspects what this is about. I don't know what my expression must look like, but I can imagine. This is what I had hoped for before. That we wouldn't need to talk. That we both knew what the other wanted to say.

Now, even as the unspoken words hang between us, I know I still need to do this. Officially. Before I wimp out yet again.

"Marcus, I think we should break up."

I need to get the words out, finally, before they can jump way back inside my chest and remain stuck for the rest of the summer, or longer.

I never considered how Marcus would react. Which says even more about our ghost of a relationship. All I thought about was my own feelings, my own consequences. Marcus was a phantom image in my head, a stand-in. For a few seconds after I've said the words, I already feel guilt edging through me as I cautiously glance up at him.

Instead of sad or enraged or confused, he looks mildly irritated.

"Addy, be serious."

I furrow my brows, straightening in the plastic bench seat of the outdoor table beside the food stand. "I am. I don't feel the same way I did three years ago. I've changed a lot, and so have you. I don't think we're a good fit anymore. You're wanting something I can't give, and I'm wanting something you can't give."

Marcus leans back, scoffing as he aims his disbelieving gaze out at the gas pumps. He hasn't looked me in the eye since he got here.

"I'm sorry, I should have done this earlier, before—"

"Is this about that drugged-out reject, Jackson Lowell?"

I startle and feel my face burn at the mention of Jackson. It shouldn't have surprised me. There were some kids who saw what happened last night at the barbecue. Naturally the word spread. Marcus either saw himself or would have heard from one of his friends by now.

But no one saw me. They couldn't have seen me, right? Someone would have said something to me by now if they had.

"This is about us," I tell him firmly, pushing away the fear and the even bigger sense of guilt that his words bring up. "I don't want to be with you. Maybe I don't want to be with anyone for a while. I don't really know what I want."

"That's for sure," he scoffs. "God, you have got to be kidding me, Addy. You're so disgusted by me, and yet you're ready to throw yourself at someone like that complete loser? And you say I'm the one with a problem?"

I narrow my eyes, anger rising through me as Marcus finally turns to look me in the eye with a glare.

"Do you know how ridiculous you sound?"

"No, here's what's ridiculous, Addy," he says with a sharp hiss, making me jump. He leans forward across the table, holding up a stern finger as if he were a parent scolding their teenager. "Ridiculous is you embarrassing me every chance you can get, making all my friends, our parents, think there's something up since my own girlfriend does everything she can to be as far away from me as possible. It's bad enough you live all the way across the country, how the hell am I supposed to convince people I *have* a girlfriend when you won't even let me touch you when you're here?"

I stare at him, letting out a small laugh as I shake my head. "Wow. I think that about sums everything up between—"

"Tell me, how many of the trailer trash have you screwed so far? I'm assuming you started before we got together, right? Since they're so much better company than I am?"

My hands shake against the table. I feel my eyes burn, but I refuse to cry in front of him.

I stand up, my fists curling at my sides as I curb the jolting ache to smack him across the face. "Let's get this straight if it wasn't abundantly clear already. We are done, Marcus. I'm embarrassed to say I ever went out with you. And that's without knowing whatever the hell you must be like at school and every other moment I'm not here. I'm embarrassed to say I even *liked* you."

These words seem to register with him. But they only make his eyes turn icier with rage, his hands curling against the table before he shoots up just as I turn and walk back toward the street.

"And by the way, they're my *friends*," I add, turning around but not slowing my pace. "But what I do is none of your business anymore."

I hear his footsteps following behind me as I step onto the empty street, heading back into town.

"It's that scrawny kid from the diner too, isn't it? *Danny Macklin*. Hah! I always knew there was something off with you, Addy, but this is just priceless. You've been dying to get with him ever since you saw his broke ass squabbling around the Roller Dollar that night. You got a thing for homeless punks now?"

"Just *fuck off*!"

I've stopped to face him, surprised at the strength of the words that have shattered through me, satisfied to see Marcus pause in momentary shock as well. We both stand still and silent in the middle of the empty street for a few seconds before Marcus shakes himself off, narrowing his eyes again.

"This is crazy, Addy. Do you know what you're doing? Without me, you're nothing around here."

"What a tragedy," I muse as I continue walking away, thinking he'll finally begin losing steam. But still he follows me.

"You're gonna be sorry, Addy. And your pathetic little crush Danny is gonna get what's comin' to him."

My stomach drops as my footsteps pause again. I turn toward Marcus, who stands behind me, a horribly satisfied smirk on his face. His face that looks so different now. Not handsome and kind and gentle like it was when we were younger. Now it's twisted and smug and wrong.

"You leave him alone, Marcus, do you understand me?"

"I don't really have to care what you think anymore, do I? That's what you said, isn't it?"

I feel an anger shake through me like never before. Something that makes my insides feel like they're burning, clawing at my skin. I can't tell if it's anger directed only at Marcus, or everyone here like him, or at myself for taking so long to see this.

"I don't ever want to see you again. So stay the hell away from me."

"You're a little bitch, you know that?"

"Great," I laugh bitterly. "Something we both finally have in common."

I turn to leave again. But his hands lock around my arms, yanking me back. I shove away from him, but he holds on with a steel grasp that makes me feel he's as blindingly angry as I am.

"Let go, Marcus, I'm serious!" I shout, thrashing against his grasp as he attempts to crush his arms around me to hold me still.

"You're not going anywhere until we talk, you little—"

I don't hear anything as I put every bit of my focus and effort into wriggling out of his grip, trying to throw my head or feet back to land a hopefully painful blow against him, but he manages to keep me well out of aim. Neither of us hear the car pulling up alongside us until a booming voice scares the hell out of us both.

"Hey, hey! What the hell is this?"

Marcus's hold immediately loosens and I take the chance to jerk away. We both stare at the large dirt-splattered pick-up truck that has stopped in the middle of the empty street and the man who has jumped out of the driver's seat and is stalking toward Marcus with an infuriated glare.

Marcus has gone pale, and I can see why. The man is a foot taller than him, his loose-fitting blue tank top showing off an impressive array of muscles that Marcus couldn't hope to have, even despite his football playing. The man stands with a wide gait, his hands on his hips as he glares at Marcus through his crop of messy ginger-shaded curls that match the stubble across his stern face.

"Do you wanna explain to me what the hell I'm seeing right now?" the man asks in a tone that even has me feeling reprimanded.

Marcus attempts to puff up his chest, but the effect beside the larger man is laughable.

"S'none of your business," he answers with a lot less conviction than he's had so far tonight.

"Oh, is that so?" the stranger asks, taking a couple steps forward and sending Marcus skittering backward. "I've seen you around, you little punk. Let me tell you somethin', if I see you puttin' your hands on a girl like that ever again, you and I are gonna be having a little conversation. You understand me?"

Marcus continues to stagger backward away from the man, shooting him a deadly glare. His eyes move to me briefly before he turns away.

"Whatever," he mutters before sauntering off back the way he had come, where I suspect Deran or Eddie or one of his friends is waiting at their car, eager to hear all about what went down with Marcus and his wacky girlfriend. A story I'm sure Marcus is already thinking of how he'll edit.

The stranger doesn't turn away or lower his He-Man posture until he's watched Marcus turn the corner at the end of the street. Then he turns to face me.

He doesn't look scary now. He has a kind expression, wide eyes, and an almost shy stance now that he's dropped his brief persona.

"You alright?"

I nod, still dumbfounded as I stare at the man.

"Headin' into town?"

"Yes, I... I'm meeting my friend," I answer shakily.

"Where at?"

"Uh... that bar, Johnny-Jay's?"

The man nods, his brows raised in surprise before he seems to work something out. "Same here. Need a lift?"

The car ride is silent at first, with just the sound of the truck whirring along the road into town accompanied by the light rock playing softly from the radio speakers. I discreetly glance into the back seat and see an array of what looks like carpentry or landscaping tools. He must have been on his way back from a job.

I don't think he's a big talker, so I decide after a couple minutes to finally speak.

"Are you Ted?"

The man looks vaguely surprised as he casts a quick glance toward me. I watch him solemnly.

"Nice to meet you. You must be Addy."

Now it's my turn to be surprised, and embarrassed. I'm hoping it was Danny who told Ted about me and not Jackson. Either way, I feel like I have to apologize for something, but for what, I don't know.

"Thank you," I decide to say instead. "Thank you for stopping."

Ted gives a quick nod. "It's not the first time I've come across that... kid." He seems to swallow down a different word he wants to call Marcus. I don't think I'd be offended if he did. "He's been causing trouble with his buddies for a lotta people around here."

I look down at my hands in my lap, feeling more guilty.

"You shouldn't ever let a guy grab you like that, Addy."

I look over at him. His gaze is still focused on the road, but his eyes look sad.

"I know," I assure him.

"I'm serious," he says, his voice more severe. "You don't ever put up with anything like that, from anyone. No one's worth that."

"I broke up with him," I blurt out, sounding as if I'm trying to convince him of something. "That's why he was so angry."

Even I don't like how it sounds. I don't know why I said it. Like I'm trying to defend him. But I am, in a way. Because I've known Marcus for so long. Because I never imagined he would even think to do anything like what he just did.

Ted doesn't respond. He doesn't need to.

It doesn't take more than a few minutes to arrive at Johnny-Jay's. We can hear the music thumping from outside and see a stream of people buzzing in and out, the flashy pink and purple lights glowing from inside the old building.

I spot Ellen huddled against the building beside the bar in a bright turquoise dress and white heels, half her hair piled in a messy ponytail atop her head, and her arms close to her body as she clutches her purse like she's afraid any one of the people jovially moving in and out of the bar might snatch it from her.

"Thanks for the ride," I tell Ted as he parks the truck across the street. "And, I'm... I'm sorry if I caused any trouble or anything..."

I don't know what I'm trying to apologize for or how to say it. I can't read Ted's expression as he throws open the door and hops down onto the street.

"Don't worry about any of that, Addy. Go have fun tonight."

He pauses before he can shut the door and head across the street.

"But not too much fun," he affirms, his eyes narrowed. "Don't start tryin' to sneak any beers or anything. Benji'll try to get you to, but don't follow his example."

I hold back a laugh as I climb out of the truck, landing down on the street before turning back to nod at him through the window. "You don't have to worry about me."

Ted heads inside while I hurry to meet Ellen.

"Oh thank God," she groans as she rushes toward me. "What took you so long?"

"I... lost track of time."

She must not have seen me show up with Ted. And I'm not in the mood to talk about anything that happened in the last half hour. Ted's right. Right now, I just want to have fun.

"This is insane," Ellen breathes as we approach the door to the bar. "Are you going through a rebellious phase?"

"I don't know."

There's someone at the door. A bearded man with an elegantly curled mustache but a no-nonsense demeanor who stops us before we can walk inside.

"Uh... we're with... Danny invited us?" is all I can think to say. Ellen presses her lips together, staring at the bouncer as if he might attack if she makes the smallest movement.

"Heyyyy, look what the cat decided to drag in!"

We both turn to see Benji stumble toward the door, his spiky hair wet and plastered against his forehead, the multiple pins on his beat-up leather coat flashing under the lights, and a glass of something swinging in his hand. "Let 'em on in, Roy, it's okay."

Roy doesn't question Benji's decree, stepping aside and letting us into the crowded, stuffy bar.

The place is a lot bigger than it looks on the outside, even when filled to the brim with a collection of dancing, laughing, sweating bodies moving all throughout the space. I can hardly make out the bar in the center of the room amid the crowd. The amber glow of the regular lights mixes with the harsh white and blue stage lights bathing the band currently playing a rock tune that pulses through the entire building.

It's louder and rowdier than anything I've ever been to before. It sends a thrill of adrenaline through me and I'm unable to keep the smile from my face.

Ellen, on the other hand, looks as if she'll be quietly counting down every minute we spend here.

Danny runs up beside Benji, calling out a cheerful greeting we can barely hear over the noise. I'm relieved to see him. We embrace like old friends, and even Ellen moves forward to throw an arm around him in greeting.

I find myself scanning all around the bar, expecting Jackson Lowell to pop up somewhere next. I don't find him.

Which is probably good. After what happened yesterday at the barbecue, I'm not sure either of us are eager to see each other right now.

There are small tables set up throughout the room that Danny leads us to through the crowd. Benji misses the chair the first time, but we're soon all seated at one of the circular wooden tables before Danny disappears to get us all some food and water.

It's still too loud to talk, though my ears are slowly getting used to the noise level. Instead, I sit back and watch the band as they start up their next song, this one slower, but the crowd is still energized, swaying along merrily to the upbeat ballad.

Being in drama back at school, I used to sing and act in most of the productions throughout elementary and middle school. But this is something different.

Watching the lead singer strum along on his shimmering emerald green guitar, the sweat dripping down his face and through his longish blond hair as he sings with his eyes closed, a song I don't recognize that might be an original, I feel like a magnet, captivated by the scene. Imagining myself in his place, all those eyes and ears on me, able to command an entire room full of people just with the sounds I make on the guitar, the words I string together.

My cousins and I used to pretend we were performing in the biggest stadium known to man when we played our instruments in their garage or in their backyard. It seemed inevitable at ten years old that we would take over the world one day.

To be honest, I don't think the dream has entirely faded for any of us. Even if it's been some time since the three of us played together like that.

I don't realize Benji has left the table until he's hopping up onstage, one of the guitar players patting him eagerly on the back as he walks up to one of the microphones. Cheers ring from the crowd as the familiar opening chords to "Highway to Hell" fill the bar, and Ellen and I look at each other incredulously. The lead singer fondly ruffles Benji's mess of already sweaty hair as he steps back, joining in on his bass as Benji begins to belt out the lyrics in a less than polished singing voice.

It's a performance meant to get everyone singing along and dancing together, and it certainly does that. Ellen and I clap along, Danny collapsing into Benji's empty seat as he sets a plate of fries and burgers down on the table before us.

I turn my head, reaching out for one of the glasses of water Danny had got for us, pausing when I catch sight of a familiar figure at the edge of the bar behind us.

Jackson Lowell is standing with his hip leaned against the bar, turned mostly away from me so that I can't make out his expression as he glances over at the woman a few feet away from him. It's the same girl from the alleyway. The one he had been arguing with. The tall one with the gorgeously perfect smooth hair and long legs.

She's hanging off the arm of a guy who looks at least five years older than both her and Jackson. I'm not sure if she notices him until she casts him a quick glance over her shoulder, a smirk spreading over her lips. She turns back to the man beside her, pulling him in front of her before planting her lips firmly on his mouth. Her leg goes to wrap around the back of his, her hand curling roughly through his hair before she pulls away with a satisfied breath.

She turns to throw Jackson a pointed look before turning away again. "That's Brenda."

I startle as I turn to look back at where Danny has followed my stare. He's close enough that I can just make out his words over the noise. Ellen is still engrossed by Benji's performance. Ted appears out of the crowd, pulling out one of the chairs at the table and sitting beside Danny, sipping from a beer bottle.

"Jackson was with her for a while," Danny continues to explain over the booming of the music, "then she got with some guy who works at the bowling alley. He had to find out the hard way."

"Boy's too gullible." Ted shakes his head before taking another sip of his beer.

Danny gives a fond smile. "It's not a bad thing to want things to work."

"It is when you think so low of yourself, you'll take a girl cheatin' on you rather than, God forbid, bein' single," Ted calls out over the music.

I look between them, beginning to understand, recalling the sort-of fight I saw yesterday. "She cheated on him but he doesn't care? He still wants her back?"

"I don't think he cares if it's her," Ted replies. "Long as it's someone."

"Brenda's better than Annie," Danny says, leaning back in his chair and scooping up a handful of fries. "She was with someone else when she and Jackson first got together."

"Nah, Trish was still the worst." Ted shakes his head again. "She may not have cheated on him for a while, but she made sure we all knew what she thought about him every minute she saw us. Couldn't have one conversation without lettin' him know she was downgrading herself bein' with him."

"Was Colette the one who stole money out of his drawer that one time?"

"Think so."

The conversation fades as I turn to look back at Jackson, who's still at the bar, now turned away from this Brenda person and her new boy toy. His expression looks uncaring as he sips from a glass, casually looking out at the crowd. But even from here, I can see his mind is somewhere else.

I don't imagine Jackson Lowell to be the type of person to get angry about things like this. I pictured him to be the type who goes around with as many girls as he can. The type who wouldn't care enough about any relationship to feel bad if a girl constantly degraded him to his friends or cheated on him in front of his face. He's someone who would simply move on. Someone who doesn't have the capacity to care that much about a relationship to be hurt. About anyone.

That's what I think, because that's what he wants people to think. That's the persona he desperately clings on to, I realize as I watch him now and think about how desperate he had been yesterday when asking Brenda if they could still be a thing. Even if she wanted to go around with someone else.

Instead, when I look at him now... really look at him... he seems passive. Like Ted had said.

Like he thinks it's all he deserves. The best he can get. Even though maybe... he does want something more.

It's sad. Pathetic, maybe. But we're all pathetic when it comes to figuring out relationships, if there's anything I've learned so far this summer.

I sit at the table a bit longer, watching Benji conclude his spontaneous guest performance, cheering and hollering with everyone, before standing up. None of the others follow me, and I'm glad. Maybe they sensed I just wanted a moment. A moment to move on my own through the crowd, slowly but steadily, until I've reached the stage.

I just watch at first. Daydreaming again. Knowing how obnoxious it is to be standing here while everyone else around me is trying to dance. But also knowing that he saw me come up here. That he won't be far behind.

There's a hand on my wrist. A hand that spins me around briskly until I'm facing a pair of brown eyes that reflect the white and blue lights of the stage.

I don't smile, but I stick my chin up teasingly. Jackson takes the invitation.

His hands pull me forward. My chest crashes against his as his arms curl around my waist.

We dance. Not the jumping and twirling most everyone else does along to the strong beat of the song. Something slower. Looser. Something closer to what a few other couples are doing.

And I don't mind. I'm having fun. I sling my arms around Jackson Lowell's neck and move along to the beat, the both of us smiling under the stage lights. And it might be fake because we hate each other and he's probably still pissed at me for yesterday. But right at this moment, it's what we both need.

Chapter 12

Jackson

Addy disappears, extracting herself from my grasp and slipping away into the crowd after the song ends. I'm so thrown off-balance by the lights and the heat and the noise that I lose her in the blink of an eye.

I pause to glance back at the table where Danny, Ted, and Addy's friend are still sitting. Seeing she's not there, my eyes trail along the path she had disappeared down until they meet the side door at the other end of the bar that is just falling closed.

The outside air is refreshing after the heat inside the bar until it becomes instantly freezing with the sharp absence of warmth. I've never been good at adjusting to quick temperature changes, obviously.

Her silhouette stands against the sunset in the patch of grass behind the bar, the breeze whipping her hair at her shoulders. She's waiting for me again, like she had up by the stage.

"I never take time to notice how beautiful it is here," she says as I walk up behind her and she continues looking out at the mountains in the distance, swallowing up the sun. "Even though I've been coming here for years."

I step closer, twisting my shoe against the dirt. Why am I out here? "That's kinda sad."

She finally turns around to face me. She looks indecisive, biting her lip as she stares at the ground before looking up. "Do you really hate me?"

The way she says it makes me laugh, but not because it sounds pathetic or pleading. It sounds concerned. Why should she give a shit if I hate her or not?

"I'm sorry," she says when I don't answer. "About yesterday, at the barbecue. I should have done something."

I sigh, my hands in the pockets of my jacket against the chill as I look away from her, not knowing where the hell to go with this.

"I guess it's only easy for you to be charitable when it's convenient."

Or only to Danny.

It's the only thing I can think to say even if I can't muster any bite behind it. It's exhausting, being constantly frustrated with this girl. And yet here I am.

"I don't want to be that way. Like them."

I look back at her. Her hair looks auburn, shaded against the sunset. I want to believe her.

"That only counts if you do something about it."

She nods, not arguing.

"What's up? Seriously."

She stares at me, knowing what I mean, but still not answering.

"Is this real? Are Danny and Benji and me all just a joke to you? Something to rile up your boyfriend? Some excitement to spice up your kind?"

Her brows rise incredulously. "My kind?"

I shrug. "Your group, your posse, your affiliation, whatever."

She shakes her head, her expression sinking right back to the typical angry grimace that hadn't been present so far tonight until now. "Grow up."

"You're so tired with your boring life that you wanna have a thrill with the poor kids?"

"You've got some nerve, Jackson Lowell."

"So do you." I move closer. She tenses, but doesn't move away. "You do whatever your parents, and your boyfriend, and all your little friends want you to do. You don't care if it's wrong or not what you want, you just do it. Even if they treat everyone else like shit. I've known your type and I'm not interested in playing this out with you. So tell me what the hell your game is here, or go run back to Daddy."

"Jackson, you don't know a thing about me or my family, so shut your damn mouth!"

Her voice trembles with the same rage it has all the other times I really push her buttons. It instantly makes me feel better.

"There she is." I grin as she blinks furiously at me. "There's the gal who threw a milkshake in my face and told her boyfriend to piss off."

She continues to stare at me oddly, the rage on her face melting into confusion, until she eventually looks away. A laugh shudders through her as she raises an exhausted hand to her face.

"I don't understand you at all."

"Why don't you try?"

She turns to give me a look. "Nice try, but I'll pass."

"No, I'm serious." I nod, stepping closer to her. She stiffens again, but still doesn't shift away. She holds my gaze, the gentle breeze whispering around us, the noise from the bar still humming distantly behind us.

She turns away, taking only a few steps until she is leaning up against the back wall of the building, looking out at the now hidden sun.

"Where do you live?"

I try to cover my surprise at her question, following her over to the wall. "Here and there. My old man lives back in New York. I mostly crash at this guy Ward's place, above his liquor store. Sometimes Ted's. Danny's or Benji's now and then."

"New York? Where in New York?"

"White Plains. Kinda boring part of town, but close enough to the urban center for somethin' to do every now and then. And I was able to run away to New York City a couple times. Can't find anything like that around here."

She's quiet for a while. I finally look over at her and see her about to laugh.

"What?"

She turns, her nose high in the air as she stifles a grin. "I'll give you three guesses."

"Huh?"

"Three guesses of where I live, Jackson Lowell."

I stare at her, her meaning eventually hitting me.

"You're kiddin' me."

"Nope."

"You live in White Plains, New York?"

It comes out sounding angry because... I am angry. I don't know why, but I am.

"Born and raised," she confirms. "Small world, isn't it?"

I lean back against the wall again, my mind turning in disbelief. "No shit."

"Maybe you and I aren't so different after all."

I roll my eyes, hiding my grin from her. "Sure."

"Were you born there?"

"No. Think I was born in Bridgeport. My mom moved us all down to Paterson when I was two or somethin', then to White Plains when I was five, and then... yeah."

Something twists in my stomach. I wish we hadn't started talking about this. I hope she'll change the subject.

"When did you leave?"

An image forms in my mind before I can stop it. A town so different but somehow so similar to this. Different friends. A cop who'd look at me with more hate than Sheriff Nulty could muster up with his entire body. The heated glares from any adult I passed on the street.

Then another image. Holding hands with a girl. Staring at a wooden box decorated with dying flowers. Two times. Two boxes.

"When I was twelve," I manage to answer in a normal voice. "Saved up some money... stole a bit from the old man, but he'd never notice... hopped on a plane and then a bus, and ended up here. Not exactly my plan, but it hasn't worked out too bad."

The grand plan in my twelve-year-old mind being that I would run away from my zoned-out father, a beat-up shack of a house, and a bor-ing-ass life to the golden beaches of California, bask in the luxurious Hollywood Hills, smoke the best marijuana every day, fall in love with a glamorous movie star, and never look back.

Instead: Greydon.

A minute improvement due only to Danny, Benji, and Ted.

"Are your parents... looking for you?" she asks carefully. Like she senses the dangerous ground she's treading on.

"Nope."

"Don't they care that you left?"

"My old man loaded me up with a cigar to smoke when I got to California before I left. My mom's dead."

Sure, the silence is uncomfortable like I knew it'd be, but shit, at this point, we gotta get it over with already.

"Oh."

I shrug, reaching into my pocket for my packet of smokes.

"When?"

"I don't know, like twelve years ago now, or somethin'."

The lighter clicks and the cigarette lights, easing the chill. Until I have to strangle myself to stop from coughing since I inhaled too fast. These fucking things...

"My dad died when I was four."

I pause, the cigarette halfway back to my lips. I gaze out at the empty patch of grass in front of us. She doesn't say anything else.

"Your... your dad's dead?" I say it thankfully without choking on the smoke filling my lungs.

She nods. "It was a little after my sister was born. She doesn't remember him at all. But I get fragments every now and then."

I wait a beat before turning to look back, the cigarette still held frozen in front of me.

"He was a piece of shit," she says then, making me almost choke again. "I think he and my mom were close to getting a divorce. He had a drinking problem. And he... he was into a lotta stuff. Bad stuff."

"What, like drugs or somethin'? Coke?"

Her eyes widen pointedly as she crosses her arms over her chest. "As a start."

"Shit."

"Yeah."

It's quiet again for a while. My cigarette lets out a small, unending streak of smoke.

"What happened?"

"Car accident. He was high out of his mind and drove right off the road."

She says it with so little emotion. I know the feeling. I hear the barest cracks in her voice, any major thing she is supposed to be feeling covered up by the words she's probably said a hundred times to who knows how many different people. Strangers. People who ask about her dad, where he is, or talk about him like they assume he's alive, what I had to go through almost every day back home. People whose assumption is like a knife twisting in your gut.

Like I had done to her. How many times have I mentioned her father, like I knew anything about her family?

"One good thing to come out of it is that I'll never touch drugs in my goddamn life," she says, brushing a strand of hair behind her ear, covering up something in her expression. Another gesture I know well. "My father gave them enough attention without me ever having to add to the mix."

"That's…"

What do you even say? People saying sorry used to piss me the hell off. People saying how horrible it was made me even angrier.

"What a fucking dumbass."

It seems to be the right thing. She laughs. Because surely no one else has said that in response to her so far.

"Cancer. Pancreatic."

I answer her unspoken question. She leans her head back before turning toward me again.

"We're a pretty sad teenage angst story, aren't we?"

Her musing makes me laugh, and I shake my head as I take another puff of my smoke. Inhaling it properly this time. "Everyone's got somethin'."

She and I stand there for a long while. Sitting against the wall. Being alone. Thinking about whatever it is that's going on in our brains.

"My dad smoked like a chimney," she says, watching the smoke from my latest puff go by. "That's one of the clearest things I can remember about him."

For whatever reason, her words make me drop the thing to the ground and stomp it out.

"You outta show me how it's done," I tease. "Like I said, I'd be open to a lesson any time."

She sighs, rolling her eyes despite the smile threatening her lips. Lips that look soft against the glow of the bar and the distant street lights blinking to life.

"Oh, come on. You know you want to."

A sigh heaves out of her as she pushes away from the wall. "I've had enough of you for one night."

I stand back and watch her head back toward door.

"It's locked on this side," I wait to tell her just as she yanks on the handle and finds the heavy door completely unmoving. She looks like she could curse me out as she spins around and begins to walk all the way back to the front door. I laugh to myself, staying up against the back of the building, nothing but the low hum of the bar and the loud chirping of crickets filling the air after Addy is long out of sight.

A feeling comes back to me. A memory. Feeling like this only once before in my life, when I was barely old enough to be in school. When I had a friend I felt like this with. Who I talked like this with, even though we were small. Though I felt old beyond my years even back then. Especially back then.

I stay outside behind the bar for a while longer until I can get the memory to go away.

Chapter 13

Addy

"**A**drienne?"

I slide back before I can reach the front door, poking my head into the living area. "Yeah?"

My mother looks up from her task of folding a large pile of purple pearl-beaded napkins on the coffee table in preparation for her brunch she's hosting today, her eyes sweeping me over with concern.

"Is everything alright?"

"Fine."

I try not to be overly nonchalant. I'm momentarily worried that one of her friends said something to her about Marcus and me breaking up. Until I realize that if that happened, she'd be a thousand times more animated than this.

Instead, she's looking me over as if I just climbed out of a mud pit.

"What happened to all your new clothes?"

I look down at my plain blue jeans and cargo jacket. "It's gonna be chillier today, Mom."

Her eyes go to the guitar strapped across my back. The same black and bronze sprayed one I got for my tenth birthday from my guitar instructor who was tired of me not having one to practice with at home. The one I usually keep confined to my room while I'm here.

"What's going on?"

"Just heading down to the creek to work on some stuff," I tell her breezily, heading to the door. "See you later, Mom."

I rush out of the house before she can ask anything else. Mainly who I'll be with.

I'm winded by the time I make it all the way into town and then toward the far west side neighborhood, past the rickety chain-link fence and into the tree line, all while lugging the guitar on my back. I am used to carrying it on a short bus ride and walk to school, but not all the way across an entire town.

This is where I nearly get lost when I realize I've only ever been here once, in the dark, with someone else leading the way. But thankfully, the sound of the creek rushing leads me the rest of the way until I break through the thick of the trees and into the clearing where the circle of trailers sits on the other side of the water.

Danny meets me outside, leading me to one of the picnic benches. I give him my guitar, first helping him tune it up, and then teaching him to play a few simple notes.

I've never taught anyone anything like this before. I have no idea if I'm doing it well. Danny is paying attention as if his life depends on it, and I try to go as slow as I can while not talking down to him like he's five years old. Some music teachers I've had in the past would take multiple lessons before even letting the class play a string of notes all together, and that was no fun.

But after taking a moment to get used to the instrument in his hands and how each string sounds against his fingers, Danny's a natural. I can tell it's like me, Jenny, and Heather. Something within us that's ingrained from spending thousands of hours listening to all kinds of music that allows him to find the rhythm until his hands start to play of their own accord.

"I told you!" I praise him as he finishes up a near perfect rendition of the three open chords I taught him only about ten minutes ago. "There's a musician's blood in your veins."

He laughs bashfully, adjusting himself again on the wooden picnic bench, letting the soft rushing sound of the creek fill the air once more as he pushes back tufts of his light brown hair that have fallen over his eyes. It's a perfect day to spend outside practicing, the air warm enough but with a crisp breeze, the sun glowing through the thin layer of clouds that have filled up the sky and seem to be here to stay for a while.

No one is around. It feels as if Danny and I have fallen away from the rest of the world, into this little cove, with no one watching, just him and me and the slow, gentle strum of the guitar every now and then mixing with the whisper of the creek.

"Why don't you take any music classes at school?"

"Our school doesn't have things like that," Danny answers, leaning back against the picnic table, adjusting the instrument on his lap. "If you want to, you can ask the gym teacher to teach you how to play the trumpet. But music got cut sometime in the sixties."

"That should be illegal."

"I wish."

"Don't you at least have drama?"

"We have a club that does improv shows sometimes."

Danny relaxes his shoulders, his fingers dropping away from the strings. I glance at the familiar shiny red marks already forming on the pads of his fingers I used to get after every lesson when I was first learning how to play.

"What got you into music?"

My eyes widen at the question. It's not a strange thing to ask. It shouldn't be. And yet I don't know how to answer it.

"I don't know, it wasn't one specific thing."

I try to think back to such early days of childhood, the time when cranking up the sound of a record or a radio would begin to not only provide an escape, but a different sort of thrill. A hunger to be a part of it.

"My cousins and I, we'd listen to music together all the time, just to have a way to get away from everything. Their home life wasn't always great. My uncle left the state with some makeup saleswoman when they were little, and my aunt... She likes to blame everyone she comes across for it."

It should feel wrong to talk to someone I met only a few weeks ago about something I'd never dare discuss with anyone. But something about where we are, something about Danny himself, the way he listens like he wants to hear me, not because he's anxious to learn some juicy gossip that he can save for later, makes it easy to be honest with him.

Though not honest enough to tell my side of the story. That the scars my father left on my entire family felt so overwhelming that drowning out the noise in music was one of the only ways to feel like I was moving forward, like my life wasn't stuck in a bog I was slowly sinking away into. Plus, I figure Jenny and Heather won't ever meet Danny anyway, so they'll never know.

"First listening to music was the escape, and then pretending to perform along with it, and then actually performing along to it. It brought the three of us closer together. Now, for me, it's a place I can go to with them. Somewhere we don't have to talk if we don't want to, but still get everything out."

I look back up at Danny, who's leaning over the guitar so naturally, it's as if it's been apart of him his whole life.

"It was like that for me too." He nods.

It's all he has to say. Every kid's life is messed up in some way. All of our parents have done something unforgivable at some point. Something has driven us to do the things we do to try to escape. To just try to get by.

I stay the entire day, taking breaks teaching Danny to play by grazing along the creek with him. Talking. Staying in this little space away from the rest of the world.

Toward the evening, Benji appears, followed by Ted and his friend Jay, who runs the bar we went to. I'm preparing to head back, but Danny asks me to stay. It's a Friday night and Ted and Jay are going to grill up some hot dogs and have a campfire outside.

Now I'm sitting on a plastic chair around a warm crackling fire in front of Ted's trailer, the smell of charcoal and ketchup and mustard thick in the air, and Jay the Bar Owner strumming like a pro on my guitar. Apparently he was in a small country band when he was a teen and still knows how to play.

"Shit, Jay, we need to start up a group!" Benji exclaims after Jay finishes off a delightfully sped-up version of "Sweet Caroline." "We get you, Danny, and Addy on guitar, Ted on drums, Jackson can play a triangle or somethin', and I'll lead with my incredible vocal chops."

"We'll start that up when we're ready to cause a stir so bad, all of Greydon gets burned down tryin' to get their time back." Jay nods, his black-browed eyes narrowed as he stares down at the guitar. "Now, here's a little somethin' I picked up down south when Terry, Blue, and I were living on the road in '69."

He clears his throat and begins another crisp tune against the strings, a song I've never heard before but sounds like a mix between a road trip drinking song and a mournful ballad about a woman named Bobby Lynn who "broke his heart on a bottle of gin."

"Here, girl," Benji sighs, collapsing onto the grass beside my chair, shoving a bottle toward me. "I ain't seen ya sip anything stronger than water in the whole time I've known ya."

I laugh outrageously at the beer bottle he holds out to me, looking back at the group. But Benji keeps his arm extended, blinking a set of tipsy eyes pointedly at me, the flames from the campfire flickering against his spiked hair, making it look like knives.

I glance around at the others. Jay's engrossed in his song, his hands moving across the strings so fast, they're a blur of shadows in the darkness. Ted's holding his own beer looking apprehensive. And Danny's trying unsuccessfully to hide his snickering at my expression.

"Uh…" I take the bottle from Benji's hand and he rolls away so fast, it looks as if I've released him from a paralyzed state.

"You don't have to if you don't want to," Danny assures me quietly, leaning closer to me as I stare uncertainly at the amber-colored bottle, the condensation chilling my hand against the heat of the fire. "But one should be fine. It won't get you hungover or anything."

I look back to Ted. As if looking for permission.

"Hey, you didn't get it from me." He shrugs after a reluctant sigh. "That's Benji's shit. Keep it to just one though. And you're not about to go driving anywhere after this, are ya?"

"No."

Ted shrugs again, raising his own bottle back to his lips and taking a swig.

"I trust you to be responsible more than any of these yahoos anyhow," he says after another uncertain sigh. "Don't go makin' this a habit though. It's hard enough trying to wrangle this one." He nods to where Benji's now collapsed on the grass, beer bottle raised toward the sky.

I look down at the open bottle. Well. Sixteen years was a good run while it lasted without taking my first drink. And I feel much better about doing it here than at any other teen party I've been to where underage drinking was rampant. Here, it's just us. A relaxing night at the campfire.

I take a quick breath and raise the bottle to my lips, swallowing a tiny sip. It tastes mostly like water, with something bitter that makes my face scrunch up. Benji guffaws like it's the funniest thing in the world. Ted rolls his eyes.

"Hey, I think Jackson might have been pretty impressed with this, wouldn't ya say?" Benji nudges me as he rises to his feet again then moves to the other side of the campfire. I don't think I have ever seen this boy sit still for more than thirty seconds at a time.

"Where is he?" I ask casually after steadily swallowing down another mouthful of beer. It feels like I'm getting used to it until the aftertaste hits.

It goes quiet, Jay slowly picking at the guitar strings, everyone's expression dropping.

Something in my chest seizes in panic, though I have no idea why. I worry for a moment that something happened, like he's back in jail. Or worse.

"You never know about Jackson, do you?" Ted wonders aloud, looking down into the dying fire. "Can never tell if he's just in a rough patch or not. Most of the time it's like he can't stand being alone, and the next, you don't see him for a couple days."

"Yeah, but you can guess what he's doin' with all that time." Benji nudges playfully at Ted's shoulder, letting out a drunken laugh. Ted raises his brows knowingly. This makes me sick for a different reason.

"Does he really get into trouble a whole lot?" I ask, the half-empty beer bottle in my lap, my fingers running along the damp label I can't make out in the dark.

"Depends," Danny answers with a shrug. "Sometimes he hates the world and wants to fight everything in it. Other times he seems..."

"Sad," Jay answers across from us. He shakes his head, his dark bearded jaw in a slight grimace. "Fucked-up kid."

"Not really," Ted reasons. "Not yet, anyway."

I bite my lip as I continue staring down at the beer bottle. Wanting to ask if they know what Jackson told me the other night. About his mother he never really got to know. His father who doesn't seem to care where in the world he ends up.

"Alright." Jay clears his throat again, sitting up straighter. "Enough of this heavy talk. This is one my brother, Gerald, and I came up with for our old man's funeral to honor his banjo band roots."

He takes a deep breath before his hands are strumming on the guitar strings fast as lightning once again.

"Ohhhhhhh
You hear banjos strummin'
While birds are hummin'
This is life in the banjo world
With a puppy on my shoulder
Oh, yes, indeed'er..."

Danny and I look at each other, the tension ebbing as we both stifle outrageous laughter while Jay's voice carries away into the night along with the floating embers from the dying campfire, Benji rocking out to the acoustic guitar tune as if he's at a Led Zeppelin concert. Ted watches all of us like he's already regretting allowing me my gateway beer.

Ted drives me back to my street, insisting that I can't walk all the way back to the rental cottage on the edge of town at ten o'clock at night.

I don't argue with him since I don't want to carry my guitar the whole distance. I do insist he not drop me off in front of the house in case my mother's still awake, which he thankfully understands.

The light's still on in the living room when I get back in, and Lorry is sitting on the couch, a pile of ice cream sandwich wrappers piled beside her as she clicks through the news stations wrapping up for the night.

"You're home late," she mutters suggestively. "Another riveting night with Marcus and the gang?"

I pause in the hallway beside the entrance to the living room, leaning up against the wall.

"I broke up with him."

Lorry isn't thrown off by much, so to see her whip her head toward me, her brows raised in surprise, brings with it a sense of satisfaction.

"Wow. Thought the day would never come."

I don't know what it says about me that I get such satisfaction from knowing I've impressed my little sister.

"So who've you been rollin' around with, then?"

"God, Lorry."

"What? I meant in a totally nonsexual way."

"I met this guy, Danny Macklin. He's nice. He likes music and movies. His friends are cool. It's been fun."

"Danny who?"

I jump as my mother patters down the hallway from the bedroom. She looks like she's been trying to sleep but has been waiting up for me, her hair frizzled, her crisp white robe wrapped around her even though it's stuffy in here. I take a few hopefully casual-looking steps back, wondering if the beer I drank was strong enough for her to smell it on me.

"Danny Macklin," I answer, praying she didn't hear the earlier part of the conversation. Her eyes narrow suspiciously as she steps into the light coming from the living room, and I will my breath to come more slowly. "I met him this summer. We're friends. He's super nice, Mom."

"I've never heard of him."

"He lives in... in a different part of town."

I can't tell if she knows where I'm talking about. I guess if she did, she'd be livid by now. If she knew I've been anywhere near people like Danny or Benji, or...

"Hmph," she sighs sleepily, rubbing at her forehead, the tension leaving her ever so slightly. "The name isn't familiar. I haven't heard any gossip about him, so I suppose that's good for something."

I allow myself to feel slightly relieved.

"Unlike that *other* boy I've been hearing about lately." She rolls her eyes in disgust, her arms crossing over her chest. "Jackson something. The one who broke into the Lensens' house to play some outrageous prank during the barbecue."

I can thank the natural progression of gossip in this town that the story got warped enough that Jackson Lowell being anywhere within my vicinity that day seems to have gotten buried or ignored entirely. But still, my mother must see the look on my face as soon as she brings up Jackson's name.

"You know him?"

"I... I've heard about him." I nod maybe too quickly as my face gets hot and my palms feel sticky. It just makes me talk faster. "That he gets into trouble a lot. He just got out of a night in jail. I think he went to juvie a while ago. Everyone's talking about it."

I hate myself with every word I say, but I can't stop, desperate to convince her all I know of Jackson Lowell is the same small-town gossip traveling around her friends' circles.

"And yeah, everyone was talking about him crashing the barbecue. It was a huge thing."

My mother scans me cautiously with tired eyes, waiting for me to say anything else that might reveal how well I do know Jackson Lowell. "Yes, well, you know to stay away from boys like that. There's something not right with them, you don't need to be anywhere near any of that trouble. You could end up getting yourself seriously hurt, and not to mention what people around here would say about you..."

I hear Lorry give a dramatic sigh somewhere behind us.

"Danny's not like that," I promise her. "He never gets into trouble. He's got a summer job, he's polite, he's... he's okay, Mom."

She stares at me for a moment longer, but I can already see her posture relaxing. "Alright. What about your other friends?"

"They're not her friends, Mom," Lorry deadpans from across the room. "They're Marcus's friends. Ellen is her friend."

"Everything's alright," I assure her, giving a sincere smile that does nothing to calm her. "I'm gonna head to bed."

My hand circles around the strap of my guitar as I step around my mother and head back through the hallway toward the bedrooms. Her eyes follow me as I go, and she calls out to me once more just as I turn the corner at the end of the hall.

"And just because it's cold out doesn't mean you can't put a bit of effort into your clothes, Adrienne."

Chapter 14
Addy

I hardly make it into town the next day before seeing Marcus and his friends. They're all piled in Deran's car outside the street leading down to the rows of sprawling columned homes, looking like they're waiting for someone. Sounding already obnoxious and possibly drunk.

I'm not in the mood for whatever confrontation will arise if they see me. And Marcus's behavior from the other day hasn't left my mind. He might have just been angry, but given the way Danny is wary of him enough to desperately avoid any contact, I wonder if Marcus and his friends are more prone to violence than I would have ever given them credit for in the past. And there's no one else around, no Ted to stop gallantly in the road to assist. I get the feeling the kind of people driving around this neighborhood wouldn't want to stop and get involved.

I decide to move off the road, walking deep into the brush sprawling along the sides of town, keeping it sequestered from from the rest of humanity. Though I wonder as I move through the abandoned strips of field and dead grass if this was the smartest idea. I may have looped around Marcus to avoid him, but I could be dragged off by a wild wolf. Are there bears around here?

Probably not, but there are small ponds. Ponds that pop out of nowhere, their edges hidden away by bunches of weeds and bushes. Like one such pond that I sink into after my foot falls straight through what I had thought was a solid patch of brush.

My life flashes before my eyes as my body drops several feet down into a cold puddle of disgusting water that thankfully splashes only to my chin before I manage to kick myself up, rescuing myself from choking on a mouthful of swampy water at least.

The peaceful silence of nature is broken apart by my desperate splashing and gasping as I clamber against the damp marshy ground to extract myself from the pond, my clothes soaked through and already sticking to me like clingfilm as I crawl back out into the hot sun.

It isn't until I'm back on my feet, shaking myself off like a scandalized wet dog and yanking bits of unidentified debris clumps off me that I hear laughter echoing merrily from somewhere above me.

"I love that we've crossed paths this way today."

The world might just hate me.

"What the *hell* are you doing here?" I ask, the outrage clear in my voice as I yank a string of something from my hair.

"Could ask you the same thing," Jackson answers from his spot perched against the trunk of one of the trees above where I have been dipping down a path deeper into the fields, hence the pond I succumbed to.

"I asked first."

"Waitin' for Shelly Criston," he calls to me as I clumsily stumble my way back out of the hole and onto steady ground. I should be annoyed that Jackson doesn't lift a finger to try to help me, but it would feel condescending if he did. And I wouldn't accept his help anyway. "We've got some business."

I stop a few feet from him, still shaking the now warm water from my body. I give him a pointed glare.

"Are you serious? You're gonna have a fight out in the middle of nowhere?"

"Where would you prefer, in front of the Roller Dollar?"

"That's dangerous. Someone could get killed out here."

"Actually, I'm hopin' Criston'll fall for the same trap you just did. Thought you were him 'til you popped up just now."

"Very funny."

He hops down from his perch on the trunk, looking me over after running a quick hand through his dark gold hair that is sticking out in a couple different directions today. "You're dressed different. Less girly."

"I didn't want to intimidate you any further."

And I'm relieved I decided to wear jean shorts today, because I would have ruined any skirt I own by falling into that pond.

He laughs, my insult not landing. "Your turn."

"My turn what, I already gave you a comeback," I remind him.

"No, your turn to tell me what you're doin' all the way out here on your own."

I sigh, reaching over to begin squeezing the water out from my hair. "Wanted to take another way into town."

"Oh, yeah?" His hands go to his hips. "Who're you avoidin'? Your boyfriend still?"

I glare at him, straightening myself up with as much dignity as I can. "None of your business." I brush past him, eager to get out of here as fast as I can. "And he's not my boyfriend anymore. I dumped his sorry ass."

It feels as therapeutic to say it out loud now as it did last night when I told Lorry. And when I told Ted. Actually, it feels more and more freeing every time I think it. Strange, when I feared it might only make me more and more sick with regret.

Jackson is uncharacteristically silent, and I think he's stopped following me until I hear his steps start up again, clomping through the dry grass.

"You serious?"

"No. I'm lying just to have a thrill. That's what you always say I'm trying to do, right?"

"Damn." I can hear an appreciative smile in his voice. I don't know why it makes my stomach suddenly flip, but I ignore it and keep walking. "How'd you do it? Public humiliation? Throw a milkshake in his face? Any of the classics?"

The sound of a car roaring up along the side of the road makes us both pause. The car stops beyond the tree line, the sound of doors wrenching open and slamming closed following before a group of guys barge through the brush.

Shelly Criston and his gang. Four people this time instead of two. Jackson's fighting all of them?

I look back at him and see a troubled look on his face as he gazes at the group descending toward us. And realize no, he hadn't been planning on this. Shelly Criston cheated.

"You should beat it," Jackson tells me without looking at me, his entire demeanor changed, but his tone strangely soft. I look back at Shelly and the guys approaching, their faces twisted into ugly sneers all focused unflinchingly on where Jackson stands, backing slowly away from me. And a sudden urgency strikes through me. What if they have weapons? What if they came here to...

"Jackson—"

"Go." He looks me in the eye now. A different look. One that tells me he's not playing around. That this is serious. And something I have no business being anywhere near.

My mother's warning from last night flashes in my mind. And without another word, I turn away and start walking in the other direction, breaking back out onto the road. I move across the street to the other side, and don't stop until I reach town. Before I have to hear a moment of whatever is about to happen in the hidden cover of the brush.

***

"We should have a movie night. I've decided."

"When?"

"Soon."

"Where?"

"Ted's got a TV at his place."

"What movies?"

"Hey, Danny!" Benji calls out to Danny before answering me. "You remember that night we rented *Cannibal Holocaust*?"

"I wish I didn't," Danny answers from across the store where he's in the middle of trying to help a lady find the Greta Garbo romance movie she's looking for.

"Poor bastard didn't eat anything for two days straight," Benji sighs as he twists around the aisle to join me in the action movie section.

"I thought I was going to go to jail just for watching it," I tell him, pulling out a copy of *The Road Warrior*. "How about an action movie night? Then we won't have to traumatize poor Danny with horror."

"Ah, but it's so fun! And horror flicks are the best for movie nights."

"How about action-horror?" I suggest. "*Alien. Dawn of the Dead.*"

"Hell yeah."

I peruse through the lines of VHS tapes, Benji trailing along behind me as he scans the opposite side of the row.

"So you're a music gal, huh?"

"Meaning?"

"You're into music. You have a guitar. You're *cool.*"

"Sure, if you say so."

"I've been tryin' to get Danny and the guys to learn how to play a tune so we can play at the summer carnival. They think it's a shit idea, but maybe you can join my one-man band and they'll all follow 'cause they'll be so jealous."

"That sounds terrifying," I tell him.

"Ah, come on!" he insists, hopping on his feet. "It'd be bitchin'! Having a girl in the band might get people to actually listen to us."

"How flattering."

"Hey, a girl who's *good*. That's what I meant. Do you sing?"

"I know how to sing, yes."

"Damn, even better!"

I shake my head, smiling. "I'll think about it."

Benji pulls out a copy of *Assault on Precinct 13*, turning to lean against the shelf and face me. "You like movies or music better?"

"Both. Can't have one without the other."

"You think so?"

"Of course. Music is what gives movies half their life. And you can't listen to or play a piece of music without feeling either epic or depressed enough to be starring in your own movie, right?"

Benji stares at me, his eyes flickering upward. "Huh. Deep."

"Shut up," I laugh.

Danny finishes helping the woman and rushes off to answer the phone after she leaves with her Greta Garbo movie.

"Don't tell Danny this is a horror movie," Benji mutters, passing me a copy of *Rolling Thunder*.

I open my mouth to argue that it's more of a revenge movie than anything before the sound of something crashing through the front window of the store makes me yelp.

Both Benji and I instinctively duck to the ground as the glass shatters, whatever had blasted through it slamming into one of the shelves in the front showing the new summer releases, and sending it crashing backward. VHS tapes of *Rocky III*, *Cat People*, and *Annie* spill across the floor.

The sound of tires screeching and a distant howl of laughter echoes somewhere in the distance before a still silence fills the store.

Benji is quick to jump back onto his feet while I stay pressed to the ground, my heart thundering in my ears, certain I'm about to hear gunshots at any moment.

"You okay, Dan?!"

I hear Benji leap over the shelves, his feet shaking the ground as he runs toward the front desk. *Oh God, Danny...*

I crawl to my feet, hurrying through the aisles toward the front desk where Benji is helping a terrified-looking Danny to his feet on the other side. Danny's still clutching the phone in his hands, probably with a baffled customer on the other end, as he gazes in shock at the obliterated window. His face is a sickly shade of white.

My gaze moves from the shattered window, trailing along the collapsed shelf, all the way to the corner of the front desk. Where a pale red brick lies amid the mess of glass and VHS tapes.

I sprint toward the hole that is the front window now and leap down onto the sidewalk, my shoes crunching against bits of glass as I run a few paces, just far enough to catch sight of the only car at the end of the street speeding at least thirty miles over the limit.

I can easily make out the familiar car right before it disappears around the corner. A green Buick I've ridden in countless times, ever since Marcus's parents bought it for him last summer.

Chapter 15

Jackson

Shelly Criston's surprise posse shouldn't have been too much of a surprise. I nearly got into it with him in the middle of the back lot of the shopping center last night after having to rip him off his dopey girlfriend who for some reason keeps hanging around him even when I've seen him smack her around more than once. But fighting someone on the ground drunk isn't my idea of a good time, not to mention the fact that Sheriff Nulty could have rolled up on us at any second. Instead I told him to meet me out off Keeley Road so we could finally have it out, no distractions, no nosy cops, no interruptions.

And of course, he decided to bring his merry band of idiots.

While I took a good beating, two of the boneheads went down immediately when they chased me down to that hidden pond I watched Addy fall into a couple minutes earlier. I really didn't know the pond started there until I saw her fall into it, so I might have to thank her for that. Shelly was easy enough to knock out after a while, but the bigger guy he brought with him, his cousin's friend's ex–jail mate or something, really knew how to throw down. Still, while it wasn't a fight with a clear winner, I think I placed pretty high if we were comparing.

Now, I would love the rest of the night to lie like a corpse in this bed, a cold beer in one hand pressed to my throbbing right eye and a sack of ice on my ribs that I don't think is helping anything, but feels nice against the heat that always gets stuck up here in this bedroom above Ward's store.

Unfortunately, my peace is interrupted by the sound of feet scurrying up the stairs and someone's little fist pounding at the door.

"Oh my fuckin' God," I groan in disbelief as my head throbs in time to the rapid beating rattling the door, shaking the entire damn room.

It can't be Ward—the man doesn't move that fast. If it's Shelly or one of his cronies, they'd be stupid to want to go for round two. They got just as socked as I did and are probably still pulling themselves up out of the pond and back to their car.

So it might be an emergency. Goddamn it.

I roll off the bed, catching myself before I can faceplant onto the floor, dropping the ice pack onto the bedside table but holding on to the beer can. I crack the door open, blinking through my bleary vision to try to make out the figure standing in the hallway.

"The fuck is it?" I mumble, my tongue tripping over my busted lip that's already swelling.

"Jackson?"

Addy's voice is breathless and panicked, but she stills as soon as I peek my head out the door. She shoves it open wider, and I stumble back, wincing at the light from the shop down below.

"What do you want, Addy?"

"Are you alright?"

"I was until someone started hammering on my door like the goddamn cops."

She blinks. "Oh. Sorry."

I huff out a laugh, leaning against the door frame. I'd be lying if I said I didn't enjoy how worried she is about me. It sort of makes me want to play it up, just a bit.

"What the hell are you doing here?"

She shakes herself off after a moment of continuing to gaze at me with that concerned little frown. She's still in the same clothes from earlier today when she fell into the pond. Dry now.

"Benji told me where to find you. He's back at the video store with Danny." She presses her lips together, her eyes looking down shamefully as her face turns red to match the rage beginning to glow on her expression. "Marcus and his friends threw a brick through the store window at him."

The cops are inside talking with the store manager by the time Addy and I arrive, and Benji runs over to pull us toward the side of the building, away from the small crowd that has gathered. Danny looks up as we approach, and I can see the terror in his eyes that he only just manages to squash down once he sees us. Kid will never admit when he's scared if there's more than one person around.

"I say we get 'em back tonight," Benji starts as I stare over at the shattered window by the front desk. Where Danny had been standing. Where the brick easily could have smashed into his face. "Slash their tires, pour paint on their car, light up their fuckin' gas tank. We gotta do somethin'."

"Why don't we just talk to the police?" Addy suggests desperately, sounding as if she's brought this idea up a few times before I got here. "We know who did it, Danny and I both saw Marcus's exact car..."

Danny laughs humorlessly, leaning against the side of the building, looking only mildly shaken and thankfully completely unharmed. "I'm sure they'd take my word for it."

"There were tons of witnesses," Addy insists, gesturing around the street. "I'm sure we could find someone who would have seen—"

"You don't know this town too well, hun," I grumble, giving Benji a firm pat on the back to stop him from teetering on his feet, looking as if he's preparing to take off and sprint a marathon. "No one around here's gonna wanna get involved. Especially with somethin' like this."

"Teen antics aren't exactly a desirable topic," Danny agrees. "Besides... you know who the sheriff is. You think anyone's gonna believe me over people like Deran Burth and Marcus Tanner?"

Addy looks like she wants to argue, stubborn as ever. But even she can't dispute that logic.

"I could talk to them," she offers, her voice smaller. "I saw it too. Sheriff Nulty knows me alright, he knows I wouldn't lie about something like this. He might—"

"You really ready to go against all the good ol' boys on this?" I ask her, my hand resting on my hip as she turns to give me a determined stare. "You? An out-of-towner? A *girl*? A girl who just broke up with the hailed scholar, athlete, golden boy Marcus Tanner? How well do ya think that's gonna go over?"

She takes a breath to prepare to argue, but the determination is melting from her face. She knows I'm right.

"Besides that, you ready for your mother to know the kind of people you've been hangin' around?"

It might be a low blow, but I can't help it. I want to see her reaction. Almost because I want to see her prove me wrong, like she does every so often. To stare unblinkingly back at my face and say she doesn't care. That she isn't ashamed of being friends with people like us, let alone standing up against her jackass ex-boyfriend, even when it's a losing battle. To see her march over to the cops and tell them what really happened, that it wasn't hooligans from the bad side of the neighborhood where Danny lives. To not care if it gets back to her mother at all.

But she does what I expected. Lowers her head, a look of fear flashing across her face like her mother knowing is the final decision made for her.

"Who gives a shit about cops?" Benji interjects again, his energy rising. "Let's get these bastards back. I say revenge outweighs justice every time."

"Forget it, Benji," Danny sighs, leaning his head on the wall, blinking against the harsh late evening sun. "They're not worth it."

"He's right." Addy nods solemnly, still looking at the ground, my words obviously still weighing on her. "All you're gonna do is make them angrier."

"Who gives a shit? Jackson, ya gotta have my back on this."

"Actually... I have to agree with the squares on this one."

Both Addy and Danny turn to look at me at the same moment with a comically surprised expression. Benji's head falls back in a frustrated groan.

"C'mon. You're killin' me."

"Think about it, Benji," I begin, forcing myself to be reasonable only because I don't need Danny to get himself into any more trouble over this. "These assholes won't even get a slap on the wrist for shit like this. But we'll get worse than that if we go messin' around their neighborhood."

"We've done it before," he argues.

"Deran and Marcus will be expecting us to come lookin' for some payback. They'll point us out to Sheriff Nulty the moment one leaf is out of place in their fancy little yards. Not to mention, they'll come lookin' to get some revenge of their own."

Benji can't argue with that. I'd like nothing more than to go up to Marcus Tanner himself and beat the crap outta him for what he could have done to Danny. There'd be nothing holding me back at all if it was just me I had to worry about. But them targeting Danny makes this an entirely different thing.

And it makes me even more pissed off.

I can't help but kick at a discarded Pepsi can on the ground, sending it rebounding off the wall with a sharp clang that makes Addy flinch before it tumbles across the sidewalk and out into the street.

I told him this would happen, stupid kid...

Danny's boss lets him off the hook for the rest of the night, and doesn't fire him, even though the cops conclude it must have been some of Danny's friends trying to pull a prank. It's useless for Danny to try to argue. Not like the cops care about tracking down who's responsible anyway. And Danny's manager is satisfied that the insurance will cover the window.

Benji heads back home with him to make sure he gets there without any trouble. Marcus and his gang are no Shelly Criston, haven't been known to jump people in the dead of night on their way back home. But they also, as far as I know, haven't been known to chuck bricks through store windows, so I'm not taking any chances. And we all know Danny isn't able to step on a bug, let alone throw a punch or defend himself in any way.

Addy lingers near the store after the others have left and I'm ready to head back to Ward's to try to get some sleep and fight off this migraine that's right on top of me.

"I'll stay away."

I pause and look back at her. Her face never lifted from the frown it had sunk down into after I made it clear to her she's not willing to risk anything for Danny. And I do not feel bad. I don't.

I really don't.

But for whatever reason, her dejected, resolved face makes me pissed.

"If it helps," she continues, looking up at me earnestly, trying to hide the hurt in her expression. "I'll stay away. This all happened because of me."

I laugh. "Please. That's a coward's way out."

She looks surprised, stepping back as I walk toward her, but her eyes continue to hold mine, even as I stop a few inches from her face, close enough to see the slight smudges of dirt still streaked across her left cheek from her jaunt in the pond earlier.

"And the reason I like you is because I know you aren't one," I tell her, my voice lowering, strands of her hair fluttering against my breath. I shrug. "Not really."

Finally, her usual countenance begins to return, her eyes narrowing at me. "I thought you wanted me to stay away."

Herbal. She smells like something herbal, like some kind of tea. Beneath the lingering aroma of the pond water, anyway.

"I did. But you hate it."

"Hate what?"

"Being told what to do. Being treated like a delicate little doll. Having to sit by and watch all the injustices of the world and not being able to save everyone you can."

She's about to retort, but I hold up my hands, taking a step back. "Hey, it's not exactly a bad thing. You may be a little out of touch at times, but I admire the spirit."

She shakes her head as she stares at me with incredulous eyes. "You're one of the most confusing people I've ever had the displeasure of coming across, Jackson Lowell."

My lips curl in satisfaction after she's turned away. I hope I really do get on her nerves as much as she makes it seem.

Chapter 16

Addy

"Does Jackson Lowell get in fights like that often?"

Danny and I have hardly gotten more than a few words of conversation in since I arrived to meet him at Ted's house this afternoon. Our guitar practice today was destined to be rudely interrupted by a rogue beagle puppy running rampant throughout the trailer.

Jay's going off on a road trip to pick up a new stereo for the bar a couple towns over and had to leave his dog, Skerritt, with Ted while he's away. Of course, Ted has to work most of the day, so Danny is staying here and watching over the little demon. He's already nearly escaped into the woods four times, got into a bag of cheese puffs hidden in one of the kitchen cabinets, and gnawed a puppy-sized hole through one of the quilts in Ted's bedroom that he then ran around wearing as a cape for several minutes before we could catch him.

"Oh, they aren't too rare," Danny answers, catching the flailing puppy with one hand as it attempts to leap from the couch onto one of the curtains. I'm convinced this dog thinks it's a cat. "And not too rare that Shelly cheats either. Most of the time he does."

Skerritt ambles out of Danny's grip and shoots toward me next.

"Shelly's a wannabe," Danny says. I catch Skerritt like he's a football when he stumbles on slippery legs and slides several inches right into my grasp. "Always tryin' to be a big bad gangster, but he comes off as a washed-up high school dropout who still thinks he's fifteen. That's why he only picks on people younger than him."

The front door swings open and Benji lands in the room, wielding a spray bottle. "Alright, you think this will work?"

"I think Jay will sue us for animal cruelty," Danny says as I wrestle to keep the squirming dog in my arms. "He loves this dog, Benji, we can't go spraying him in the face."

"We can't have him eatin' all Ted's food either! That's for us to do."

"What food did he leave you with?" I ask, gritting my jaw as tiny puppy teeth nip at my hands and arms.

Danny's face scrunches with uncertainty. "Uh..."

"Shit, Dan."

"Hey, Jay left Ted with the instructions!"

"What about you, Addy?" Benji turns desperately to me. "Aren't you supposed to have a natural motherly instinct or something?"

"Excuse me?"

"Aren't girls supposed to know how to... take care of things?"

I cock my head at Benji. "I'm sixteen years old, genius, I can hardly take care of myself. My little sister's more responsible than I am."

The next second, the mongrel leaps from my hands, crashes down onto the floor, and skitters up onto its legs before careening toward the front door. I nearly bite all of my fingernails off as I see the screen door whip open right as Skerritt dashes toward the open world, far too fast before either Danny or Benji can dive after him.

"Shit, Addy. You better not let your mother hear you talkin' like that. How're you supposed to give her any grandkids if you have no natural motherly instinct?"

Jackson had been the one to sweep in through the front door, scooping up the runaway puppy with one hand. He curls it against his chest as he steps inside, a self-satisfied smirk on his face as he holds the little demon dog as easily as if it weighed no more than a tiny box of milk. Though he has it easier than any of us have had, because miraculously, Skerritt has decided to stop squirming entirely in Jackson's grip, instead sticking his tiny pink tongue out to lick all along his hand.

"Damn, Jackson," Benji speaks first as the three of us stare in stunned silence. "Where've you been all day?"

"We coulda used *your* motherly touch this entire morning," Danny agrees, slumping down onto the couch tiredly.

"Ah, dogs are easy." Jackson shrugs, staring down at the white and gold patterned pup that continues eagerly licking his hand. "Skerritt and I are old pals. I play with him at the bar all the time while tryin' to get Jay to slip me a whiskey. Haven't been successful yet, but this little beast sure likes me givin' him some attention every now and then."

"Jay's abandoned him for three whole days," Danny explains, hauling my guitar up from where I had laid it against the couch. "Ted's gotta watch out for him. Which really means *we* do."

"*You*," Benji points out. "You're the responsible one of this ragtag team, my friend."

"Hell of a summer," Danny mutters, strumming along the guitar as he begins to recall the last notes we had gone over. He's managed to play through an entire song so far.

"These animals tryin' to tame you, little man?" Jackson asks, lifting Skerritt up in both hands to gaze at him nose to nose. "You wanna come hang with me at Ward's place instead? Much more fun than these stuffy jailkeepers."

"Yeah, he can join the revolving door of gals stayin' the night up there," Benji jabs. Jackson laughs. I roll my eyes and join Danny on the couch.

"How's the band comin' along?" Jackson calls over as Benji throws down the spray bottle and starts raiding the kitchen cabinets.

"I can play without hurting my own ears," Danny reports. "So that's something."

"But you shouldn't be in here all day," Jackson decides, settling Skerritt up on his shoulder, who of course obediently remains there, gnawing lightly on the worn edge of Jackson's loose green tank top. "The sun's out, it's the middle of summer! We've got a creek right there."

"We can't go out with the dog." Danny nods to the tiny beast perched on Jackson' shoulder. "He'll take off and we'll never see him again. Jay says he's pretty dumb, he won't know how to get back."

"If he even wants to," Benji adds, taking a long sip from a can of Pepsi.

"Ah, little man'll be fine," Jackson says, nudging his shoulder up. "He'd never take off on me. Come on, let's go."

"Jackson!" I call warningly as he whips the screen door open again and jumps down onto the grass outside. Danny, Benji, and I follow, watching as Skerritt leaps from Jackson's shoulder, bolts about five feet, and then stops, turning back toward Jackson before doing an endless twirl of clumsy circles.

"See? He's fine! He just wants to play out in the sun. Live a little, guys, we're still young!"

Benji lets out a relieved laugh before running along behind Jackson as they both amble toward the creek, Skerritt in tow.

Danny and I glance at each other. I'm already kicking my shoes off.

The ankle-deep water of the cool creek feels like a healing balm against the glaring afternoon sun and the stuffy inside of Ted's trailer, and I trail my toes through the smooth pebbles coating the bottom of the waterbed.

"Hey, Addy!"

I turn toward Benji's voice, enthralled in my reverie enough that I forgot about the first time I waded into this creek with these boys.

Before I can do anything, Benji is throwing a handful of ice-cold creek water at my face.

I shriek and gasp, bringing my hands to my face as I stumble backward, gooseflesh chilling pleasantly along my skin. I hear Benji laughing and splashing away, Skerritt barking happily as he repeatedly splashes only his front paws into the water, and Jackson guffawing somewhere in the background.

Whipping my soaked hair out of my face, I see Benji now standing in the water next to Danny, who has clasped his hands over his mouth, trying not to laugh as well, pretending to be horrified on my behalf.

"You think it's funny, boys?" I ask, leaning down to scoop water into my own hands.

"Shit, run!" Benji shoves Danny before splashing off in the other direction, toward where there are several larger rocks. Skerritt lets out a sharp bark and runs after Jackson toward the tree line, while Danny stands in front of me, frozen, not knowing where to turn. I grin at him.

He squints his eyes shut, raising his arms in preparation as I dive toward him, using all my momentum to splash a large wave of water straight at him.

It's war for a while. The sound of running and yelling and splashing and barking, the strain and sweat of playing so hard under the hot summer sun easily washed away by the icy water. I do manage to get Benji back, sneaking up behind him while he's busy tripping over Skerritt after trying to exit the creek and hide in the tree line with Jackson.

Later on, I discover Jackson kneeling down behind one of the rocks, looking out at where Benji and Danny are in a temporary duel (Benji at some point acquired a huge branch and is now waving it threateningly in a circle around himself). Skerritt sits on top of the rock, jumping up and down and barking madly, cheering... one of them on.

I move slowly, the sounds of my approach drowned out in Benji's and Danny's shouts and splashing as I scoop up a handful of water, prepared to throw it down the back of Jackson's neck and finally have some well-earned revenge. The suspense is maddening, and I'm concerned I may be slightly psychopathic for how badly I want to be the one to take him down.

And I think I succeed, for a moment.

Meaning, I do manage to throw a handful of water down his back, but in the same breath he turns, grabs my arm, and twists me around, dragging both of us down into the water until we're completely submerged and temporarily paralyzed by the cold.

I don't hurt anything, since his arm and hand press against my spine and the back of my head so that I don't fall straight onto the rocks. But I do take in a breath of water that I gladly spit into his face the moment he pulls us both up.

A mix of emotions flutters through me as I hear him laughing, inches from me, his lower body still pressed against mine, his arm is still wrapped around my back, his hand holding my head, his other arm touching against my waist. It's outrage first, then relief as my body unwinds against the surprisingly refreshing full-body dunk. And then it's... something else.

Something that pauses my own laughter as I look at him, water droplets dripping from his soaked hair onto my face; something that sits heavy and pleasant in my chest. His laughter calms into a snarky grin that begins to look only half-teasing the longer I become lost in his deep brown eyes, his face framed against the harsh sunlit sky behind him that sends sparks through his dark blond tufts of hair, inches from touching my cheek.

The moment lasts... I don't know how long. Then I'm being yanked back up, the water sloshing around us, and I'm in the air until Jackson places me firmly back onto my feet. I tilt as the pebbles shift under me.

And then he's gone, marching over toward Benji and Danny, joining their game. I remain standing by the rock, staring at some point past the three of them, Skerritt watching me from his perch, his wet ears flopping as he cocks his head.

Ted grills up some burgers for us when he gets back from work. Jackson sticks around so that we can all remain outside without having to worry about Skerritt running off. Although it looks like we've finally entertained the feral puppy enough that he's not thinking about running anywhere else for the time being.

The sun begins to set. Danny plays the Beatles song I taught him for everyone. And I don't want to leave.

It's almost dark as I'm sitting on the edge of the creek, the air still warm enough for the water to feel nice on my bare feet. Benji's out in the middle of it, wading back and forth, the water illuminated by the full moon. I watch him mindlessly.

Something flies over my head, landing in the water a couple feet from Benji with a huge splash. He jumps with a loud curse, looking behind me at whoever had thrown the pebble. He raises his middle finger.

I don't turn around when I hear Jackson's soft laugh. I stay frozen, my heart picking up fearfully. And also with a strange eagerness.

I expect him to saunter back toward the trailer where Ted and Danny are cleaning up from the burgers. Instead, I hear him move closer. And then he's sitting beside me.

"Something botherin' you?"

I'm glad it's dark so that he can't see how red I turn. I must have heatstroke.

"I don't want to go home."

I don't know why I say it. I don't know why Jackson Lowell would ever need to know about my weird, nostalgic feelings. That I've so suddenly changed my mind when all I've been feeling this summer is entirely unimpressed with Greydon. Surely he'll only make fun of me.

But he doesn't.

"You don't go back to New York until the end of the summer," he reminds me in an unemotional voice.

"It's a month away."

"That's a long time."

"Not really."

"You gonna miss this?" he asks, leaning back on his hands, his gaze still feeling like a weight settling on me. "Lettin' your hair down with a bunch of dumbass boys who throw rocks and swing sticks at each other?"

He says it like it is indeed as ridiculous as it sounds. And yet...

"Yes," I reply, unashamed.

Jackson is quiet for a while. I still don't look over at him, even though I want so badly to know what he's thinking. Why he's so quiet.

Benji leans down over the water, clapping his hands together as if he's trying to catch something he sees in the rocks.

"You'll be back next summer. Won't you?"

He says it as unenthused as I feel. And with something else in his tone too. A reluctant surrender. An anger. Not at me, but at something.

Finally, I turn to him. Under the glare of the moonlight reflecting off the water, I can see the look in his eyes matches his voice.

"Yeah. As long as you all don't forget about me."

My expression is intentionally lighter, desperate to drag us away from whatever tense place the conversation is going. Thankfully, when he turns to look at me, the ghost of his familiar smirk is in his eyes.

"Oh, don't worry about that, princess. And I already know we're unforgettable."

"That's one way of putting it."

I know it's time for me to head home. I asked Lorry to cover for me and say I was with Ellen if our mother asked, but I still don't want to push it. I'm never out with Ellen this late.

"Hey," Jackson calls to me after I've said good-night to everyone (including Skerritt, who has eased up on nipping at me and even graced me with one tentative lick). I turn back before I can walk off toward the tree line and head to the road. He follows behind me, taking something from his back pocket.

"I've got Ward's car with me," he says, jangling a set of keys in his hand. "I can drive ya home."

"Oh, you don't have to..."

I can't even finish the sentence. Though I decided to leave my guitar here with Danny so he can practice more on his own, the long walk back to the rental cottage doesn't sound as enticing tonight as it usually does.

"Sure. Thank you."

Jackson doesn't move though, once he's standing in front of me. He grins, an idea stirring.

"Or we could take a drive. Somewhere."

I say nothing. I'm afraid to. He notices, turning his head knowingly.

"You don't want to go home, right?"

I finally shake my head. "Where did you have in mind?"

Chapter 17

Jackson

There are some places around Greydon that are nice. Shocking-ly, none of them are within the populated areas of town. It's out on the edges of town, in the open fields. Not the dead brush and pond-infested areas either. No, the place I have in mind, where I think Addy might like, where it would be nice to get away from the noise, is somewhere where there's nothing but openness, a view of the hills on one side and a view of the road to Greydon on the other.

Addy seems to enjoy the drive in Ward's convertible. I'm not the biggest car guy myself, but it's a pretty sweet ride. He keeps the old '59 Chevrolet in pristine condition. He doesn't have a wife or a family, so this baby's his pride and joy.

He lets me take it for a spin only when he's shitfaced and doesn't even know who he's handing the keys to.

Addy's hair flies behind her on the drive, her face relaxed into a numb bliss that I've never seen from her before. But it's similar to what she's looked like all day. Unwound.

"Lookin' good, Audrey Hepburn," I comment as I slow the car down as we approach the open field on the other side of the road. We're far out from where she needs to go to get home, but she doesn't seem to mind.

She runs a hand through her now-messy hair, her eyes still closed. "My friend hates driving with the top down."

She opens her eyes and looks around as I drive the car straight onto the plain of empty grass that stretches on for miles and miles in the darkness, the shadow of the mountains hovering beyond us.

"Is this someone's property?" she asks as I park the car in the middle of the grass, the engine quieting until there's nothing but the dead quiet of the field.

"Probably. But I've never been caught before." I unbuckle my seat belt, heaving myself up onto the top of the seat and looking out at the utter emptiness all around us. "But there's a first time for everything."

She gives me a look, but unbuckles her seat belt too and sits on top of her seat. She takes in the vastness of the empty field, the miles of space around us. The feeling of being completely hidden away, and yet out in the open.

"I never would have pictured you enjoying a place like this, Jackson Lowell."

"I'm full of surprises." It's true that I usually hate the quiet. But there's something about this place, something about being away from any prying eyes, from any sound of town, especially alone here with someone else...

"I hope you haven't taken me to your hookup spot."

I laugh, throwing my head back and gazing up at the clear indigo sky. "Look, it's a nice place to talk, alright? With the occasional fun time."

She snaps her gaze to me.

"I promise I'm not tryin' anything!" I insist, holding my hands up. "Cross my heart. Hope to die, stick the needle in my eye, however it goes."

Her eyes narrow, but she seems satisfied.

"So what, then?" I ask, resting my hands against the top of the seat, reaching over to nudge her with my elbow. "Why can't someone like me enjoy a touch of nature every once in a while, huh? What, because I like trouble, 'cause I like sleepin' around?"

She looks considerate, turning back to look out over the quiet field.

"You like for people to think you're a tough guy. But not like Shelly Criston." I frown at the mention of that jackass right now. Way to bring a mood down. "Not like you're insecure and need a bunch of children to think you're a badass."

She turns to face me, and it feels strangely intimidating. But I make sure not to flinch away, meeting her stare goadingly. Mostly because I like looking at her face.

"What is it, then? Why am I the way I am?"

A small grin appears on her face. An equal challenge. A game.

"Because you're hurt. And afraid. And sad." She leans back, tossing her hair dramatically, continuing before I have the chance to process what she said. "And I bet you haven't even slept with that many girls."

I can't help but laugh. She joins me.

"And what about you?"

She jumps down from the car, lands on the grass, and walks a few steps before sprawling herself out on the ground. "What do you want to know?"

I follow her down from the car, collapsing beside her on the grass, landing on my side. "Why do you like horror movies?"

She stifles a grin, staring up at the sky. "Why does anyone like horror?" She turns toward me, a mischievous grin on her face. "I like being scared."

"What scares you the most?"

She looks like the answer will come to her easily. But she pauses, her eyes drifting, her mouth quirking.

"In movies, or in life?"

"Life. Duh. That's the more interesting one."

She sighs. "Damn you."

"Okay, what *does* scare you the most in movies? Start with an easy one."

"Anything body horror."

"Really?" I snort.

"Yes. Have you ever seen *Shivers*? *The Brood*? That is the epitome of terror. And why I don't ever want to have kids."

"Yeah?"

"Yeah," she half laughs. "Not having control of my own body? Have the definition of a parasite growing in me and feeding off me? You do know some people can go blind or become paralyzed, or have their uterus fall out when..."

She pauses when she sees my face.

"Sorry. My sister read this book on all the unknown horrors of pregnancy. Her stories have stuck with me."

"I don't think I expected the word *uterus* to be spoken tonight."

"Maybe it should be spoken more."

"So... your real-life fear is pregnancy?"

She shakes her head. "No. My real-life fear would be that same idea. Not having control over myself. Having something or someone else decide what's going to happen to me."

She sighs, looking back over at me.

"Or the classic: ending up like my mother. That keeps me up at night often."

I laugh again. We both look back up.

"Your turn." Her knee nudges against mine for just a second.

"Ghosts, for movies," I answer without pause. "Possession shit. Haunted houses."

"Really?" Her laugh at least doesn't sound teasing.

"Yep. *Amityville Horror* scared the shit outta me. You never know, that shit could be real, and we aren't even seein' it, ya know?"

"Huh. Alright, fair. And real life?"

"Real life..."

I know exactly what my real-life fear is. It's something that's already happened. Something that could happen again at any moment. But for whatever reason, even here in the dark alone with someone I feel wouldn't make fun of me or talk about anything we say here tonight with anyone else, it feels more embarrassing than my first admission.

"That I won't ever get to see a beach in California."

"Oh, come on," she groans. "I was honest with you. You can't leave me hanging."

"What? It's true. It may not be a lifelong fear, but it's a current one."

"Jackson."

"What?"

"Tell me."

I can feel her looking at me. I know if I meet her gaze, I won't be able to keep it to myself.

"This was your idea, by the way," she reminds me.

"You wanted to psychoanalyze my 'bad boy' tendencies. I wanted to return the favor."

She turns away, sighing heavily. "Fine. I'm going to assume your real-life fear is also ghosts."

"It's a good one."

I turn fully toward her again. She looks at me. Her hair looks soft, sprawled out against the grass and along the side of her face. She's not glaring at me or analyzing me or looking like she wants to slap me. Her eyes instead look like something I don't think I even recognize, but it has some kind of knot forming in my abdomen.

"I'm gonna kiss you now, Addy."

She laughs. Loudly. "No you're not."

"Why not?"

"Oh my God." She shakes her head, her hands going to her face. "Jackson, you promised no funny business."

"What's wrong with a kiss?"

She lifts herself up from the ground. "You're taking me home now. And you're parking at the end of the street so my mother doesn't see some random boy dropping me off."

"What?" I ask in mock astonishment. "But I wanted to meet her!"

***

"What's the deadline for this carnival thing?"

"You gotta enter by tomorrow," Benji explains eagerly while Danny homes in his laser focus on the next round of Asteroids. "I'm headin' to town hall tonight to sign us up."

"You are *not*."

"Too late, Dan my man. I'm planning on askin' forgiveness, not permission."

"I'm already not giving you permission."

"Come on, Danny, you should consider this," I argue, nudging his shoulder lightly with my fist currently gripping a cup of Coca Cola. "We all heard you play last night, you're not half-bad. Next to Benji, people'll think you're David Bowie."

"Hey! Who's the ringleader of this operation?"

"Unfortunately you," Danny answers, struggling to keep up with the controls and the screen in front of him.

"Does that mean you officially defer to me?"

"Sounds like I won't have much of a choice."

Benji claps loudly. "Yes! That's you and Jay down. Next I gotta convince Addy, and we'll be all set to debut our band. D'ya think it might be better to just throw her up onstage, day of? She seems more likely to agree if it's on the spot."

"Why don't you ask her?"

I nod toward the propped-open doors of the arcade that face out to the courtyard of the small shopping center.

Addy and her friend with the big curly hair are walking across the plaza, pausing in front of the beauty salon to organize the array of plastic shopping bags the friend has acquired.

I watch Addy silently as she helps her friend, the furrow in her always-furrowed brow, her hair pulled back neatly from her face to show off her small lips and her sharp eyes that glint underneath the sun.

I'm brought back to that moment at the creek. When I'd tackled her down into the water. When something seemed to shift as I held her close, both of us staring at the other's lips. Something that maybe was there the whole time and didn't shift at all, but just became obvious.

That I am very attracted to Addy Moreno. And I think she might be into me too.

If I thought I couldn't get her out of my head before because of how much she frustrated me, it's nothing compared to now. Especially after the night we spent alone, out in the middle of nowhere, a place I've never once wanted to take anybody just to talk and do nothing.

"Hey, not a bad idea," Benji nudges me, rudely yanking me out of my contemplation, before he jogs toward the exit of the arcade, calling to Addy and her friend. Danny turns from the game as his last ship finally gets shot down, following my gaze toward where Benji has run off to meet the girls.

"It wouldn't be so bad if she was there," he contemplates, walking up beside me. "She might not make us look half-bad, right?"

I wipe the look from my face before he can notice anything, turning to him as I slap him on the shoulder.

"Bud, I don't think anyone's gonna be lookin' at either of you if you bring a rich girl onstage with ya."

Danny and I step out of the arcade into the baking afternoon sun, approaching the small group.

"... don't know," Addy is saying to Benji as we walk up behind them. "I can't perform onstage like that."

"Why not?"

She whips around at my question. I had time to coolly control my reaction, but her face rushes with color the moment her eyes land on me, her mouth falling open. I can't help but give a gloating look. Her friend gives her an odd stare, looking between the two of us.

"I... I've never performed like that," she replies once she's clumsily gotten herself together. Only now she's way too obvious, turning herself pointedly away from me to face everyone else. "I do school drama performances, I've only ever pretended to be a rock 'n' roll singer alone with my cousins. And in front of all those people..."

"Ah, hell, not *everyone* will be watchin'." Benji waves his hand. "It's a carnival, there'll be fifty hundred different things going on all around us. I bet we get a crowd of twenty people at best. To everyone else, we'll be background noise."

"You don't have to play guitar or anything," Danny offers. "Jay's gonna rent an electric one for me. I can learn the chords real quick on the guitar now, Jay's gonna be on drums, and you can sing with Benji. That way you won't have to do anything on your own, and Benji's squawking won't ruin the song."

"Hey, are you kiddin'? My squawking *makes* the song, Danny."

Addy grins, her arms crossed over her chest as she looks at the ground. Clearly she wants to. And I can guess what's holding her back.

"I don't think the Sheriff Nultys of town will even notice you," I say to her back. "They'll see it's Benji and Danny and Jay playin' the music and not be bothered to stick around."

I step around beside her, my shoulder intentionally brushing along hers. She jumps, but doesn't move away.

"Plus, the carnival doesn't seem like the scene for your old friends," I point out. "By the time you get up to play, I bet they'll have taken a hike to find somethin' else to do."

She can't argue with that.

"Come on, princess." I meet her warning gaze with a smirk as I raise my soda up to my mouth, entirely innocent. "You know you'd look pretty cute up onstage."

I think for a moment she might lunge at me. Her friend is now whipping her head back and forth between us, like she's waiting to be let in on the joke.

"I..."

A smile is already creeping over Addy's face despite her indecisiveness. She glances at her friend, who gives her an encouraging smile and a small shrug.

"Oh, just go for it, Addy!" she begs. "It'll be fun, and your cousins will be so jealous."

"Alright," Addy finally sighs, running a hand through her hair as Benji punches the air in victory and Danny looks to have taken a heavy sigh of relief. "What songs are we doing?"

Chapter 18

Addy

"**Y**ou and Jackson."

I look up in the bathroom mirror, watching Ellen's reflection standing in front of the door, her hands on her hips. Her eyes are narrowed in her best attempt to be a hundred percent serious.

"Huh?" My voice shakes.

"You. And Jackson. What's going on?"

"What do you mean?" I attempt to laugh as I dry my hands, though it comes out sounding nervous.

"Uh, what do I mean? There's *tension*."

She moves toward me eagerly, her voice not lowering despite a woman walking in and heading to one of the open stalls. "What happened? Last week you despised him and today you're looking at him like you used to look at Cole Waters in fifth grade."

"Oh, come on," I scoff, leaning against the sinks where she's practically trapped me.

"Mm. You're right. This is way more intense." Ellen raises her brows pointedly. "You *flushed*. He couldn't keep his eyes off you the whole time we were talking. And you liked it."

"Ellen, please. How could I ever in my life be attracted to Jackson Lowell?"

"Uh, because he's hot?"

I startle, my eyes widening as if her words sent an electric shot through me. She shrugs.

"What? It's the truth. He might be a total creep, but he's got the whole sexy bad-boy look down."

"He's not a—"

I cut myself off, but it's too late. Ellen already caught it, her eyes brightening gleefully as she points one of her pastel blue manicured fingers at my face.

"Ha! I knew it! Not only are you insecure that I called him hot, but you're *defending* him!"

"We talked a few times, alright?" I relent, dodging away from her to exit the bathroom. "Turns out we're all misunderstood. Big whoop, who cares?"

"You care, because whatever chitchats you two have been having have led to *stirrings*!"

"We're done talking about this," I affirm as we return to our table. I slide the menu toward me, pulling it up over my face, pretending to read.

"Fine," Ellen sighs, plopping down in the seat on the other side of the booth. "Clearly you haven't admitted it to yourself yet. But I have to be the first one to know about all the gory details the minute you accept this and go full good girl/bad boy love story, alright?"

My eyes peek warily at her over the menu. She blinks at me innocently before leaning over her own menu.

Typical Ellen. Being completely dramatic and over the top. Just because Jackson Lowell and I don't hate each other now, just because I wasn't prepared to see him today so soon after the creek and the field and the weird feelings happening whenever we talk. Just because of course he's attractive, which I already noticed long ago, thank you very much. Just because we might be something close to friends, or at least have an understanding after all we talked about and revealed to each other in a random moment doesn't mean anything more.

And any girl will think about kissing any boy who's tackled her playfully into the water and hovers inches above her lips for a few seconds. It means nothing.

It's around seven p.m. by the time Ellen and I conclude our day of shopping around town. Ellen's family has always had more money than mine, giving her permission to not have to be picky about what she buys. And since there's not much to do in a town like Greydon, our summers here consist of her ending a day with armfuls of shopping bags filled equally with things she's picked out for herself, I've picked out for her, and that random salespeople insisted she has to have.

Now that I am going to perform onstage, Ellen and I decided I needed some new clothes as well, so I walked away with a brand-new outfit and snazzy heeled leather boots.

Ellen goes to drop our things off in her mom's car that she's borrowing for the day and get a smoothie from the Fruit Juice Bar while I head to the movie store to drop off the copy of *Hell Night* I rented the other day. Lorry read some biography about *The Exorcist* and is now fascinated with the filmography of Linda Blair, so she set aside her reservations about teenage slasher movies to watch it with me last night.

I glance at the boarded-up front window with a slightly nauseous feeling when I enter and exit the store. Danny isn't working tonight, but he and Benji were talking about grabbing some tapes for the action movie night they're planning.

I head down the alleyway between the movie store and the light fixture repair shop next door to find the less crowded path back toward the Fruit Juice Bar when I see something that makes me pause.

A car parked back along the empty gravel lots isn't strange, even at this time of the evening. But it's a car I recognize. The same one that I've ridden in dozens of times. The same one that had whipped away from the movie store seconds after the brick flew through the front window.

Marcus's pristine green Buick would never be anywhere near one of these back lots, where no one but employees at the various shops will park and the occasional lone smoker will linger.

I march toward the vacant car, parked at a haphazard angle as if someone had whipped into the lot and screeched to a stop before jumping out. The other side of the lot appears abandoned, the only sound coming from distant cars and the occasional shouts of other kids getting ready for the long summer night.

My ears tune to the sound of muttered voices nearby as I move farther down the lot, my eyes catching on a boy who looks vaguely familiar, perched in the archway of a bricked-up alley.

Jeremy. One of Marcus's friends. He's bigger than all of them, the best on their football team, so I've heard.

My shoes crunch against the gravel as I move toward the archway, stopping outside the alley where I see a group of boys piled in the space, all crowded around someone.

"... gonna steal my girl, huh? Think you can get away with whatever you want, you homeless little bum?"

"*Marcus!*"

The sound of my shout thunders loud enough through the alley that the entire group of boys jump, whipping around to face me. They step away from where Marcus stands, one hand locked around Danny's throat, his other arm pressing his chest against the wall.

Danny's right eye looks red and swollen and a small line of blood drips from his split lip. His chest is heaving against Marcus's arm, his hands scrambling to push the other boy away. But Deran, Jeremy, Eddie, and

Steven Nulty cage around him, ready to pounce if he does manage to escape Marcus's hold.

I run straight into the alley, ignoring the aghast looks of the other boys. I push against Marcus with every bit of strength I can muster, nudging him roughly so that his grip on Danny loosens. "What the hell do you think you're doing?"

Marcus shoves away from Danny, who stumbles to the side, gasping for breath. Deran steps forward and pushes him back into the wall while Marcus glares down at me.

There's a glint in his eye, a sadistic grin on his face that is foreign to me. Something that makes him appear warped. Like I'm looking at Marcus Tanner in a funhouse mirror that makes him purely menacing.

I realize that I'm now just as surrounded as Danny. Alone in an alley a good enough distance away from anyone who would bother to come and help, encircled by a group of boys who all look eager to start a fight.

"Look who decided to show her face," Marcus taunts, stepping closer to me as he cocks his head to the side. I don't flinch, finding it easy to keep my courage despite the unfavorable circumstances purely through the anger that burns through me.

"Do you think this makes you tough, Marcus? Do you feel like a man, ganging up on someone in an alleyway?"

"Run back to your shopping spree, little girl," Eddie's voice drawls condescendingly. "This doesn't concern you."

"Oh, so you're a badass now, are you?" I ask Marcus, ignoring Eddie. "Trying to be like that pathetic brute, Shelly Criston? You think this is gonna impress me and get me to come running back to you?"

"You think I want *you* back?" Marcus laughs, his face sneering in disgust. "Get over yourself. After where you've been, I wouldn't touch you with a ten-foot pole, honey."

I slap him. The sound snaps through the small space. My hand stings as Marcus's head whips sharply to the side and he stumbles, the self-satisfied smirk gone from his face in an instant.

I've never hit anyone in my life. It should feel scary. Wrong.

But it doesn't feel scary. All I can feel is rage.

I grab Danny's hand and pull him along behind me. But Deran moves forward, yanking Danny by the shoulder and throwing him back against the wall.

"Hold up, this little prick's not goin' anywhere." He glares down at Danny, stepping closer to him with his chest pushed out, forcing Danny to shrink against the wall. "We're not done teachin' him a little lesson, are we, boys?"

"Hell no," Eddie spits, pushing past me to shove Danny in the chest. "This son of a bitch thinks he's better than us, doesn't he?"

"If your pride is that hurt, Eddie, why don't you go cry to your mommy," I suggest, stepping in front of Danny again, shoving Eddie back with both hands. He's shorter than all of the other boys, probably why he has the loudest mouth and will only step up to a fight when it's five on one. "That's all any of you small-dick assholes know how to do."

"You stay the hell out of it, bitch!" Eddie snaps, his eyes wild with anger as he dives for me. I feel myself flung toward the other side of the alley, my body and head smacking into the brick wall before sliding to the ground.

"*HEY!*"

We all startle at the shrill voice that shatters across the lot beyond the alley. Two figures are barreling straight for us. The first one, the one who had shouted, is revealed to be Benji, who I swear leaps several feet into the air before crashing down on top of Eddie, bringing him straight to the ground. The second figure is Jackson Lowell.

Jackson leaps on top of Eddie as well, both he and Benji twisting into a tangle of limbs, swinging, punching, and kicking, until Deran joins in an attempt to fight both of them off.

Jeremy and Steven Nulty, however, now look concerned with the arrival of the other boys, both of them edging back out of the alleyway.

Benji scrambles to his feet, tackling Deran into the wall, the both of them holding each other by the collar of their jackets, trying to aim kicks at the other's ribs.

Jackson slams Eddie into the ground before yanking him up and pressing him into the opposite wall. Jackson's face is distorted into a fit of rage, his jaw locked into a growl as he leans closer toward Eddie's face.

"The next time I see you around here, you're fuckin' dead."

He throws Eddie back to the ground. The boy barely catches himself on his elbows before scurrying after the group now running back to the car.

I rise back to my feet and find Marcus, who had conveniently slithered out of the way at some point when the fighting began. He takes a brief glance at Benji and Jackson before his gaze lands on me. His eyes narrow. A warning. A promise. Something that makes my stomach churn.

"Hey! What the hell's goin' on here?"

The boys have already scattered as Ted rounds the corner, surveying the scene before running full speed toward the alley.

"Danny, you good?" he pants as he slides to the ground where Danny is slowly rising to his feet, one hand pressing against his head.

"I'm good, Ted," he mutters, reaching up to wipe the blood from his lip.

"Yeah, fuck off, scumbag!" Benji shouts, aiming one last kick at Deran, who then runs to join the others. Benji turns to Danny, slipping on the gravel as he runs over. "Dan, you alright, bud? What the hell happened, we left ya for five minutes!"

"They were waiting round the corner," Danny answers quietly, wincing in pain as he rolls his shoulders back. Ted hovers around him like he's waiting for him to break apart into pieces. "It's fine, guys, I'm alright."

"I swear, I'm gonna kill those bastards," Benji grumbles, still buzzing with adrenaline from the fight as Ted walks with Danny out of the alley. "They threw Addy around too, Ted, we saw as soon as we came around the corner."

Ted casts a glance toward me. I haven't moved from my spot, shifting back and forth on my feet but unable to do anything else. He's pale as a ghost, his eyes wide with a fear that chills me to my bone.

I look away. "I'm alright."

"You shouldn't wander off on your own anymore," Ted is saying to Danny as they head out of the lot. "Not around places like this. Now come on, let's go take a look at that eye, I don't like the way it's swellin' up."

I let their voices fade, staying silent and still, hoping they'll forget I'm here. It seems like they do, thankfully, they're so worried about Danny.

But one person stays behind long after the other footsteps have faded around the corner. Someone I'd forgotten about, who had stayed as silent and unmoving as I've been, who doesn't speak until the others are out of earshot.

"You sure you're okay?"

Jackson's voice no longer sounds as dangerous as it had when he had growled his deadly warning at Eddie's terrified face, but there's a trace of it.

He's only a few feet away from me. I can tell he isn't looking directly at me either.

"Yeah," I answer, running a hand through my hair as I finally unlock myself from the spot I'd frozen to. I don't look up at him as I walk past, only sneaking a peek through the corner of my eye. He's more rigid than

I had been, his hands shoved into the pockets of his ragged denim jacket. His eyes are narrowed down at the ground, as if a spot somewhere in the gravel has personally offended him.

"You have a ride home?" he asks before I can continue walking.

"Ellen's driving me."

I'm not sure he's heard me until he finally nods. He doesn't say anything else. Not that I hear. I turn and walk fast out of the alley, away from the lot, my feet crunching loudly against the gravel.

***

"So... you're gonna be singing. A rock song. In front of tons of people."

"Not tons. Benji said it won't be more than twenty people. You know what the carnival's like, everyone's busy doing something."

Lorry makes a face.

"Benji's one of the guys in the band," I explain.

"Oh my God."

"What?"

She sighs, walking from the doorway of the bedroom to fall down onto the other side of my bed, jolting me where I'm sitting trying to brush out my hair. "I need to keep up with you more, Addy. It's been two weeks and you've broken up with Marcus, decided to sing onstage somewhere that isn't a school musical, and are hanging out with guys named *Benji*."

"Just promise you'll keep Mom distracted and away from the music stage for one hour?" I insist again, lowering my voice as I glance out into the hallway, even though I know our mother is still out in the living room talking on the landline with Mrs. Burth about the latest gossip going around. "I told her I'm going with Ellen, and if she sees me up on that stage with a bunch of boys she doesn't recognize, she'll think—"

"—that you're hanging around a bunch of strange boys, I know." Lorry nods as exaggeratedly as she can with her neck scrunched against the pillow. "I wish I could see this though. And I know Mom hates rock music, but she'd want to see you perform."

"No she would not."

"She cries every time we see you in the school plays."

"That's because I'm dressed in a bunch of prairie gowns singing ballads about the old west."

Lorry reaches over to my bedside table, snatching up the letter and Polaroid photo our cousins send us every summer. Heather clearly took the photo, her long face and shining bleach-blonde hair that matches her blinding smile taking up most of the frame, while Jenny's reluctant face is covered mostly by her sheet of frizzy brown hair at the corner of the square photograph.

"Heather and Jenny are gonna be jealous."

"We don't have to tell them."

"You tell them everything that has to do with music. This is big, Addy. Your rock 'n' roll debut."

I say nothing, pulling my fingers through my hair and setting my brush down on the nightstand. I feel Lorry roll over onto her side, her eyes gazing intensely at the back of my head.

"So what else? You should be way more excited than this."

I don't know how to tell her everything else. I should be excited about the show. But I still haven't forgotten about Marcus and his friends attacking Danny the other day.

Neither Danny or Benji seemed concerned about it at the two rehearsals we've had since then, content to move on with life, despite Danny's face still hosting several light-colored bruises that make me sick with shame any time I look at them.

I've been trying to work up the courage to not only back out of this performance, but find a way to keep myself out of sight of any and all people for the rest of the summer until I'm safely back in New York and away from this ridiculous small-town teenage boy drama.

But if it were that easy, I would have done it weeks ago now. The truth is, I've felt happier and more myself around Danny and Benji, Ted, and even Jackson this summer than I have in a long time. And getting to sing Elton John, Fleetwood Mac, and Alice Cooper covers with the thought of being onstage at the carnival, surrounded by excitement and noise and music, with Danny, Benji, and Jay playing up there with me makes me buzz with a shot of adrenaline that I haven't felt in a long while.

Something hitting the window makes us both jump before I can think of how to answer my sister's question.

We stare at the glass that shows nothing but the pitch black outside. I'm about to let out a small laugh, figuring it was a bird, until another sharp crack sends us jumping once again.

"Is it hailing?" Lorry asks in her typical deadpan as I get up to my feet and approach the window, peering out into the dark.

"Can you get the light?"

Lorry stands up from the bed and switches off the lamp in the corner of the room, sending my bedroom into darkness. The yard outside is illuminated underneath the dull glow of the moon in the cloudless sky.

I freeze in terror when I see the outline of a figure standing a few feet away from my bedroom window, looking positively nightmare-inducing in the darkness. But my fear melds into irritation as my eyes adjust to the familiar outline standing beside the maple tree.

"You have got to be kidding me," I mutter, tossing my head back with a groan as Lorry approaches, leaning on the windowsill beside me to look out into the yard.

"Ooo. Who's this? New boyfriend already, Addy?"

"*No.*"

"What's he doing throwing rocks at your window?"

"Being an asshole."

Jackson Lowell waves his hands over his head like a maniac, knowing that I'm watching him from my now-dark bedroom window.

"How does he know where we're staying, Addy? Have you snuck him in before?"

"Like I'd be able to sneak anyone in past you," I point out, turning and walking to the other side of the room to switch the light on again. Lorry takes it upon herself to slide the window open, letting the cool night air spill in along with the sound of Jackson's approaching footsteps in the grass.

"You must be the little sister," his voice rings out as he arrives at the window. I freeze again, this time with an entirely different sensation of fear. My skin prickles at the sound of his voice resounding with a soft richness through the same bedroom I've slept in every summer for years, and I become very aware that I am standing here in my nightgown.

"Lauren Moreno," Lorry introduces herself, probably extending her hand for a formal greeting. "Lorry preferred. Spelt with an *O*, double *R*, *Y*. That's important."

"Yeah? Why, don't wanna be confused with Laurie Strode?"

Lorry pulls a face. "The one who spends both movies crying, cowering, and running while the man saves the day? Definitely not."

"Huh. Well, nice to meet ya, Lorry. I'm Jackson."

"Jackson..."

"Lorry, can you give us a minute?" I ask as I finally turn around and walk back to the window, shuffling my little sister toward the door before she can put together that this is the same Jackson who crashed the Lensen barbecue.

"Use protection, please. I'm too young to be an aunt."

I slam the door behind her after shoving her out into the hall.

I run back over to the open window where Jackson is waiting casually, like he's getting ready to order at a cafeteria window.

"What in the actual hell do you think you're doing?!" I hiss at him with all the fire I can muster. "Are you trying to get me locked away for the rest of my life? My mother could have heard you!"

He raises his brows, and I try not to think about the glow that the warm light from my bedroom casts over his face, making it look softer, his dark hair framing it in a perfect tangled mess...

God, what the hell?

"And throwing rocks?" I ask, shaking myself out of whatever that was. "Really? I'm not even on a second floor."

"I thought it would be a better option than walking up to the window in the dark and knocking. I know I'm shockingly handsome and everything, but I would have given you both a heart attack."

"You could have cracked the glass and my mother would have had to pay for it. And I still had a heart attack, by the way."

We both stand there in silence for a few seconds, me begrudgingly calming down while he waits for me.

I haven't seen him since the incident with Marcus. And... I missed him.

Alright I can admit that to myself. Never out loud, but to myself.

Jackson raises his brows, his hands rising up from the windowsill questioningly. "So are you gonna come outside, or what?"

Chapter 19

Jackson

While I spent much longer than I'll ever admit debating if showing up at Addy's house in the night might be considered a stalker move and completely turn her off toward me, I can safely say it was worth it the moment I saw her reaction.

I've gotten good at treading the fine line of irritating her in a way that doesn't actually piss her off. At least not enough to never talk to me again.

And I had to see her. Not in public around everyone else, not around the guys. I need another moment like this, alone in the dark, hidden from the rest of the world. And giving her a slight heart attack in the process just so I can see her sheer exasperation with me is a bonus.

Not to mention seeing her in her PJs.

I try to help her crawl over and out the window, since it's obvious she's never done it before, but she slaps my hands away multiple times as she struggles to lift herself over the windowsill and gracefully land on the grass while keeping her nightgown from flying up. And she does accomplish the task all on her own, impressively enough. Though she's not winning any athletic awards, that's for sure.

She keeps her sweater pointedly wrapped tightly around her chest as she stands and leans against the maple tree in the yard. I swing myself up to sit on one of the branches. It's quiet. Dull lights glow from the inside of windows from the surrounding rentals, a murmur here and there from an open window. But she and I are tucked away in the sprawling branches and leaves of the large tree, hidden within a temporary hovel in the yard.

"I know what you're thinking."

I hear her snort a soft laugh. "You always seem to, don't you?"

"You're thinking of not doing the show."

She stays silent and I have my answer.

"You need to stop letting other people control your life, Addy. Especially your numbskull ex-boyfriend."

"Danny got hurt, Jackson. Danny got hurt and it was because of me."

"Danny got knocked around by a group of chickenshit pansies who were lookin' for any reason to pick on someone. And he didn't get *hurt* hurt, because we were there. And that includes you."

She doesn't have an answer for that. She knows it's true. She bought him a hell of a lot of time before Benji and I showed up.

"Ted looked so scared…"

I frown, reaching up to brace against the branch above me as I lean forward. Addy turns, her face gentle and stunning in the moonlight. Waiting for an explanation she knows I have.

"Ted's older brother got killed."

It's clearly not an explanation she was expecting.

"He was just like all of us, as Ted likes to remind us. I don't think he was in a gang or anything, but he got into a lotta trouble. Normal shit, you know? When there's not much else to do in a place like this, we get bored."

I watch the slow realization and pain begin to fill Addy's eyes. The same pain we all feel for Ted.

"What happened?"

I want to make something up, or at least adjust the story. I don't know what it will make her think. But I can't lie to her.

"He got with this girl. Someone's ex. A guy he used to get into it with a lot. Harmless stuff, from what I hear. But one night, it just... it went too far. Guy pulled a blade on him, jabbed him in the right spot, and that was it."

Addy looks away, her arms curling tighter around herself. I can't blame her. It's not a new story to me, but it still sends something uncomfortable down my spine that I have to physically shake away.

"Ted was only ten at the time. His brother was sixteen. It screwed his whole family up. That's why he is the way he is with us. Why he kinda took us all in. And I give him a lotta shit, but I know he just wants us all to stay on the right side of the dirt. Until we're adults at least."

Addy still says nothing. But she's not running away, so that's a good sign.

"The other day reminded him, I guess. And he's closer to Danny than to me or Benji. Danny practically lives with him most of the time."

"I never knew things like that actually happen," she says. "Somewhere like this, somewhere..."

"Somewhere that's a part of you?"

I try not to say it accusingly. But from the way she shifts slightly, I can tell she picks up on some of the heat behind my tone.

"I hate to break it to ya, but bad shit can happen anywhere, even if you are a perfect goody-two-shoes who does everything right all the time. Sometimes the world just sucks."

"You're right." She turns against the tree, looking up to face me again. "A lot of the time, I just ignore it. Anything bad. It's what my mom does. What she taught us to do. Anything that doesn't have to affect us doesn't have to be our business."

I'm about to come up with some snarky remark to that, until I really think about it. Is it not what I do, to an extent? I don't care about anything outside of my own world either. It's just a different world from hers.

"Is this why you had to see me at eleven o'clock at night?" she sighs before the silence can become too overbearing, a gentle levity in her voice. "To beg me to grace you and the town with my tremendous singing skills this weekend?"

I grin down at her, thankful for the change of subject. "Partly. And to ask something."

"What's that?"

I hop down from the tree, landing inches in front of her. She shifts back, but I don't move. "They're having a Herschell Gordon Lewis double feature at the drive-in next week. I thought we could go. Together."

I expect her to pull a face, or scoff, or tell me to fuck off. Instead, she cocks her head, and I swear she's trying to hide a grin as she leans back against the trunk of the maple tree.

"Hm. That depends on the movies for me, Jackson Lowell."

"*The Wizard of Gore* and *Blood Feast*."

She sighs dramatically, looking off over my shoulder. "Oh, I don't know. *Color Me Blood Red* is my favorite..."

I lean closer, still gripping the branch above. "They'll have that next summer." I look down at her lips. "Guess you'll have to come back."

"Guess so."

I move forward the rest of the way. My lips are a breath from hers when she turns her head away.

"Jackson..."

She says my name like a whisper, as if she's run out of breath. It makes me want to kiss her more.

"Yeah?"

Thankfully her expression is still light, her voice not affronted, even as she ducks out from under my arm.

"Don't push it."

I can work with that.

"Alright, alright. But as for the date...?"

She smiles. It makes something in my chest move so suddenly that I can't help but return one back.

"It's the only date I would have accepted with you."

"Because you're gettin' free movie tickets out of it?"

"Exactly."

I'm holding my breath, waiting for the punchline. Waiting for her to laugh in my face, drop the facade, tell me that of course she's not going on any date with me ever. That there is no way in this life she would ever want to be seen with me.

But she continues to smile. Something genuine and glowing and private that I've never seen from her before.

And it's all for me.

"The next time I try to kiss you, I think you're gonna let me."

"A presumptuous prediction."

"I'd bet everything."

She rolls her eyes. "Well, you're always right, aren't you?"

"I'm gonna wait," I promise her. "For the perfect moment. You won't even see it comin', but you're gonna think, *Damn, he's right, I really do wanna kiss that devastatingly handsome troublemaker now.*"

She tosses her head back as I wave my hand dramatically.

"And then the magic happens."

She leans back up to give me another incredulous grin before shaking her head and turning back toward her open window.

"Good night, Jackson."

I watch her go, my smile dropping only slightly as she hops back up onto the windowsill.

"And tell your sister that Laurie Strode stabbed Michael Myers in the face, like, twice before Loomis even showed up! I think that's pretty badass."

She hops down into her bedroom, much more gracefully than when she climbed out. I need to give her an excuse to practice more often, and she'll be a pro.

"I'll see you this weekend." She waves pointedly before sliding the window closed and throwing the curtain shut over it.

"See you."

The ridiculous euphoric feeling in my stomach doesn't last much longer as I begin making my way from the street of vacation rentals and down the long road back into town. I grab a cigarette to distract me, even though I know it won't work.

This is possibly the stupidest thing I've ever done. Sure, I've been with plenty of girls, girls who I knew from the first moment we made out didn't give a damn about me. Girls who I, for whatever reason, would have dropped everything for whenever they called. Who I held on to some deluded fantasy for, thinking that this time, *this time* it might work out. That something deeper would grow. That I'd have someone to go to to talk about anything with. Someone who felt like a natural part of me, like a limb I'd been missing my entire life.

Someone like... her. The girl I held hands with back in New York. The girl I talked to. The girl who went to my mom's funeral with me.

The girl who's gone now, I remind myself sharply before I can keep thinking about it. Again.

I knew it would never work out. With any of them. But I didn't care. A part of me likes self-sabotaging.

And this is the worst yet. Because Addy is leagues above someone like me. Because she doesn't even live here and will be gone in a month.

Because I'm asking for trouble from all angles by being with someone like her.

And because I'm suddenly more attracted to her than I've been to anyone in my life.

I snatch the key from under the fake rock in the patch of dirt beside the liquor shop and open the side door, slipping into the stairwell and up to my room. I can hear Ward snoring from here, even after I close the door.

I don't get changed or shower or do anything but collapse onto the bed, staring up at the popcorn ceiling.

Follow her back to New York, an unhelpful voice prods in my head. *Get away from this town. See what happens there instead.*

It'd be the same, I'm sure. There are still snarky cops and disapproving parents in White Plains. Plus my father. Plus everything else that happened that made me leave.

I roll over onto my side, flipping down onto my face so I can groan helplessly into the pillow.

I'm doomed.

***

The day of the carnival is hotter than all hell. It always ends up that way, no matter how many times the town has changed the date in the past few years to try to catch a day with at least a cool breeze. But it's like whatever higher power's out there wants to make sure that the one day half the town of Greydon all gets shoved in together in one space at the fairgrounds is the hottest day of the summer.

Maybe Greydon is actually Hell, and we're all here paying for the sins of our past lives.

I decide to be nice and get up early to help Jay and Ted set up Jay's drums on the stage, even though setting anything up at the Greydon Summer Carnival at nine in the morning is its own form of psychological torture. I'm gonna make up for it by skipping homeroom for at least a week when school starts.

I notice Benji, the self-proclaimed ringleader of this damn thing, has elected to sleep in this morning.

After they're mostly good to go by noon, I head off back into town toward Roller Dollar to get something to eat.

The nice thing about carnival day is that most people in town are either setting up, or getting their parking spots early, so there aren't too many yahoos roaming around who will give me any trouble.

When the diner comes into view as I turn the corner of the street, I see Addy leaning up against the shaded side wall of the building, the cool cement no doubt a nice relief from the already beating sun.

Her shiny hair falls all around her shoulders in bouncy curls that frame her face as if she's a 1950s movie star. The bright red lipstick on her mouth matches the vibrant shade of her tight-fitting shirt that barely reaches to cover below her ribs, leaving a strip of skin showing between it and her equally tight-fitting dark blue jeans. One of her black leather boots kicks back against the wall as she tosses her head back to sip from a bottle of Coke.

I am perfectly content with standing here for a few seconds enjoying the view, even though I'm sure I look like a drooling idiot. Whatever it is about this girl that makes me not care how the hell I look to anyone else, I'll never know.

I'm about to finally cross the street when a group of guys walk around from behind the diner, along the side toward Addy. I don't give them a second glance until I see the one leading them pause as he does a double take in her direction, moving his group back until they're standing before her.

Shelly Criston. Looking as hungover as the rest of his group.

"Hey, look who it is," he drawls as Addy casts a confused and then unamused glance in their direction as they surround her. "This that gal who's goin' around with little Danny Macklin?"

"Jackson Lowell too," one of the cronies snickers as he nudges the guy beside him. "She gets around fast for a new gal, huh?"

Addy ignores them, looking unbothered as she continues to sip on her Coke. It's pretty sexy.

"Word on the street's, she's a spy," Shelly stage-whispers to his crew, who all chortle obnoxiously in response. "That she's lookin' to bring the sheriff down on all of us lowlifes."

I move slowly across the street, looking around the ground for something I can use as a weapon. Looks like I'll have to use old-fashioned fists if this gets outta hand. The odds aren't in my favor with the four guys Shelly's got in his crew today, but I've survived before.

Shelly steps closer to Addy, getting close enough in her face that she's forced to acknowledge him. It's now that I see she's about an inch taller than him with those boots on.

"You wanna tell me why you've been snoopin' around here lately?" He licks his lips, leaning one hand against the wall as he presses closer to her, his ridiculous silver tooth, which I know for a fact is just his regular tooth painted silver, glinting in the light. "Or better yet, why don't you give me a little of what you've been passin' around town?"

"Why don't *you* go fuck yourself?" Addy states, the curse rolling off her tongue effortlessly, even though I can tell she's never said anything like that out loud before in her life. She leans forward and lightly shoves Shelly back a few paces. "It seems like none of you have anything better to do."

I hold in my laughter as I creep along the outside of the little circle formed around Addy, who still looks to hardly be batting an eyelash. I have Shelly in my line of sight, getting ready to dive forward and tackle the prick at just the right moment as I slide along the side wall of the diner.

Shelly scoffs, trying to recover himself as the others chuckle among themselves. "You've got some nerve talkin' to me like that, bitch. Do you know who I am?"

Addy blinks at him. "Yes. I do."

He steps closer again, his mouth turning to a pouting frown. "I'm not someone you wanna mess with around here."

"Oh, is that right?" she asks in an exaggeratedly innocent voice. "Well, I'm sure all of the school kids you bully will agree."

She takes a long sip of her Coke, not taking her eyes off him before turning and nudging him out of the way again, walking toward the front of the diner.

"Oh, you wait just a minute, honey, I'm not done with—"

Shelly has hardly grabbed on to Addy's arm to yank her back, his other hand snaking around her waist, before she whips around, smashing the near-empty Coke bottle against the wall of the diner. It doesn't work the way I think she hoped it would. Most of the bottle breaks off, leaving her with just the rim in her hand. Still, it's a sharp piece of glass that she waves menacingly in front of her and that makes Shelly take a step back.

I finally let my laugh ring out loud, causing the group to turn around and face where I now lean casually against the wall. "I'd back up, Criston," I advise, nodding at the bottle rim. "She'll use it."

Addy glares at the little weasel when he turns around, silently telling him that, yes, she definitely will.

"Hey! What's goin' on back here?"

Shelly and his gang scatter at the sound of the diner manager's voice as he appears around the corner.

"Get the hell outta here, you hooligans!" the burly man huffs as he waves a dirtied dish towel. "I'm not dealin' with your shit today!"

The Criston crew books it across the street like five-year-olds caught messing with the neighbor's cat, while I continue to lean comfortably against the wall to watch the view, finally the one not being reprimanded by a grumpy adult in this town.

Shelly is across the street before he turns around again, his goons tripping over themselves to dive out of sight of the diner. But he twists his face into an ugly sneer as he aims his finger in my direction.

"You're gonna get yours, Lowell. I know it was you who tried to pin that little revenge prank on me. You ain't gettin' away with that, just you fuckin' wait!"

He walks backward a few steps, and unfortunately turns around to chase after his buddies before he can trip over the curb. I don't know what he's smoking, but it must be some heavy shit. I have no idea what the hell he's talking about.

The diner manager shakes his head, muttering loudly about the future going to hell, before he vanishes around the corner again and Addy and I are left alone.

My eyes trail down to the pathetic piece of glass in her hand. She drops it to the ground. Sticks her chin up and tosses her curls over her shoulder.

"It worked in all the movies I saw that in," she tries to defend her sad bottle-smash move.

"I've never seen that work for anyone in real life."

She laughs, crossing her arms and shaking her head at herself. My chest tightens when she looks up at me through her shiny curled hair.

"What revenge prank is he talking about?"

"Beats me." I shrug. "The guy's paranoid as hell. Probably did a line this morning for breakfast and made up a story in his head."

Addy brushes some of her hair behind her ear. My blood gets hot and my eyes travel to the strip of skin showing beneath the hem of her top.

"Did you get all dolled up just for me?"

Her brows rise. "Oh, of course. It's all I ever do, Jackson Lowell, make myself look divine, all for you."

I know she's joking, but still, the way her voice dips to a husky tone as she moves closer has me entranced, her bright red lips practically begging me to kiss them.

"Uh-huh." I nod as I move closer until we're a couple inches apart. I gaze at her for a moment, uncertain. She stands with her arms still crossed. Daring me.

I reach out to pull her closer. She doesn't pull away. My hands slide up her back, catching on the hem of her shirt. A shirt that I now feel is incredibly thin.

My blood turns to fire when she presses her hands against my chest, leaning closer against me. The side of her mouth turns up.

"How scandalous, Jackson. Imagine if anyone sees."

She laughs, pushing away and out of my grasp before turning and heading toward the front of the diner. I follow behind her.

"Tell me something."

"Like what?"

Addy shrugs, using one of her fries to push the remaining ones around the plate. "Anything."

"I'm gonna need direction."

She sighs, looking up at the lamp hanging above the table as she quirks her red-painted lips to the side in thought. "Like... when did you first get in trouble with the police? Ever."

I nod, leaning back in the booth. "Hm. Well, I was seven years old when—"

"*What?*"

She looks like she's about to choke on the fry she just swallowed. I grin.

"Some jackass in school said I wasn't man enough to swipe a milk carton from the supermarket. I did. Only got caught after I'd made it down the street a ways."

Addy gives me a look.

"What? I was gonna give it back! Just had to prove I could do it. Anyway, I got the typical lecture from the officers, you know."

"No, I don't."

"These guys were cool," I recount, remembering the incident well. "Tried to scare me with juvie and all that, but they weren't fightin' to lock me up for a night like some would. It didn't matter though, 'cause my life of high crime only grew from there."

I sigh dramatically and Addy shakes her head.

"Cute."

"What, you aren't impressed?"

"No. It makes you look stupid."

"I know, for getting caught?"

"No! It makes you look like you have nothing better to do than waste people's time by getting into trouble for no reason."

"What's the trouble?" I laugh. "So I loiter around places I'm not supposed to and slash an occasional tire. And swipe a carton of cigarettes now and then."

"What, are you too good to pay for anything?"

"Hey, money's tight sometimes. I don't have a nice fat allowance to go on a shopping spree with every week."

"Why not get a job?" she questions, ignoring the jab.

I laugh so hard, I curl up in the booth. "You think anyone around here wants to hire someone like me?"

"They're gonna have to at some point. What about when school ends? What are your grades like?"

"Should I even answer that?"

She shakes her head after a moment, obviously deciding not.

"Look, I'm not exactly the kind of guy who dreams of becoming a lawyer or a forensic scientist or whatever when I grow up. I take it as it goes."

Addy raises her glass of ice water to her lips. "Terrific."

"Well, what did you wanna be when you grew up, then?"

She gulps down her water and tilts her head. "Are you serious?"

"Yeah," I challenge, straightening up in my seat. "All this talk about wantin' to do somethin' to change the world, or whatever. What was your big dream?"

When she's quiet for a short moment, I can tell she's debating whether or not to tell me the truth.

"When I was little... I wanted to be a rock star."

I can't help but give a quiet laugh.

"I'm serious! I thought I was gonna be real famous too, until I realized how average I was."

"You still play," I point out. "With your cousins, right?"

She gives a small shrug, going back to her water.

"What, they're not any good either?"

"No, they're great. They're the ones who convinced me to take guitar lessons in the first place. It's just..."

"Just what?"

Her eyes widen, her hands gesturing as if it should be obvious to me. "Come on. Everyone has that dream when they're little."

"I didn't."

"Okay, normal people do, then. But it's unrealistic. There's a one in a million chance of making it and an almost guaranteed chance I'll end up homeless on the streets of New York playing for change." She shakes her head again, stirring her water with her straw. "That fantasy is long gone."

"What do you wanna do now, then?"

She doesn't look up from her water. I can guess why. I can see the same glassed-over, dissatisfied look that I have in the few moments I'm ever forced to think about my future. And come up with nothing worth spending a moment thinking about.

"Probably work in an office somewhere. A secretary or something. My mom works in a real estate office, I could find a nice job there."

I shove myself back in my seat, already regretting this conversation. This is why talking about the future is pointless. We're all gonna end up depressed adults with shit lives one day, why waste time imagining it when we still have our youth?

"I like the singing idea better," I tell her, just to attempt to get that regretful look off her face. It seems to work, based on the sly grin she gives me.

"For the record, I think you'd make an excellent lawyer, Jackson Lowell."

I scoff. "Why?"

"You love to argue and you love to defend the downtrodden."

If the idea weren't so ridiculous, I might admit she has a point. "If that were all there was to lawyering, then you could have somethin' there," I allow, gulping down the rest of my orange juice and reaching into my jacket pocket to plunk down the small handful of change and crumpled bills I have on the table. "But I ain't wastin' ten years in an overpriced institution for that. And me going into any profession that has law in the title is a laugh."

There's some time before Addy has to be at the carnival. At least that's what I tell her so that we have another hour to kill, just me and her. I'm sure the guys need help figuring out how the hell to set all their shit up, but Benji's the one who got them into this mess, so as far as I'm concerned, he can work it out.

Addy and I walk around town, talking about more random things, our voices and footsteps the only noise we can hear since most places are nearly vacant now that the carnival is open. I even venture to sling my arm over her shoulders and pull her casually to my side as we walk. She looks up at me and laughs quietly, but there is a light blush high on her cheeks. She doesn't pull away, doesn't worry about who's looking, because no one's really here. I know otherwise she would, but I'll take what I can get for now.

After a while, I don't pay attention to where we walk. Through town, along the outskirts, across Cropsy Park (where the playground practically rings with the heat from the beating sun today, guaranteeing second-degree burns at least should anyone attempt to place a finger on it), along the abandoned train tracks at the edge of Benji's neighborhood where I don't think a train has rolled through since the early 1900s, and who knows where else. I'm hardly paying attention.

We talk. And it feels nice. We talk about our first horror movies and the absolute best death scenes. We talk about how much our parents suck, but also the okay things they do every once in a while. We talk about the pets we had when we were kids (none) and the pets we would have wanted to have (also none after having to take care of Skerritt, but the idea of hanging out with an iguana or a turtle every now and then sounds alright). She tells me one thing about her dad. A vague memory of reading with him on the couch when she was barely two years old. I tell her one thing about my mom. The Christmas Eve when I was five and she let me help her bake buñuelos from a family recipe she'd learned from her grandmother.

It's exactly what I needed. And maybe she needed it too. Talking to someone, someone new, about serious things, stupid things, random things. Just wandering.

And I realize I don't want her to leave. And that maybe I really would follow her back to New York if it could be like this all the time.

Chapter 20
Addy

It's past five p.m. by the time Jackson and I arrive at the carnival. Spending all day in the completely dead town swept us away in a temporary time warp that is now loudly broken once we enter the Greydon Summer Carnival filled with screaming children, popping water balloons, and various bells and alarms trilling from different games.

Our set starts at seven, so I find the music stage where it looks like the boys have gotten their instruments all set up. Benji jumps down from the stage, almost toppling over, before pulling me up to the side steps, and my panic is immediate as I'm suddenly on a stage with a small crowd of curious people already staring at us getting ready.

But it's us. It's not me, alone. Benji sets up his own microphone next to the one he directs me toward. Jay is behind him getting the final parts of his drum set tuned, and Danny is behind me, strumming a couple chords on the electric guitar Jay rented for tonight from a music store a couple towns over from Greydon.

I turn around to glance at Danny. He has a pair of ripped jeans and a nice burgundy button-down, the top open to reveal a crisp white shirt. His hair is mostly slicked back, though several strands of his sandy brown locks jump forward to escape.

He smiles at me, nervous too. But ready.

I turn back, my eyes focusing down at the dinged-up black grille of the microphone before rising up to our minuscule audience.

Just like I always pictured. Just like I'm back home, in Jenny and Heather's garage, playing our hearts out for an imaginary crowd. Not a lick of fear, just the music. The adrenaline of playing together and the excitement of celebrating with a largely unhealthy meal afterward.

I can do this.

And when it's time, we do it. After we're finished tuning and warming up, Benji introduces us as the Skerritt Wranglers (a name I don't think any of us were made aware of until now), and then Jay is leading us into "Don't Go Breaking My Heart," and we're off.

It's ridiculous. I forget about any nerves I had, any doubts during our brief and mostly unfocused rehearsals, any sobering thoughts I'd had earlier today during my conversation with Jackson. Right now, I'm singing with my friends onstage, the audience is clapping along and dancing, and I feel on top of the world.

Benji is by far the showstopper, a beacon I can focus on to lead the way in his hot pink sleeveless shirt and dark black jeans, performing a barrage of wild, if unrefined, dance moves that get the crowd whooping and roaring with laughter. He tries to swing me into his moves, but I'm far too stiff, and dancing has never been my strength when it comes to performing. I'm perfectly content to sing beside him while he leaps and spins and drops into half splits across the stage. He's in his own world.

I'm sure we don't sound like a cohesive band, but that's not the point. The point is to get people dancing and singing along. And I lose myself in the feeling as I always thought I would, despite the crowd being infinitely smaller than I would picture while staring at the empty street through my cousins' open garage door. Still, the feeling of leading them through the lyrics that they all recite with us, the blare of the electric guitar pulsing through the speakers, the shock of the drums thumping through the ground, mixing with the beat of people's feet and hands... it feels just as powerful as I imagined a gigantic stadium would.

Lorry was right. Heather and Jenny are gonna be pissed when I tell them.

There are a ton of teens in front of the stage dancing with each other and jumping along cheerfully to the music. I see Ellen in the crowd, waving madly and jumping up and down as people bump around her. Ted is dancing with an attractive young woman who I had seen slyly eyeing him when we were setting up, and Jackson is standing on one of the bleachers near the back, trying to look cool as always, but grinning and nodding along to the music.

It couldn't be more perfect.

After closing out our set with a well-received rendition of "School's Out," the Skerritt Wranglers take a final bow before we join Ted, Jackson, and Ellen to walk through the carnival.

I'm nervous at first about walking around so openly, where not only could Marcus and his friends run into us, but my mother or any of her friends could see me with the guys. But there's so much going on, and Ellen's with me, and Jackson makes a point not to stand too close to me, that I quickly let loose most of my worries.

I know Jackson will give me crap for it later. And he should if we're supposed to be...

I don't even know anymore. I don't want to think about it. I don't want to think about how time doesn't matter when I'm talking to him, that more and more I find myself yearning to have his time all to myself, if only because it feels like he's closer to himself without all of the eyes on him, without the need to impress anyone.

No. I don't want to think about it. Right now, I just got off stage after getting the closest I've ever been to my little girl rock 'n' roll fantasy, and I want to have a fun night with my friends.

"Come on, come on, three more tries for one dollar, son!" the carnival worker cheers, waving three rings in front of Benji's face as Benji bounces excitedly on the balls of his feet. "Better luck than the last four times, eh?"

"I'd quit while you're behind, Benj," Ted advises from the small crowd we've formed behind Benji, the last one standing at this ridiculous ring toss game that's clearly rigged. "You've burned through all your and Danny's money now."

"Fuck that, Benji, don't let this guy hound ya!" Jackson eggs him on.

"Do they know they only let little kids win these things?" Ellen whispers to me.

"Can't believe I'm bein' shown up by first graders!" Benji protests as he snatches up Jackson's dollar bill that he hands him and throws it down on the counter. Jackson snickers behind his back as we all prepare to watch Benji lose yet again. "Alright, pal, get ready to pay up with that giant dinosaur stuffy, 'cause this is gonna be all net!"

None of us know what that means, but he misses every one of the bottles again.

On the bright side, Ted and Jay are able to win a nice handful of tickets from the high striker. Ted tries to let Benji pick a prize with his tickets, but Benji's pride won't allow it.

"The only stuffed animals I bring into my house are ones that I've earned, damn you."

"Ah, Benji," Jackson sighs, throwing his arm over Benji's shoulders as we all head to the hot dog stand, "if only you had a girl who could win a huge stuffed animal for ya at these things. It'd be the only carnival prize you'd ever be able to earn."

Benji nearly shoves him straight into the blow-up fishing pool.

It's right after that, as the boys begin playfully wrestling one another, that I catch sight of Marcus.

My chest seizes when I make eye contact with him. He stands near one of the tents across from us, alone, oddly enough. I begin counting down the seconds before he comes over here and tries to make a scene.

But he does nothing. He stands there, his arms crossed smugly over his chest, giving me a conniving grin before he turns away and heads in the opposite direction.

It makes sense that he doesn't want to start anything here. A lot of witnesses means... well, a lot of witnesses.

Whatever. I don't want to think about him anymore.

After perusing the carnival for a while, the boys get bored and want to head somewhere else where they can drink and be rowdy without the threat of the cops looming, most of whom have their eyes on them throughout the park. I hardly think it's fair, but I'm also not sure I trust Jackson or Benji to have not caused a riot by now without the presence of police officers.

So we decide to cause a riot somewhere else.

Ted and Jay stay behind (plausible deniability, they say) and Jackson leads the rest of us across the street and down a ways to the liquor store, heading under a small overhang on the side of the shop and ripping the cover off the Chevrolet.

"Jackson's stealin' Ward's property yet again," Benji giggles, already tipsy off the can of beer he downed on the way over here, tossing two six packs he somehow obtained without me noticing in the trunk before hopping in the passenger seat.

"Borrowing," Jackson corrects him as he starts up the car, casting a nervous glance at the store as Ellen, Danny, and I climb in the back. "I'm borrowing it. He's cool with it. *Borrowing*."

"Addy, does this make us accomplices?" Ellen asks worriedly, looking as if she's ready to jump out of the car until Jackson pulls out from under the makeshift garage and we take off down the empty street.

Jackson drives out to the field he took me to the other night, parking the car out in the middle of the large patch of grass, keeping the head-lights on, and cranking up the radio.

Benji hollers loudly as he leaps out of the car, running around to the side. I'm sure Ellen is about to ask me the same thing I asked Jackson the other night, if we're on private property right now, before Benji throws her door open and yanks her out with him. She shrieks as he spins her around.

And I feel the same high that Benji seems to be on, to be honest. I dance with Danny, and then Benji and Ellen, even accepting a can of beer Jackson throws to me. It tastes awful, but I hardly notice.

And then Jackson is swinging me into his arms, and we spin around and around in the empty field, singing and screaming along to the car radio at the top of our lungs, my stomach swirling with dizziness and a sense of levity. Like the weight of something I wasn't aware of is lifted away, never to be thought of for the rest of the night.

Jackson does a good job of holding me up so I don't topple over, somehow acting more sober than me even though I've had nothing but half a can of beer, and I'm sure he's had at least three.

I catch Ellen trying to give me a pointed look, but she's currently twisted up in Benji's arms and doesn't look too upset about it, so I'm certainly not explaining myself to her at this moment. Danny is sprawled out on the hood of the car staring up at the stars.

I'm not sure how long we spend out here. Or how we don't get caught with all the noise we're making. But we don't. We're left alone to just... be.

Even Ellen takes a sip of beer at some point.

"What the hell's even going on here?" Jackson asks me, finally sound-ing a bit drunk. The radio is slightly dulled as we walk along a calm creek in the darkness, far out of reach of the car lights. I crane my head up to gaze with wide eyes at the shadow of the mountain stretching above us.

"What?" I ask, laughing as he pulls me along the edge of the creek. The laughter from Benji, Danny, and Ellen sounds far away, but close enough to be comforting.

"How the hell," he continues, pulling me closer, his hands around my waist, "did I end up in a summer fling with someone way outta my league?"

I laugh, blinking up in the dark at where I think his face is supposed to be. Then I throw my head back, leaning so far that the only thing stopping me from falling into the creek is Jackson's arms keeping me pressed against him.

"Jackson Lowell, that was a *compliment.* A compliment without any sarcastic edge."

"Yup."

"Are you feeling well?"

"... Mostly."

I throw myself up again, my chest colliding against his, some of my curls flopping over my eyes. I can feel his breath warm on my face. I think I know where his lips are.

"Summer fling, you say?"

"Is that not what this is?" he asks teasingly. "A summer fling with the bad boy?"

"Oh *God*, you're so dramatic."

His hand moves up my back until I feel his palm warm against the back of my neck.

"You think I'm... attractive, Jackson Lowell?"

"Oh, yeah. Especially when you use my full name for no reason."

"Do you think I'm... intelligent?"

"Probably more than I am."

"Do you think I'm funny?"

"Hilarious. But only when you're trying to be serious."

"Do you think I'm the greatest singer in the world?"

"You're better than Benji."

"I'll take that."

"Your first big review," he says, swinging me around and making me gasp before he sets me down again, holding me close to his side. "Addy Moreno: a great new talent shining a thousand times brighter than That Doof Who Sang Next to Her."

When we finally decide to leave, we make Ellen drive the Chevy, being that she's the only one not currently tipsy. She only does it once all the guys agree to sit in the back so no one distracts her. Danny has to practically hold Jackson and Benji down in the car as Ellen makes her way back into town, having to make several circles to find the liquor store, since everything looks different in the dark.

We dump them off, sloppily covering the car up again. Jackson heads up to his room, Benji and Danny hobble off together to crash at Ted's place, and Ellen and I walk across the street to where she had parked her mom's car.

The carnival is dead by now, most of the cars in the lot long gone, not one sound of music, or laughter, or ringing bells from games to be heard.

Like once again, time has warped while we were away.

"That was... fun," Ellen laughs quietly after she pulls up in front of my rental cottage.

"I know," I agree, stepping out of the car. "I told you, they're cool."

"And Addy?"

I lean back into the car before I can close the door. Ellen tosses her now-tangled mess of ringlet curls out of her face, giving me a small grin. "For the record, I thought you and Jackson looked adorable together tonight."

I want to roll my eyes, or deny it, or tell her she's being delusional again. But then I remember Jackson's arms around my waist, the feeling of him holding me close several times today. The flirtations that I've been telling myself are just a joke between us, nothing actually serious. And I can't help but smile, tossing my friend a relenting head shake as she laughs.

I'm not sure what I expected to be waiting for me when I walked inside the house. I don't think I was expecting anything. I'm not even sure what time it is. My thoughts are still whirling from the performance, the carnival, the field, Jackson's touch on my skin, the feeling of his voice vibrating against my body as we stood practically glued together...

I am not expecting to walk into the living room to see my mother standing with her arms crossed and her eyes narrowed practically down to slits, Lorry standing nervously behind her, turning to look at me with wide eyes as soon as I enter the room.

"Sit down, Adrienne."

Chapter 21

Addy

I don't move. Neither does my mother. Neither does Lorry. We all stand still for a few long moments, the silence unbearable.

My mother finally lets out a frustrated exhale, tossing her head sharply with a roll of her eyes before focusing her sneer back on me. A sneer that is subtle enough to show rage, betrayal, confusion. I don't know what to say.

"You've never lied to me before, Adrienne. Ever." She huffs again, a disbelieving sound that makes my blood go cold. "I really thought... I didn't want to believe it..."

I don't want to ask what she's talking about. I don't want to assume. But what else could she be upset about?

"*Why*, Adrienne? What in God's name has gotten into you?"

My mouth opens, but I still can't make a sound.

"Look at yourself!" She raises her voice so sharply, I jump. "Dressing like a... like a slut, then throwing yourself up *on a stage*?! How long have you been parading around town with those boys?"

There it is. I knew I had to wait only a bit to get confirmation. Still, the only thing I can do at the moment is awkwardly curl my arms around myself, the clothes that I had hardly even thought about at all tonight feeling suddenly like needles poking all over my skin.

"They're not what you think," I protest, my voice coming out meek and pathetic-sounding, but my mother waves her hand sharply as she steps forward.

"Don't even start with me, Adrienne. Jackson Lowell? That boy you swore to me you knew nothing about and were going to stay away from?"

I'm sure my face says it all, even if I had the energy to deny it.

"That's what you've been doing all summer, is it? Running around with criminals, singing in rock bands, and lying to me?"

I want to break out in a laugh at the term *rock band* in reference to the Skerritt Wranglers' one-night-only performance, but I manage to keep myself together out of the sheer horror of the thought of my mother knowing all of this.

Lorry sees the question on my face from where she's still standing behind our mother, looking as if she's been waiting impatiently to get her piece in.

"Your ex-boyfriend decided to tattle on you," she tells me as she gives my mom a disbelieving look.

"Enough, Lauren," my mother snaps back at her.

"*Marcus* told you all of this?" I question her, unsure of whether my hot spark of rage is toward him or my mother for actually listening to all of this from my jealous ex-boyfriend. However true it might mostly be.

"You may not care either way about him, but he's very concerned for your well-being, Adrienne. He found me tonight and told me every-thing, how strange you've been acting all summer with him, *breaking up with him*, and now this. Hanging around a bunch of rowdy delinquents, getting up on a stage in front of everyone in this town looking like that—"

"Marcus is a sexist, elitist prick, Mom." Lorry raises her voice now, her fiery glare matching my mother's. "He doesn't care about Addy, he cares that he has no one to boss around anymore."

"Lauren, go to your room now!" my mother orders as she turns on Lorry, pointing down the hall. "This conversation doesn't concern you."

Lorry casts one more guilt-ridden look at me before angrily brushing past my mother.

"I don't want to see you for the rest of the night!" she calls out after Lorry's pointedly stomping footsteps echoing down the hall followed by the slam of a door.

She turns back to me. I'm still trying to process everything I've learned tonight. Wondering if meeting Marcus, previously one of the greatest moments of my life, might be the worst thing that's ever happened to me.

"You are not to see any of those boys ever again. Especially Jackson Lowell."

I can't help but scoff lightly to myself.

"You are not leaving this house for the rest of the summer unless it's with me."

I stare at her in disbelief. "You can't keep me locked up here."

"You're insistent on embarrassing yourself and our family, so yes, you'll be staying inside at all times unless I'm with you," my mother assures me. "Tomorrow I'm going through your things, you're going to hand over any more clothes that look like *that*"—she gestures to my skinny jeans and crop top—"and I'm making sure there is no booze or drugs or cigarettes or anything illegal you're hiding from me."

She pauses, her face sinking into distress for a brief second as she rubs a hand against her face.

"God help me, if I find anything in there, Adrienne..."

"That's it, then, huh?" I ask, my voice shaking as it rises with a fury that makes my hands curl and my skin feel a million degrees. "Anyone who doesn't live in a big fancy house or go to your pathetic little luncheon every Sunday must be some kind of drug dealer? I must be breaking into houses, stealing from my parents' liquor cabinets, or throwing bricks through store windows because I'm not the same person I was when I was thirteen years old?"

"Adrienne May, I swear—"

"'Cause let me tell you something, Mother, the only people around here who do that are the creepy, controlling, psychotic boys you've been shoving me toward every time you drag us down here. They're the troublemakers, not—"

"Troublemakers?" she questions as she tilts her head, her stare still like ice. "Really? Last I heard, your new little friends hid dead rats and poured rotten fish water in every car on your boyfriend's block last night."

"*What?*"

I'm bewildered, ready to declare the story a lie that Marcus and the others must have made up, until I think about it for a moment.

Jeez. Benji.

"Okay, there's a reason for—"

"That's enough. You're handing over your guitar as well, and if this little attitude hasn't improved by the time we get home, you're not seeing it ever again, do you understand me?" She takes a breath, her eyes looking as if, just for a moment, they're blinking back tears. As if she's just a second away from breaking down in an entirely different way. But the look is covered by her anger in the next second. "God, I would have expected behavior like this from your sister at some point, but *you...*"

Me. Perfect, docile little Adrienne Moreno. The girl you can walk all over and she'll do nothing about it.

As much as I hate the image, I can't help but wonder why I couldn't have kept it up. Because right now, this feels worse.

"Mom, if you knew what Marcus and Deran and the rest of them did—"

"Adrienne, I don't want to hear another word blaming this all on Marcus. He's been nothing but a perfect gentleman to you, and I'm shocked he's bothered to continue to care for you with the amount of disrespect you've shown him these past—"

"Mom, he's crazy!" I finally scream, my voice making her flinch back sharply. "I broke up with him and he flipped out and he started grabbing me, and if it weren't for one of those boys you hate so much who you don't even know, I don't know what he would have—"

"I've had enough of this display." My mother shakes her head tiredly, her arms falling to her sides, still focused on me with an incredulous look. A look I've never before seen directed at me. Like she's learned one of the most disgusting types of people she could ever imagine has been living under her roof all this time. It's a familiar look, one I haven't seen in years, one that I can recall only in the furthest corner of my mind.

It was the way she used to look at Dad.

"Go to your room, now. You need to be up bright and early tomorrow to go through your things."

She heads into the hall while I stand frozen to the spot in the living room.

"You think I'm like him now, right?" I can't help but say, my voice softer as it steadily begins to lose its fight. "Is that what you're afraid of?"

She pauses but doesn't turn to face me. I expect her to scream something, to shoot me another outraged glare. Because I never do this. *We* never do this. We never bring him up. But how can I not after she looked at me like that?

Like the person who ruined her life?

How could she ever think I would be anything like him? That I would get involved in anything that could ruin my life the way he ruined his own. The way he almost ruined ours.

"I'm calling Ellen's mom in the morning" is all she says, still not turning back before she continues on down the hall, muttering one last thing as she goes. "I can't believe you got your best friend into this mess too."

I look after her, a cry stuck in my throat, wanting to beg her to leave Ellen out of it, to insist she didn't do anything wrong. But it's useless.

I'm no longer trustworthy. I'm one of them now.

Troubled. Mean. Soulless. Whatever other association my mother and everyone like her throws in with kids who haven't had the luxuries in life they have enjoyed.

I march down to my room when I'm certain my mother has gone to bed. Anger flashes through me first. Anger that makes me want to trash the entire bedroom. To go out and do something reckless. To be exactly what my mother fears I'll turn into if I stay away from Marcus Tanner too long.

And then it's something else, as I pace mindlessly around my room, my hands ripping through my hair, destroying the rest of the bouncy curls I had forced it into this morning with Ellen and Lorry's help.

Ellen... God, I've gotten her in trouble too.

Guilt, shame, embarrassment, horror all ripple through me now as I obsessively think back to the first moment I met Danny and Jackson, the moment when I began to realize why I felt so distant from Marcus. I must have done something wrong, somewhere. My mother is wrong, without a doubt, but there must have been a point where I made a mistake. When I could have done something, when I could have told my mom everything before Marcus got to her, when I could have let Marcus down easier so he wouldn't...

I lift my head from my hands, finding that I have collapsed onto the floor at some point, leaning against the bed.

No. I can already hear Lorry, Ted, and Jackson all berating me for thinking like that.

Jackson...

A pain pierces my chest that makes me wince, the tears that had been burning behind my eyes finally spilling over.

Will he come back here? Once I stop showing up to see him and the others in town? Will Danny and Benji wonder where I've gone?

Will I leave here at the end of the summer and never see any of them again?

It feels like it's been hours by the time I finally stand up. The house is dead quiet. As dead quiet as the night outside when I slide open my window, throw my legs over the windowsill, and fall down quietly onto the lawn.

It's past midnight. I've been up since six this morning to try to get my hair looking nice for the show, but I don't feel tired. Not in the usual way. I feel drained. Like something has bitten into me and sucked every bit of life out until I'm left with nothing but a barely human feeling.

I'm sure I look like the living dead as I walk at a steady, thumping pace, my face expressionless, my eyes staring at my boots pressing against the road, my hair hanging in messy strands around my head, my makeup an ungodly mess.

I don't care. I don't care if anyone sees me. I don't care where I'm walking. I don't care if my mother happens to check my room and sees that I'm gone. I will later, but I don't now.

I keep walking, and it feels nice. Nicer than sitting in my room all night, where things feel so small, so life-threatening. Nice to feel the world stretching out in all different directions around me. Knowing I could go anywhere if I wanted to. That I could keep walking and walking, way out into the hills. Probably get eaten by a werewolf. But maybe not.

I make it into town, eventually. There's only a bit more sound. The distant murmuring from a late-night bar. A couple cars whirring in the distance. But mostly dark and quiet, the familiar buildings usually buzzing with energy during the day shuttered and lifeless for now.

My footsteps slow as I hover beside the closed-down café Ellen and I frequent. My eyes stay locked on the ground as I hear the steps of whoever had turned the corner behind me pause. It's still, the both of us standing, them staring at my back, me still looking at the ground as I slowly turn around.

Jackson Lowell is in the center of the sidewalk when my head finally rises to look back at him.

He looks so strangely perfect that I think he can't be real. He can't be here, at whatever horrible hour of the morning it is, standing there with that rare look on his face I only notice when he thinks no one is looking. A look of warmth. Understanding. The line of his mouth and his eyes not turned into a gloating smirk. Looking at me as if he somehow knows everything that's raging in my head just by taking one glance at me.

But he is real. Standing there as wide awake as I am, having stumbled upon me on his late hour journey just as I've stumbled upon him.

So I move toward him. Slowly at first. Then I start running.

He has time to take only a couple steps before I've closed the entire distance between us, his arms open and ready by the time I crash into them.

We say nothing. I know he's already seen the state of me and he can feel me crying against his shoulder. But we stand here for a moment. No one around to stare or comment. His arms hold me to him like something he's found and is afraid to lose again. And mine do the same.

I don't think about the fact that I'm in Jackson Lowell's bedroom. Or that I'm on his bed, for that matter. On his bed next to him, our shoes kicked off to the floor, me huddled in one of the thin, ripped-up wool blankets as well as Jackson's arms, since I recently realized I've been walking for an hour in sixty-degree weather with no coat.

There's no time to think about it. There's nothing I can think about until I tell him everything.

It's like taking a deep breath for the first time in hours. And Jackson listens. Just lies beside me on the bed and listens.

It's strange. In a way, it feels like it does when Ellen or Lorry and I lie next to each other in the dark and talk. Talk about everything that weighs on our thoughts that we don't have the energy to talk about in the day. Or when I'm with my cousins lying by the lake near their house, the three of us discussing whatever random thing comes to mind that we can't talk about with anyone else. Things that are spoken, heard, but never talked about much again or held against us in the future.

But it's different too. Different in that, with Jackson, it's more than words I want to share with him. I wonder how I'm going to extract myself from this blanket, from his now lighter but still warming and grounding hold.

"I don't regret any of it," I say decisively, my voice hoarse from crying and then talking for so long without a beat in between. "Maybe getting Ellen into trouble, but other than that... I don't care."

It's freeing to realize it. Scary. I used to care so much about what my mother thinks of me. About being the daughter she can count on, letting Lorry be the one who can do and say what she wants when she wants. I still do care. I can already feel the need to begin working to regain her trust, to never have to see that look on her face ever again.

But I know she's wrong. And that I wouldn't trade the time I've had so far this summer for anything.

"I'd still be stuck. If I didn't break up with Marcus, if I didn't do the performance, if I didn't..."

I stare down at our feet at the bottom of the bed, the dim light casting a yellowish glow and strange shadows around the sparsely decorated bedroom.

I know Jackson is teeming with jabs to throw at me. I can't imagine what I must sound like to him. Crying about my problems while he's sleeping above a liquor shop.

Maybe it doesn't matter to him. You'll be gone soon anyway.

"You shouldn't regret it."

His voice is low and soothing, matching the comforting aura of the room.

My voice is firm when I answer. "I don't."

We both laugh softly. Even when we're agreeing we can't help the undertone of an argument.

"I'm glad I could see you," I sigh, leaning my head against his chest. I feel him tense, surprised at my movement. "I wanted to tell somebody so, in case you don't ever see me again—"

"Ah, jeez," he groans. "Don't be so dramatic. Look, it's the first night, and you snuck out already, didn't you? You can do it again."

Huh. He's not wrong.

"Besides..." He leans back, looking down at my mouth. I look at his. "There's nothing wrong with having to be a little more sneaky."

I laugh again and turn away. Still too afraid.

"I think you can do anything."

"Aw."

"I'm serious." Jackson pulls fully away from me and crosses his ankles, his arms coming to rest behind his head as he sighs tiredly, his eyes closing. "You're a hell of a lot smarter than I am."

I roll over onto my side, gazing at his profile in the dim lamplight. "You can do anything too, Jackson."

"Hmph."

"I'll stand by it: you're a good person." I shrug, sitting up straight on the bed, the blanket falling away from me but the warmth lingering. "Look. You rescued a lonely crying girl on the street. You're a saint."

His eyes open. I smile, looking down as he sits up too, leaning forward so that his face is inches from mine.

"I should get back. The sun's gonna be up soon."

"This is true."

His eyes stay on my lips. My eyes stay on his.

Silence beats through the room, both of us refusing to move, even though we should. Even though I need to get back before my mother sees that I'm gone and decides to bury me in the basement when I return.

God, just do it already.

I move before he can, reaching up to touch his face as my lips crash on his.

Jackson's mouth moves against mine, both of his hands reaching up to hold my face, his fingers stroking through my messy hair.

It's much different than when I used to kiss Marcus. When I'd been so anxious to get it perfect, so worried I'd be horrible at it. Now, my stomach is doing flips for different reasons as I messily press my lips against Jackson's, the both of us completely imperfect at it because we're tired or we just don't care. I think it's for the right reasons this time.

It's not exactly an epic or triumphant kiss. I can hardly see him in the dark and there are still dried tears on my face, my hair is a ratty tangled mess, and I'm sure I have makeup smeared all around my eyes.

But it's also warm, Jackson is leaning back one hand on the bed as he pulls me closer to him, our heads are twisting to deepen the kiss, and something about it all makes it exactly what we need it to be.

And it feels, despite how I know things are going to feel again when the sun is up, that everything is as it should be.

Chapter 22

Jackson

"**W**ard was tellin' me you had a girl up in your room last night."

"He was, was he? Well, it's more than he's had in the past thirty years, I'm sure."

Ted chuckles as he rolls his eyes, tossing back a swig of beer. The bar is as dark as it usually is, only a few of the shutters open to let in some of the harsh eighty-eight-degree sunlight from outside. It's a Sunday, so Johnny-Jay's is closed to the public, but Jay always lets Ted in during the summer to kick back with a cold one. The guy works outside sixty hours a week cutting down branches and mowing lawns. It's the least Jay can do for him.

I'm allowed in too, so long as I'm supervised by Ted. Jay thinks I'm gonna raid all his good liquor if I'm in here by myself. I can't argue his point.

Ted leans back from the bar, gazing over to where I'm sitting in the corner of the room, Skerritt scratching at my shoes and trying to scamper up my leg with his slippery little paws while I mess around with the jukebox.

"Was it Addy?"

I feel something rush inside me at the mention of her name. Damn, I really do have it bad for a rich girl, don't I?

I don't answer, my fingers clicking halfheartedly through the records in the machine, my eyes flicking up toward Ted to give him a smirk.

Ted sighs heavily.

"Jackson…"

"Hey, but it wasn't like what you're thinkin'," I interrupt. "I couldn't sleep all night so I went out to head for Cropsy Park, and we ran into each other. She just… she was upset and we talked for a while."

Ted narrows his eyes.

"I'm serious! Anyway, it's not…"

I cut myself off at the last minute, looking away and pretending to busy myself with the jukebox again. Skerritt whimpers at my feet.

"It's not like *that*, huh?"

I don't know why I'm embarrassed to say it. Everyone has seen how pathetic I act with any girl I like even a little bit who I pretend likes me just as much. It feels like an official admission of something by telling Ted, of all people, that what I've been feeling for Addy is stronger than anything I've felt for anyone else.

Similar to a feeling I've only ever had once, years ago.

Maybe because it will feel real then. Something I care about. Something I could screw up.

I hear Ted's chair scrape out from under him. I lean back in mine, my shoes pushing against the bottom of the jukebox. Skerritt tries leaping up onto the bridge my legs form, clinging on with his front paws like he's holding on to a life raft for a couple seconds before flopping to the floor once again, deciding to nip at my hanging shoe laces instead.

"Now, I don't need the speech," I warn, though there's hardly any bite to my voice as I feel Ted standing a couple feet behind me. Looking down at me like a sad child, like he always does when we're alone and have conversations like this. "I know, she's above me, she's got her psycho ex-boyfriend already messin' with us, and her mom's probably best buddies with Sheriff Numb-Nuts. I know all the downsides, trust me."

"Do you?"

"*Yes*, Ted."

"You remember she's leavin' in a few weeks?"

I pause rocking back and forth on the rickety chair. The sudden silence pierces me like a white-hot needle, making me shoot forward, sending Skerritt flopping out of the way as I click play on whatever record is queued up in the jukebox.

"I know that, Ted."

I did know that. I just may have momentarily forgotten in the past twenty-four hours.

The light sound of a Diana Ross song thankfully fills the quiet. I lean back again, rocking back and forth. Ted walks around me until he's leaning against the jukebox, beer still clutched in his hand. I focus on Skerritt, who is now victoriously chewing apart the laces on my left shoe now that I've lowered my foot.

"He's gonna be huge," I predict as I stare at the dumb thing who already looks like he's finally beginning to grow out of his puppy years. Physically, anyway. "Do you know how many pounds he's put on since we last saw him?"

"Jackson."

I hate having Ted as a pseudo-older brother sometimes.

I sigh and finally look up to meet his gaze. "What?"

His mop of red curls frames his somber expression that doesn't look entirely reprimanding. It looks something close to happy.

"I think Addy's great."

"Thanks, Dad. Ya think I should pop the question now?"

"And she cares about you too, Jackson."

"Yeah, don't worry. I'm not gonna break her heart."

"She's not who I'm worried about."

"*Christ*," I huff as I lean away again.

"No, I mean it."

I know he does. His voice is rarely this serious. Not in this way. Not... worried like this. Like he is whenever one of us is being particularly stupid and gets themselves hurt or into trouble. Both of which I assume he's worried will happen to me.

I look at him again, dropping the sarcasm. Because I don't want him to worry. I don't want him to have that look on his face. Because it always spreads to me just as fast. Reminding me of reality in a way I can only compare to when my mom died. Or when... when *she* was gone. When I knew real bad things could happen at any moment.

"You've been trying to connect with someone for a long time. And they always end up hurting you. I just don't want you to lose yourself over this. She is gonna leave, Jackson."

I know what he means. But he doesn't know that I've already prepared myself for this. Addy was never going to be a forever thing for me. How the hell would that even work?

"Look, I get it, Ted. And you're right, okay? It is different with her. It's better than anything I've ever tried to have with anyone else. And it's gonna suck when she leaves. But I'm not an idiot. Her life's on a way different wavelength than mine will ever be."

It's just nice to meet in the middle. Even for a moment.

Ted seems a bit more relaxed.

"I know, mature response, right?"

He rolls his eyes, but I can see a grin on his lips before he takes another gulp of his drink. Skerritt moves on to him now, hopping on his hind legs like he's either begging for pets or to take a swig from the bottle himself.

It is mature. Because I am mature about this. It's just some fun, that's all. With someone who's decent, for once. Something I'll probably never find again. But it's fine. I don't care. I'm having fun, she's having fun. It's fine.

"Seriously though." Ted nods, the look back on his face. "You need to watch out. That Marcus guy and his friends are bad news." He leans forward on the jukebox that has now gone silent after the Diana Ross ballad peters out. "Don't go egging anyone on, don't go startin' anything with those boys. Do you understand?"

The fear in his voice and his eyes makes me feel a little sick as the both of us automatically think of his brother. I answer as quickly as possible so we can stop.

"I'm not lookin' to start anything with those clowns, Ted. Nothin' to worry about."

The tension lasts only a few seconds longer while I scramble to start the next record to break the silence. Pink Floyd begins to play as Ted leans away, his worry looking somewhat eased. But not all the way.

***

Addy's been stuck inside the entire week because of her crazy mother, which sucks. But I still plan on holding her to her agreement for our date to the Herschell Gordon Lewis double feature.

There's a small part of me that wonders if she might sneak out again on her own to meet me. But I decide to plan on showing up at her place again in case she needs the nudge. Who knows what brain rot her mother's been feeding her these past couple of days?

As it happens, I have my answer when a familiar girl with a mane of dark curly hair tentatively approaches me Friday afternoon while I'm hanging out with Benji at the arcade.

The way she walks up to us looks like she's about to make her first drug deal.

The girl (Ellen, I finally remember when Benji greets her jovially) tells me that she talked to Addy yesterday at some dinner party they all went to with their parents.

There's a plan set in place. Addy's mom is going out tomorrow night to some makeup party thing that sounds to me like an excuse for women to get away from their husbands and get sloshed, and Addy and her sister, Lorry, will be in the house alone. Addy will sneak out and meet me at the end of the street if I drive her into town, and Lorry will cover for her, telling their mom she got food poisoning and barricaded herself in her room for the night if she comes back early. Apparently their mom won't go near them when they're sick, so I'm assured it's a foolproof plan.

It's pretty devious for my goody-two-shoes rich girl (girlfriend?), and I'm all in.

As promised, the plan goes perfectly, and Saturday night, Addy is curled up next to me in the spacious back seat of Ward's Chevy, the giant drive-in screen flashing with cheesy neon blood and severed rubber limbs.

Both of us find it incredibly difficult to focus on the movie.

Kissing Addy has opened up an entirely new world of me not giving a shit what anyone says or thinks.

"Do you find it odd that it's a standard to make out during grotesquely violent horror movies?" Addy asks, pulling away from me to cast a glance up at the screen, where a lady's overly gigantic tongue is currently being ripped out.

"Aren't sex and violence supposed to go together?" I ask, pulling her closer to me, even though she's practically on my lap.

"Don't you still think that's weird?"

"No. They're both deviant things that people don't like to mention in polite conversation."

"Well, when you put it like that..."

"Look, if the rubber body parts are turning you off, just say so."

Addy rolls her eyes, leaning down to press her lips against mine one more time. She curls her arms around the back of my neck, holding us closer together for a few more moments before she leans away, settling back into the seat beside me with a sigh.

She tastes like peppermint and smells like that familiar herby scent I've unknowingly grown accustomed to that I can determine must be her shampoo now that I've had the luxury of burying my face in her neck with her soft hair grazing my nose.

"My cousin Jenny told me they used real animal organs for this movie."

Once I come back down to Earth, I cock my head, flicking my eyes back up to the screen. "Really?"

"Yup." She nods, popping the *P* sound. "That was a sheep's tongue we just saw."

"Okay, now it feels weird to be making out."

We watch the movie for a bit, getting lost in the outlandish plot and overindulgent gore effects (that have to do with animal guts now, I guess) until Addy turns to me before the third act begins.

"Have you ever had your heart broken?"

A laugh that is so loud it warrants me a hissed shush from the car next to us bursts from my chest. I wave the lady in the car parked beside us off. "Have you been talkin' to Ted recently?"

Addy shrugs. "Just curious."

The light from the movie screen flickers gently across her features, her bronze hair fluttering in the breeze as she leans her head against her fist. Her striking eyes are focused on me with that look she always has that seems to pierce right under my skin.

God, she's somethin' else.

Not yours, a voice has to annoyingly remind me. *Not really.*

I take a breath, stretching my arms out along the seats, looking away before turning back to her. She looks the same.

"Seriously? We're gonna talk about heartbreak at the end of *Blood Feast*?"

She gives a soft grin, placing her hand on top of mine. "Seriously. Tell me."

From the look on her face, the way she says it, or from that bizarre sensation where I feel I can already plainly see all of her thoughts, I can tell she already knows. But she wants me to explain.

I give a heavy sigh, leaning my head back against the leather seat. So we have to talk about this now.

"You already know I got around with a lotta girls."

She raises a brow.

"It was never anything serious though."

She keeps her brow raised.

"Not *serious* serious. It was just..."

I look up at her again, but she's still not letting me off the hook.

"What the hell did you ever see in Marcus Tanner?" I ask instead, hoping it proves my point. "What did *you* get outta any of that?"

I don't intend it to sound accusatory. Thankfully she doesn't seem to take it that way.

"I really don't know," she admits, her penetrating gaze turning away from me as she stares blankly at the movie screen. "When we first got together, I thought it was like a fairy tale. Back home, I'm not exactly the person I am here."

"What do you mean?"

"I don't hang out with people like Marcus. And people like him want nothing to do with me. I'm kind of a loser."

I laugh again. The lady next to us shushes me again.

"No, really. Ellen's my only close friend. Ellen and my cousins. Here though, my mother gets to relive her glory days, and everyone thinks I'm this interesting popular girl from New York. And I was always taken with the handsome rich boys in the big houses from California. So when one of them said he thought I was pretty and wanted to go on a date with me, it was the best thing that could have ever happened to me."

From the expression on her face, it sounds as sad to her as it does to me.

"Jeez. Well, glad to know I'm not the only delusional one in this pairing."

She shoves me playfully.

"So the answer is I never really liked him that deeply at all," she admits. "And God does that feel good to finally say out loud."

"I know." I shrug. "I'm the king of makin' people feel good."

"Alright, Romeo, well, it's your turn now. Tell me about Brenda, or Colette, or Annie, or whoever."

Jeez, she's certainly been talking to someone.

I frown, staring off at the corner of the screen, where Ramses, the psychotic killer, is preparing to decapitate the teenage girl lying on the kitchen counter.

"I don't know. I was lonely, I guess. They helped."

It doesn't feel as bad admitting it to her, here where only she and I can hear. In the darkness of midnight, buried within a sea of cars, part of the reason I'm sure Addy agreed to this date in the first place. Not as bad as I thought. Not as bad as it would be admitting it to anyone else.

"They weren't really what I wanted. But I didn't realize it until after I had some distance."

I keep my eyes on the screen, watching Ramses scurrying away from the police toward the trash compactor that will be his undoing.

"I get it."

There's a look on Addy's face that seems like pity. I don't think it is though. It's just... understanding.

"You do?"

"I do." She nods. "I have Lorry. And my cousins. Something closer than just friends. People who make me feel like I have a place. If I didn't have them, I'd feel alone too."

The credits roll. Applause fills the lot. Addy moves closer to me again, resting against my outstretched arm. She smiles at me when I look down at her. I pull her closer.

"I'm just saying, *Color Me Blood Red* has to be, objectively, his best film," Addy insists after I've parked Ward's car back under the overhang. "*The Wizard of Gore* can't even compete."

"I don't know," I muse as we both strain to heave the ratty tarp up over the convertible. I keep telling Ward that this mangy thing is gonna do more harm than good to his nice car, but he insists that storing it out of sight, even if everyone in this town knows what kind of car he has and where it's always parked, will keep people less tempted to steal it. "A psycho magician butchering people in a magic show is more intriguing than some yahoo who sucks at art so bad he needs to use human blood to paint."

I throw my arm around her as we leave the overhang. She casually reaches up to grab my hand, like we've done this for months. And it sorta feels that way, to be honest. Everything with Addy starts to feel that way pretty quickly. To the point where I'm starting to not remember what life was like before her.

Or how it's gonna go on after she leaves.

"How did you end up staying here?" she asks, nodding up at the old liquor shop, where we can both see Ward behind the counter. There's an open can of beer beside him as he stares down at a deck of cards spread out on the counter with a pondering look on his face, his hand resting against his bushy beard. He forgot to close down the shop again, too wrapped up in whatever world he sinks away into.

"Oh, I could tell from a mile away Ward was the type to take an old hoodlum like me under his wing," I sigh as we cross the street. "Think he had a son once who stayed up in that room, but he went off to join the armed forces, or somethin'. Ward'll never admit it, but he hates being alone. He pretends I earn my keep by helpin' out around the shop, but really I just hang out with him every now and then and swipe some of his good stuff that he pretends he doesn't notice. It's a mutually beneficial arrangement."

"With mutual gray legal areas."

"The best kind of arrangements."

We're about to make our way over to Cropsy Park, mostly because there's a definitive chill in the air now, and I know for a fact that the metal playground will still be warm. But we only just barely cross the street before the sharp chirp of a siren beeps behind us, making us both startle and turn toward a police car rolling up smoothly to the curb.

The door swings open and slams shut in one breath, and I'm amazed to see Sheriff Nulty move so fast when there aren't even any discounted donuts in sight.

"Stop right there, Lowell," he growls, pointing a triumphant finger at me. Addy pulls away from me instinctually, as if she's been shocked. Terror flashes over her face as she stares with wide eyes at the sheriff and his deputy as they approach me. "I gotcha this time, ya little shit."

"Are you *serious*?" I ask as the deputy yanks my arms back and cuffs me. "This is the biggest crime you can find tonight in this town, boys?"

I knew Addy's mom was friendly with the sheriff, but damn. Arrested for going on a date with her daughter seems extreme. Not to mention a good case I might have against the department in a world where I could afford a good lawyer.

"You just think you're so clever, don't ya?" Nulty grumbles, a grin on his face, but a look of anger in his eyes that gives me pause.

"Ah, no, sir, just goin' on a date like any normal person," I respond as the deputy pushes me toward the car.

"Wait!"

Addy runs forward, the look of terror still fresh as she faces down Nulty. He looks at her at first in annoyance, as if he hadn't expected her to say a word. And then recognition flickers over his face.

"Adrienne Moreno...?"

Addy ignores him, pushing down the panic in her voice as she speaks firmly. "What is he in trouble for? You can't arrest somebody off the street and not tell them what's going on."

"Probable cause," the nasal voice of the deputy pushing me toward the cruiser responds haughtily. "Suspicion of theft of a firearm."

"The firearm of an officer of the law, no less," Nulty continues, his hands looping into his belt as he raises his chin in self-importance. From how he's obviously referring to himself, I don't have to ask.

"Oh, right, like I'd be bored enough to swipe anything of yours, Nulty? Are you fucking kidding me?"

"This is ridiculous," Addy says, looking between Nulty and me as the deputy begins cramming me into the back seat of the cruiser.

"Ridiculous?" Nulty asks, still keeping his haughty gaze on me, an air of victory in his tone. "With a history of breaking into houses on my street?"

"He didn't break into the Lensens' house, Sheriff, he—"

"And with multiple witnesses attesting that this lowlife broke into and desecrated multiple vehicles as revenge for a harmless prank?"

Addy's eyes move rapidly as she tries to figure out what he means. I already know. I can see everything clear as day.

And goddamn it, I told Benji to leave it be.

She understands as her eyes widen in outrage. "A harmless prank? Do you mean when Marcus Tanner and his friends, *your* son, threw a brick through—"

"And multiple witnesses attesting that he's been casin' the place several times in the past few weeks."

Great. So taking a shortcut through Mansion Row to get to Addy's place saved me time, but screwed me in the end.

"This is crazy," Addy protests, her hands going to her head. "Sheriff Nulty, you can't—"

"You've been weaslin' your way outta trouble long enough," Nulty declares, aiming a stern finger at me again through the front window of the cruiser after I've been tossed inside, the door slammed closed beside me. "Once we got ya officially busted for this, I'm advocatin' for hard time in a juvenile hall far from here, you understand me, Lowell? If we can nail you with intent to use the gun you stole from my house, I'll do everything in my power to see you tried as an adult."

Addy opens her mouth again to argue, but he rounds on her, pointing his finger in her face now, making her take a step back. "And *you*, missy, will do well to get back home. I'd hate to have to tell your mother about any of this."

There's nothing more Addy can say. There's nothing I can say.

I always figured it might happen one day. I've made enough trouble for Nulty and his department with all my petty crimes, and I've made enough enemies in this town that they would gladly attest that I would do something as monumentally stupid as steal the sheriff's gun from his house.

It's already happened once in my life before I came here to Greydon.

Hell, I wouldn't be surprised if someone already planted the stolen gun in my room above Ward's shop.

I can feel Addy watching me desperately from the sidewalk as the cruiser pulls away and we head off toward the station. I look straight ahead at the back of the passenger seat.

Chapter 23
Addy

"It's *wrong*! They can't do this... can they?"

Benji shrugs, pausing his pacing to give me a look. "We're not the best people to ask about how the law works around here, Addy. Half the time, I think Nulty and his crew don't even know."

"It's gotta be Shelly Criston," Danny says from the other side of the trailer where he sits at the tiny kitchen counter. He worriedly runs his hand through his hair, his eyes filled with the same dread that's been running through me for almost an hour now since Jackson got arrested. "Right?"

"Would make sense." Benji nods in agreement, returning to pacing in front of me where I'm sat on the couch next to Ted. I came straight to his place after the sheriff drove away with Jackson. I'm not sure why. It's not as if any of us can do anything. Though for a brief moment I had a tiny fantasy of the four of us marching to the station and staging some sort of coup.

It doesn't matter that it's past two in the morning, the boys all leapt out of bed the moment I announced that Jackson had been arrested. Even though we're all sitting here now with pallid faces, frizzled hair, and raccoon eyes, I don't think any of us could be more awake.

"He threatened him the other day," I recall. "At the Roller Dollar, before the carnival. He said something like Jackson was gonna get his because he blamed some revenge prank on..."

My eyes widen and we all turn to look at Benji, who at least has the grace to look guilty.

"Well, you see... I *was* thinkin' about what you guys were saying, so I may have given an anonymous tip that I saw Shelly and his gang roaming around Mansion Row the night in question. Posing as a worried suburban mom."

"You blamed *Shelly Criston* for your car prank?" Danny questions, his eyes wide with disbelief and horror. "Why the hell would you ever do that?"

"I don't know!" Benji waves his arms helplessly as he begins pacing again. "I was tryin' to be smart! Clearly that's not one of my attributes."

"Of course he's gonna think it was Jackson, then," Danny groans, slumping onto his elbows against the counter. "Now he wants to get back at him. Shit, Benji."

"He's the only one who hates him enough," Ted agrees. He's been mostly silent since I told them what happened. Even Benji is quieter than I thought he'd be, despite the racket his pacing makes, shaking the entire trailer as we all sit in stunned and terrified silence.

Stealing a gun is serious. More serious than anything Jackson has done before, I'm certain. But it also seems serious for someone like Shelly Criston, who'd rather spend his time harassing elementary school children than risk the trouble that could come from stealing a firearm.

Then again, if he wanted to get back at Jackson, he had the perfect opportunity offered to him on a platter, didn't he?

"Damn it, Benji, why the hell would you pull a stunt like that?" Ted demands.

"I don't know, man, I was drunk one night, and it was right after they jumped Danny, and I was sick of their shit!"

"I don't need you to get revenge on anyone for me," Danny protests. "We told you, all it was gonna do is cause more trouble, and now look what happened. They're gonna blame everything on Jackson."

"Hey, don't turn all this around on me!" Benji argues, his voice rising as he pauses his pacing to point an accusing finger Danny's way. "I may have stunk up a few fancy cars and pointed a casual finger at some jackass we all hate, but I didn't bust into any of those houses and steal any goddamn gun."

Danny's face curls in disgust. "God, where did you even get a bunch of dead rats?"

"That's no concern of yours."

"Marcus and his friends have to have something to do with it," I interject quietly.

"Oh, no question," Benji agrees. "I'm sure when Nulty asked them if they'd seen Jackson creepin' around their street, they happily made up whatever bullshit they could."

"You think anyone saw you?" Danny asks him.

"Hell no. I'm nothin' but stealth when I'm pullin' off a prank, even if I am five beers in."

"They would have done it anyway."

Ted's words are meant only for me. I turn toward him, seeing the understanding look in his eyes.

If Marcus and the others did have anything to do with this, it wasn't just because of me. They've hated Jackson and Danny and Benji for a long time, long before I ever came around.

It wasn't just because of me...

"And I bet it all played perfectly into Shelly's hands," Benji continues. "He knows what those guys did, throwing that brick through the store window. He's always creepin' around Mansion Row himself, so he probably saw Jackson headin' that way to meet you loads of times. He swipes the gun, tips off the cops he saw Jackson around there, the rich boys back up his story without even knowin' it, and he gets off scot-free. With his enemy number one off the street."

Benji aims an angry kick at the kitchen cabinets, making me jump and Danny teeter back from the counter. "Damn bastard."

I lower my head into my hands, my fingers dragging against my scalp, as if that will wake me up from this nightmare. A part of me thought that coming here and telling the boys would somehow reassure me. That they would know exactly how to handle this and get Jackson out of trouble in no time.

"What the hell is wrong with this town?"

The resounding silence at my inquiry makes me think this is a question that has been asked long ago with no clear answer.

"Is it much different where you're from?" Benji asks me, having paused his pacing again, his hands on his hips as he glares at the window above the couch.

I realize I have no idea.

I don't go home. Lorry will tell Mom that I'm sick if she asks, so I don't have to worry about her checking on me. Not that she knows I have a habit of sneaking out now.

We all stay at Ted's place. It feels like the safest place at the moment. More warm and comforting than the rental cottage would be right now, where I'd be forced to do nothing but sit alone in my room and think.

Here I can sit in the dark in the back bedroom of the trailer with Danny, the two of us staring out the open window into the trees obscuring the quietly running creek.

We don't say much. But it's nice to sit here with each other.

"Danny?"

My voice sounds strained as it gently cracks through the silence.

"Yeah?"

I stay looking out the screen even when I feel him turn toward me.

"Do you feel like… Did I ever make you feel bad about yourself?"

Silence rings between us. It makes my question feel even more awkward.

"What?" There's the trace of a smile in his voice, but I still don't look.

"After we first met. Did it seem like I was condescending? Like how Marcus and his friends are to you, but… different?"

After a few more seconds of quiet, I realize he's waiting for me to look at him. When I do, there is a gentle smile on his lips. The kindness in his gaze that is so engraved in him, it seems impossible that he could ever truly be angry at anybody.

"You were nice to me. That night at the diner. You stood up for me. That's what I noticed, Addy. And it doesn't matter the reason you did it at first, to impress other people or feel better about yourself. Because it's not that way anymore. You just needed to get to know me."

There's nothing more to say about it. Because he's right. And it makes me feel easier than I thought I would.

"What do you want to do?" Danny asks, his voice as gentle as the quiet outside. "When you're on your own, I mean? When you don't have to live with your parents or go to school?"

His eyes look passive as he gazes out the window. The opposite of how I'd think anyone would look when thinking about life after teenage-hood.

What do I want to do?

Despite the circumstances, I don't want to give the same answers I gave Jackson. The realistic ones. The ones riddled with teenage angst about the hopelessness of becoming an adult and entering the real world.

I want to be hopeful this time.

"I'd like to see the world." I lean my arms up on the windowsill and feel Danny's eyes on me. "I'm gonna go all over the place and see things I don't know about, people who live differently from me, and all the things that most people don't ever get to see in a lifetime."

There's the smallest grin on his face now, though it doesn't reach all the way to his eyes. "You think so?"

I shrug. "Why not? I've got time."

Danny turns away from me, looking back out at the creek.

"What about you?"

I see him from the corner of my eye, gazing down at his hands as he leans up on the window beside me. "As long as I get out of here, I don't really care."

He leans back on the thin, creaking mattress, looking up to the tops of the tall trees shading all the little homes scattered around us, blinking past the strands of his hair that fall into his eyes. They look more blue than usual under the glowing moonlight.

"I've been in one town, in one house, around the same things my entire life. I've never even been outside the city lines, not once."

There's something more hopeful in his voice now. Something like a gasp of fresh air after being underwater for a long time as he blinks into the moonlight.

"I want a chance to go somewhere where no one knows me. Where I can be who I want. Where I can try whatever I want. Where it doesn't feel like there are all these eyes on me every second all the time, thinking they know everything about me..."

He trails off, the gentle smile that had appeared on his face vanishing. He shrinks back down, the light in his eyes quickly fading into the look from before.

Hopelessness.

"It's silly to think that, right? Like moving away would make my life so much easier? It'd be harder, right? I'd be homesick, I wouldn't know where anything is, I'd be in some unfamiliar place..."

They're words that seem well practiced, like he's said them to himself time and time again. Trying to convince himself.

"Traveling would be nice too," he adds. "Then you could always have a place to come home to. But still see... everything."

But he doesn't want that home to be here. I can see it clearly on his face. I don't know everything about Danny Macklin. I probably don't know exactly what he means when he says how trapped he is here. But the sound of his voice makes me feel like I've been punched in the chest. Because I don't think Benji, Jackson, or even Ted know either. He sounds as if he can't exactly voice it himself.

And he thinks it doesn't matter. How could he ever have the chance to leave? When everything around him is telling him that he'll never have enough to be anything more?

It makes me angry. So angry that I turn to him sharply, my heart beating fast, a breath huffing from my chest.

"You *are* going to get out of here one day," I promise him. "It doesn't matter if it's ridiculous or hopeless or if you fail or if it ends up being horrible. Which it won't. You can do it. Anyone can do it. You're going to leave here and never think about these small-minded nobodies again, and you're going to find something incredible to do with your life somewhere far away and amazing, and it's going to be perfect."

He watches me during my little speech, a grateful smile on his face that tells me he realizes that I sort of understand. Or want to. But it's not enough to come close to erasing the look in his eyes.

Not enough to tell me he believes me.

***

The day feels strange the moment I wake up. Every moment I spend wandering around the house, counting down each second that I'm not in town, that I'm not with Danny and the others figuring out what we're going to do to help Jackson.

I know they're meeting with Jay to come up with a plan. I have no idea what that plan will entail. I'm not sure if I want to know. But it can't be worse than waiting inside all day not knowing anything.

The entire day, my mother is hosting a brunch that lasts hours into the evening. An entire day of sitting in my room, lying on my bed staring at the ceiling, listening to my mother and her temporary friends chatter and laugh along with the clinking glasses and silverware while I think of Jackson getting hauled away in a police cruiser, staring stoically at the ground, like he wasn't surprised. Of Danny's face when he tried to explain whatever it is he's feeling, how scared he is that this is all his life will be.

I hate it. I want to break my window and run. Go to the station and demand to know what's going on.

The women here at my house probably know more than me by now due to whatever rumors must be flying around. I want to march into the dining room and ask them, embarrassment of my mother be damned. She's already disappointed in me.

My ears strain to catch the hint of Jackson Lowell's name in their epic gossip session, but today's not the day for discussions on rambunctious teenagers, I guess.

It isn't until the next day that my mother finally leaves to go to her regular potluck dinner at the Burths' house. And I do still have my recovering sickness excuse if I'm not here when she comes back. So come five o'clock, when I'm sure my mother and her friends are settled into their wine and card games, I'm following her path out the door, making my way into town as fast as my feet will carry me, as if I can outrun the dread prodding at the pit of my stomach.

Ellen is the first person I see once I arrive. She's sitting outside the Fruit Juice Bar at a tiny round metal table, twirling her straw through her blue raspberry slushie nervously.

Her parents have always been more reasonable than my mom, so she thankfully didn't get into too much trouble once my mother called to rat her out the other night. Just a firm warning to stay away from troublesome boys, from what she told me. Still, I feel embarrassed that I dragged my best friend into all of this drama. I've done nothing but that this entire summer. And I'm about to do it again.

"God, Addy!" she gasps in relief, as if she thought I perished at sea. She nearly knocks over her slushie and the table as she runs to me, grabbing my hands. "Did you hear?"

"About Jackson?"

She nods, her eyes growing wider.

"I was there."

I should be thankful no rumors of me being out with Jackson Lowell at midnight last night have reached Ellen, or hopefully anyone else. My mother would already have my bedroom window barred by now if they had.

"Is it true? Do you think he did it?"

"No. We think it's this guy, Shelly Criston. Benji blamed that car prank on him, but Shelly obviously thought it was Jackson. We think he stole the gun and is trying to pin it all on him. Jackson's innocent."

Something flashes across Ellen's face. Something like confusion. But she shakes her head. "They don't have any hard evidence on him. If they don't get some, they'll have to let him go."

"How do you know?"

Ellen chews on her bottom lip, staring at something across the street. I realize we're still standing here, awkwardly frozen with our hands clasped in front of the juice bar with people giving us looks as they pass by.

"I overheard Steven Nulty talking with Deran earlier today outside the arcade."

She gives me a look that makes me even more worried for some reason.

"You were right. They're bad news. The way they were talking... I don't think I want to be around any of them anymore."

"What do you mean?" I press, though I think I already know.

"Addy, I think they're all behind it. To get back at you, or to get back at the boys for the prank. It would be easy for Steven to take his dad's gun, right?"

It had been my thought from the beginning. But I didn't want to believe it. For two reasons. One being that setting someone up for a crime like that is insane. The second being...

"What would they want with a gun?"

Ellen shakes her head again. "Hopefully to just hide it somewhere and try to get Jackson in trouble. You have to understand, I didn't hear them admit it or anything, it's just, how it sounded when I overheard them... I got the feeling this isn't the end of it. That something else is gonna happen too."

It fits perfectly into place with the feeling that's been bothering me ever since sneaking out of Ted's trailer the other night and wasting away the entire next day with nothing to do but worry. That there's something we're not seeing.

"I should have said something, but... God, I'm not like you!" she huffs, her hands pressing against the side of her head.

"What do you mean?" I ask, thrown off by her sudden proclamation.

"I mean like when you stood up to Marcus and Deran for Danny," she sighs helplessly. "I've never seen you do anything like that before, but now you're all… badass and telling off these absolute morons while I was still stuck in fantasy land."

I can see the genuine frustration on her face, but I can't help but give a small smile as I stare down at my shoes.

"You make it sound like I did something good. I'm pretty sure my temper got everyone into this mess in the first place."

"Come on. That's not true and you know it."

She leans forward, making me reluctantly look up to meet her eyes.

"You're my best friend, Addy. I know you. You haven't been this happy in a while. And I don't think you would be anywhere near Jackson or those boys if you thought they didn't want you there. You've got more respect for yourself than that, give me a break."

We both laugh. Despite the situation. Despite the fear that has been gnawing at me relentlessly for the past forty-eight hours. It's a relief to be reminded that I still have my best friend at my side.

"God, we can't even go to the police," I muse, defeated, as Ellen begins to wring her hands together. "They won't believe a word we say."

"And you'll get in more trouble with your mom."

I collapse down onto the tiny stool beside the metal table. Ellen lowers back down into her chair on the opposite side.

"What do we do?" she asks meekly, afraid what my answer will be.

But I don't have one.

Chapter 24

Jackson

I've been in this exact holding cell a number of times in my five years here in this town. It's not terrible, to be honest. The bed's about as comfortable as the one at Ward's place. There's a decent amount of space. And no one from Shelly Criston's gang is locked up in here with me, which is always a plus.

The only thing I can't stand about it is the quiet. Apart from the low mutter coming from the outside hallway of the station every now and then, there's dead silence when I'm in here alone. And today in particular, it feels like it's intentionally meant to inflict psychological torture.

Having to spend a night in the slammer isn't the worst. I get out after a while, either with a warning or some community service or probation from the judge if I did something bad enough. Then that one time I had to do a weekend in juvie when Benji and I stole Deran Burth's dad's Sting Ray and took it out for a joy ride then brought it back with a dinged-up door from where Benji accidentally scraped the corner of a six pack on it. I decided to take all the heat for that one since Benji was so drunk, he could hardly remember what happened.

But this time feels different. Not only because I'm wasting time in here for something I didn't do, but because I don't know what the hell's gonna happen.

I've never been stupid enough to even think about stealing a gun from anyone, let alone the sheriff. I don't need a gun for anything first of all, and second of all, that seems like the kinda thing you'd get more than probation for. I may not give much of a shit about the law around here, but I'm not looking to get shipped off to state prison or anything.

It's my second morning waking up in here with still no word from Nulty or the deputy sitting smugly at the desk across my cell on what the hell we're doing here. Ted strolls into the station before I've even had a chance to properly wake up, heading straight to the desk where the deputy is sitting fiddling with a giant ball of colorful rubber bands.

The rubber band ball plunks down onto the desk and bounces to the ground as the deputy scrambles to grab some papers in front of him as soon as the door opens to pretend he's actually doing something, until he gets a look at Ted and deciphers who he is.

"No visitors, pal," his pinched voice squeaks out as Ted calmly approaches the desk. "If you wanna see your friend, wait for his sentence, maybe you can sign up for the visitor's list."

"Ten minutes," Ted states, his hands placidly on his hips, a seemingly casual gesture, though enough to hold his quietly intimidating demeanor. "All I'm askin'."

"No can do," the deputy shakes his needle-shaped head.

Ted takes a step toward the desk. The deputy straightens.

"Look, the kid's got no parents who are gonna come down," Ted explains. "I'm all he's got. Let me have ten minutes, you'll be here keepin' watch the whole time, right? Let me try to knock some last-minute sense into him while I can."

I swear I see him slide a twenty over the counter.

The deputy leans back, tossing a glance at me.

"My father never loved me," I call out. "Who knows how I'll behave in court after all this if I don't have advice from my big brother, Ted."

Ted gives me a look, but the deputy lets out a long sigh, sounding more whiny than any teenager I've heard in my time.

"Alright. Ten minutes, and no funny business."

He jerks his head in my direction and Ted grabs a chair from the waiting area and slides it along with him before I can ask the deputy what sort of funny business he's suspecting we're gonna get up to while I'm locked in a cell.

Ted and I stare at each other through the bars, him sitting with his hands clasped and his elbows on his knees, and me leaning up against the side of the cell, the bar digging uncomfortably into my side.

"Never thought you'd be this stupid."

I laugh in surprise. "A joke, Ted? In times of crisis? I'm surprised."

Ted's stern face melts into a gentle grin that doesn't fill his entire expression. "I'm spending too much time with you and Benji."

I appreciate Ted trying to lighten the mood, even though it doesn't last too long.

"You think Criston put on this whole shabang?"

Ted shrugs. "I wouldn't be surprised. He thinks you messed up all those rich kids' cars and tried to pin it on him."

I turn away, leaning my forehead against the bars on the side of the cell, glancing out one of the windows that doesn't show much aside from the wall of the brick building next door and a strip of crisp blue sky above.

"Somethin' tells me it wouldn't be a surprise if Marcus Tanner and his own little gang were behind it either." I say it more to the open air than anything else.

"That could be."

It could be because I'm technically in a cage while he's sitting outside watching me, but it feels like he's studying me the way someone would a wild animal, curious to what they'll do next.

"Jackson—" Ted begins, prepared to give me whatever speech he has lined up, something about how he doesn't know how I'm gonna get out of this, that I'm on my own, whatever. Like I haven't been on my own for years now.

"I've been thinkin' a lot," I interrupt him before he can continue down that path. "Couldn't sleep all night. Thinkin' about the first time I ever got arrested."

I laugh to myself, still not facing Ted directly. I can't stand the look on his face.

"It was back in New York, right before I left. It's funny 'cause it wasn't even anything that bad. I've gotten off with a warning for worse stuff. But this cop back there... he hated teens. Me especially, I think 'cause a lotta the guys at the station knew me. They knew what happened to my mom and to... Anyway, they'd always let me off easy, and he hated that. So this one time, I stayed out late on the track after school. In the bleachers, so no one could see me. I didn't feel like goin' home. Didn't roll out 'til two a.m. or somethin' and this guy was there at the gate as soon as I hopped the fence, like he was waitin' for me."

I laugh to myself as I shake my head. Ted stays silent and I still don't want to look at him.

"Threw me right in the cell, got me a court date and everything. With my record, he was able to convince the judge to hit me with a weekend in jail for some loitering charge."

It's quiet. At least outside of my head. Inside, my thoughts are racing, everything that had replayed through my mind all of last night spilling forth, like I suddenly can't wait to say it all out loud to someone.

"Rueben was his name. Officer Rueben."

"They'll let you out today if they can't get any hard evidence on you," Ted says.

I can't listen to Ted's words. I can't stop talking. I need to say everything. So someone can know.

"I've been thinkin' about my mother a lot. Or more than I ever used to, you know? D'you know my best friend when I was in preschool was a girl? This girl named Vera, she lived in the house behind mine."

My heart is going at the speed of light, my body stealing my breath away before I can continue. But I have to. I want to.

"I never thought about her much, until... now. Recently. She was my best friend for a couple years. She was there when my mom died. I remember, I ran away to her house when it happened. Her parents let me in and she and I went to her room and just... sat there. It was nice though. We didn't always have to talk or run around or play with all the toys she had. We could just sit there, all the time.

"But it wasn't just then. I'd go to her house all the time. It was better there. Her parents were nice. They never fought, not in front of us. Sometimes we'd walk around in her backyard. They had this huge back-yard. We'd hold hands a lot. I don't know why. Neither of us had siblings so we... I remember she was really small. Way smaller than me. Her mom always put her hair in these little pigtails, but her hair was so short, they'd stick straight up."

I finally pause. I shake myself out, realizing that I had started shivering as if it were freezing in here when it's at least seventy degrees, and I still have my jacket on.

"What happened to Vera?"

I knew he would ask. That's why I brought her up.

"She died. Not too long after my mom. She drowned in this fucking lake that went behind the yard at her house. She was... she was super small, so she slipped through the gate and she... I don't know, fell and hit her head or something."

Quiet again. There's not much else to say. Or maybe Ted is waiting for me to say more.

"Jeez." I heave an exhausted sigh, my hand running through my hair, starting to feel back to myself. "It's Addy, man," I tell him, even though he probably already knows. "She's got me thinkin' about all of this shit again."

At first I hated it. Now I'm not sure.

"Alright," the deputy's shrill voice calls out as he stands up from his desk, "time's up."

Ted rises from the chair, his eyes still focused on me. There's that look on his face again. That worry. That look that I hate. The look that makes me want to worry too, even though I've promised myself a million times that I would never worry that much about anything.

"I'll see you soon, Jackson."

Chapter 25

Addy

I go to the video store first after talking with Ellen. Not only does being around Danny settle me, but I'm sure he'll have an update about Jackson if there is one. Ellen's going off to try to find Deran, or Eddie, or someone she can spy on again to try to get more information.

It's strange, but she seems excited about the entire process. I've always known Ellen to be incredibly cautious of anything outside our normal routine, but I guess stepping into detective mode has temporarily eradicated that fear.

When I arrive at the video store, stepping through the front door since I can't gaze in past the square of plywood currently covering the broken front window, I see a roughly middle-aged man with silver dusted hair and a matching mustache at the front counter, sliding two tapes and a couple packets of sour gummy worms to the couple in front of him before they happily turn and waltz past me toward the door.

The grumpy-looking man with a Manager name plate pinned to his vest eyes me as I stand unmoving beside the door.

"Can I help you?"

"Um..."

I take a quick glance around the store that I find is empty, aside from a man I've definitely seen before standing near the back wall looking through the X-rated films.

"No," I finally answer when I don't see any sign of Danny. "Sorry."

My initial instinct to head to the arcade at the shopping center turns out to be correct when I hardly get within ten feet before I see Benji standing outside the door, looking to be having an intense conversation with someone.

"Come on, all I have to do is give him a plate of cheese or somethin', and he'll be distracted for at least an hour," Benji is saying to a woman at the door who has her arms crossed and her eyes narrowed as she shakes her head.

"Sorry. No dogs off the leash allowed inside."

I can see now as I approach that Benji is holding Skerritt in both arms, constantly twisting and turning his grasp to keep ahold of the slippery beagle puppy, who looks slightly bigger than the last time I saw him, but still just as squirmy.

"What if I grabbed myself a rope and made a leash?" Benji pleads. "Come on, I just want one round of Asteroids!"

"Benji."

Benji turns to me as the arcade worker heads back inside.

"Addy! Thank God, can you supervise this creature while I go in and bust out a round or two of Asteroids and some Skee-Ball?"

"What's going on?" I ask, looking down at the wriggling dog he struggles to keep from leaping out of his arms. "Where's Danny?"

"Danny's got work until ten tonight. Jay ran off with Ted an hour ago to help him pick up some tree-cutter machine from the big hardware store outside of town, and *I'm* stuck on baby-sittin' duty. But I've been antsy all damn day, and I just need—"

"Danny's at work?"

Benji twists his head at my expression. "Yeah? He started at four."

"He's not there. I checked."

Benji's expression begins to match mine, his usually jumpy body going immobile, the puppy still flopping in his arms, its paws scratching at the pins on his leather jacket.

"Does Danny ever blow off work?" I ask, already knowing the answer.

"No."

Benji steps away from the arcade, bounding across the shopping center. I follow behind him.

"*Shit!* Shelly Criston. God, I'm such an idiot for blamin' that prank on him!"

"Are you sure it's him?" I ask, my chest seizing with dread. "What would he do? He wouldn't hurt Danny, would he?"

"I don't know," Benji answers, his voice more serious than I've ever heard it, easily clutching the dog in his arms now as he walks. Even Skerritt has gone still, as if he senses the tension stringing through both of us. "Little silver-toothed asshole. Probably wouldn't plan on doin' anything serious, but... you know how these goddamn things can get outta hand."

I do. Ever since Jackson told me that story about Ted's brother.

"We've gotta go to the police, then," I say, my voice shaking. "Or we have to find him—"

"The cops ain't gonna do jack shit. Anyway, we don't—"

"Addy!"

We both turn around to see Ellen rocketing toward us from the other side of the shopping center, her purse and her mane of curly hair flying behind her.

"Oh my God, I just overheard Steven and Eddie!" she gasps after she's crashed into me. "I think Jackson will get out sometime today! There's some discrepancy with them even holding him in the first place."

"Serious?" Benji asks.

"Yes! Steven was saying his dad was all pissed because he's being accused of not having enough for probable cause. Now he's afraid the judge is gonna get on him for it, so they'll let him out soon."

The relief I would have felt otherwise is still overshadowed by our current problem of Danny being missing.

"Oh my God." Ellen's eyes go wide, her hands flying to her mouth after I tell her. "He's got to be somewhere, right? Just because he wasn't at work... maybe he was sick?"

I want to slap myself for how stupid I feel, but there is also a gracious wave of reassurance. Because that should be the obvious conclusion rather than Danny being kidnapped by an angry wannabe gang leader.

"I'm gonna check at Ted's place," I decide, already moving toward the exit of the shopping center. "Benji, can you head down to the video store and ask the guy there if Danny ever came in for his shift?"

"Already on it." Benji nods, lugging a now very invested-looking Skerritt along with him under his arm as he bounds back the way we'd come.

"Should I come with you?" Ellen calls to me.

"No, head to the police station. I'll meet you there if we can't find Danny."

It's almost dark by the time I make it through the brush, over the creek, and to Ted's house. His empty house.

I consider that Danny might be at his own house, but I don't know which of the trailer homes belongs to his parents. He wouldn't be there anyway. I know it. He hardly ever is.

There has to be an explanation. That's what I continue to silently promise myself as I make my way back through the patch of woods and out onto the run-down street surrounded by dreary houses that look to be barely holding themselves together. Some of them dark, some of them glowing with lights. Some of them ringing gently with laughter from the people on the inside, others probably containing unhappy families fighting and cursing each other, like Benji's parents in whichever of these houses is his.

The sound of a car rolling along the battered, cracked street barely registers. The glow of headlights ignites the path ahead of me, casting strange shadows from the crooked houses and leaning chain-link fence surrounding the side of the road that breaks out into endless fields of dead brush.

The car stops somewhere behind me. A door slams closed.

I turn around at the sound of quick footsteps approaching.

"Get in the car, Addy."

I don't need to see the flask clutched in Deran's hand hanging out the passenger window to know that all of them are drunk. I can see it in the way Marcus staggers as he marches up to me, can hear it in the slight slur of his words.

"What do you want, Marcus?"

I'm happy to see my glare cuts through him enough that he pauses momentarily. The guys in the car snicker.

Marcus's usually perfect-looking mop of white-blond hair is matted and wispy, some strands plastered to his forehead, some sticking up at the sides. His eyes that are usually clear and piercing now look all the more unnerving, bleary and unfocused but filled with an undeniable rage. Even his cotton twill pants and beige sweater look wrinkled and depleted.

Marcus lunges forward, grabs ahold of my wrist, and drags me back toward the car.

"What the hell is wrong with you?" I snap, yanking my wrist away and grinding my feet into the ground.

"Just *get in the car*," he pleads, reaching to grab me again.

"Marcus, I'm not going anywhere with you if you're driving drunk."

"Fine! Steven, you drive."

Steven Nulty shuffles out of the back seat of the pale green convertible, his eyes cast downward as Marcus pulls me toward the back. Deran continues laughing drunkenly from the passenger side, sipping from his flask.

"Marcus, we're done talking. There's nothing left for us to say to each other, so leave me the hell alone."

"I will after you get in the damn car," Marcus grits through his teeth, yanking me forward and shoving me toward the open door. I collapse into the back seat before Marcus slams the door behind me.

"Just listen to him, Addy," Steven sighs as I try to open the door again. I pause and stare at him through the rearview mirror. He looks bored.

Marcus climbs into the other side of the back as Steven starts the car again and we're moving down the street.

I turn my head as we pull away, the lights flashing over a figure leaning against the side of one of the houses on the side of the street. A figure casually smoking a cigarette as they watch us from the dark. The lights pass over him briefly, but it is enough to make out the permanent snarl showing off a glinting silver tooth.

Marcus sits silently, glaring out the window the entire ride. Deran keeps randomly laughing like a giddy child eager to get to our destination.

There's a horrible rotting smell lingering somewhere in the car that makes my eyes burn after a while. The effects of Benji's prank, I assume.

"What are you doing over here?" I ask. "I thought you'd never be caught dead on this side of town."

No one answers me. Deran just giggles again.

Steven breaks away from the road after we've driven along the back-roads for some time, presumably toward the center of town. But as soon as the rickety wire fence blocking off the sprawling fields disappears, Steven jerks the car to the side, bumping over the curb until we're driving along the grass, into the complete darkness of the field.

"Where the hell are we going?" I demand, coughing as the rotten smell enters my lungs. Still no one answers.

Panic rises like a block of ice in my chest. I don't know why I didn't fight harder to not get in the car. Maybe because I still feel like I know Marcus and his friends. I still see us all as dumb twelve-year-olds running around the Lensen barbecue, swimming in Deran's pool, staying out late at the diner.

Because I want an explanation. Because I trust that they would never do anything truly horrible.

We stop in the middle of a dark field, not unlike the one Jackson took me to that night, the one we all went to after the carnival. I can't tell if it's the same one.

There's another car parked ahead of us, slanted, our headlights igniting a path of wheel tracks in the grass, as if the vehicle had whipped sharply to a stop.

Steven sends the car screeching to a halt as well, Marcus jumping out almost before we stop completely. The air outside is a relief after being shut in the rot and old fish stench. If I weren't so confused and mildly terrified right now, I might take a moment to appreciate the deviousness of Benji's prank.

I scramble out of the car after Marcus, Deran stumbling out and taking another long sip from his flask before tossing the empty container back into the passenger seat. Steven is the last to exit, moving slowly as he stares over at the car across from us, where three other figures are standing ignited by the headlights. One of them is Eddie. One is Jeremy, the football captain. The other one looks vaguely familiar, another of Marcus's friends.

"Marcus, tell me what the hell is going on!" I shout, anger burning through me. He walks over to the other car, a silver Porsche that I now recognize as belonging to Eddie's parents. He doesn't even flinch at my words.

Eddie goes to the trunk, unlocking it and throwing it open.

I stare, my mouth open in horror, my blood cold beneath my skin as Marcus reaches in and pulls Danny's limp form out of the trunk, throwing him down onto the grass as the other boys laugh.

My brain tells me something unthinkable at first, something that makes my stomach lurch and an inhuman cry come from my throat until I see Danny twisting against the ground, his eyes blinking shut against the harsh light of the car headlights that ignites his bruised and bloody face.

I move toward him, unsure of what I plan to do other than throw myself over him, but Deran's arms are around me, yanking me back as he laughs drunkenly in my ear and pinning me against his chest.

"I have to say, I never thought you were into women, Danny-Boy!" Marcus shouts, kicking Danny over onto his back. "Turns out you and your buddies were sneakin' around with my girl the whole time, huh?"

"Marcus, stop it!" I scream. Any semblance of reassurance is gone as this group of boys surrounds Danny on the ground like a flock of predators.

These aren't the boys I grew up with every summer.

These boys are dangerous.

Marcus aims a kick at Danny's ribs. The boys laugh. Eddie steps forward and shoves Danny back to the center of the circle they form when Danny tries to crawl to his feet.

"You couldn't have found someone better to cheat on your boyfriend with, huh?" Deran asks as he yanks me back again while I try to twist away from the smell of alcohol thick on his breath that burns in my nose. "You had to be runnin' around with trailer trash behind his back?"

"He's not my boyfriend, you fucking morons!"

"No?" Eddie asks, a childish grin on his face as he leaps forward again, his foot slamming into Danny's back, making him cry out softly and jerk away. "You seem upset, doesn't she seem upset, Marcus?"

"He didn't listen the first time or any other times we tried to warn him about messin' with us, did he?" Deran slurs behind me, still holding me with surprising strength despite my thrashing.

"No, he didn't," Marcus agrees, moving closer to Danny, reaching for something in the back pocket of his jeans. Something that glints in the glare from the car lights.

The boys' demeanor changes instantly. Deran's grip loosens around me. But it doesn't matter. I'm frozen to the spot, my eyes focused on where everyone else's are, apart from Danny, who is curled up on the ground, his eyes still shut against the light or the pain in his swollen face.

"Whoa, Marcus..."

I turn to see Steven, who had been standing mostly silent outside the circle, step forward, his eyes wide as he stares at what must be his father's gun currently clutched in Marcus's hand. "Did you take that from the car?"

Marcus is unaware of his friends' shift in mood. Waving the gun in his hand, making us all tense and take an instinctual step back. My eyes move to Danny, my heart pounding so loud, it thunders in my ears.

I look back up to see Marcus staring at me. A triumphant grin spreads across his face, the gun clutched in his hand.

"Oh, do I have your attention now, Addy?"

Chapter 26
Jackson

I don't get anything more than a grunt and a glare from the deputy when I'm let out. I don't even see Nulty anywhere. One of the other officers warns me not to skip town anytime soon, and that's that. Until we meet again.

I should go to Ted's place. Let everyone know I'm out and will not in fact be shipped off to prison for something I didn't do.

But strangely enough, I find I'd much rather be alone. Just for a while.

I realize as I walk in the dark, finding every street I can around the edges of town, where the buildings spill off into the long fields that reach out toward the hills or the roads stretch along into the distance leading out to the main highway, that maybe I'm starting to like being alone. I do it so much. Sometimes the peace is... not nice exactly, but something like it.

It feels like space. Especially after being holed up in a cell for twenty-four hours. Especially after all of the thoughts that bludgeoned into the forefront of my brain, forcing me to think of them over and over again like a slideshow I couldn't turn off or even close my eyes against.

My mom. Vera. The girl who lived across from me who felt like my sister, my best friend, my soul mate, at least to my four-year-old self. The thought that I should stay away from Addy until she leaves. Because she'll be gone soon. Because losing anyone I want to remotely get close with, anyone who understands me anywhere other than below the surface, seems to be the theme of my life so far.

Because I care about her. Because I don't want her to get hurt by any of my bullshit.

I kick at the ground, rocks and bits of dirt scattering underwhelmingly beneath me as I trudge along the edge of the tree line along Cropsy Park. The few teens who are here at this hour are all lying along the playground, soaking up the warmth from the metal against the cold night breeze. The world feels empty. It's late enough that the rest of town is all in bed.

The only people out at this time are kids.

"Look who got outta the slammer early."

I tense at the voice calling to me from within the cluster of trees beside the pathway. I should have been prepared for this. Though I did think I'd have more than a few minutes.

My footsteps pause on the crumbling cement path. I can't help the buzz of anger as I glare at the figure moving out from the shadows, probably imagining he's the supervillain in a mafia film revealing himself in the dramatic final act.

"You're not as slick as ya think, Criston," I call out to him, doing a quick sweep of the trees behind him, but shockingly not seeing any other lumbering figures hiding there. Strange. Shelly Criston facing me all by himself after setting me up? "We all knew it was you the moment they tried to nail me."

Shelly's pinched face twists into a ridiculous chortle.

"Me? That's a laugh, Lowell. Buyin' your own lies now?"

"The hell are you talkin' about?"

Shelly steps closer toward the path lit only by the flickering streetlamp that's been close to going out for almost a year now. He glares at me through his beady eyes, his mouth turned into a comical-looking frown.

"I hear you and your little friends have been throwin' my name around, Lowell. Tryin' to pin me for this gun theft stunt. Ya think I wasn't gonna hear about it? First your little revenge act on the knuckle-head rich kids, now this too?"

I blink. Shelly stands a few feet away, waiting for me to make the first move, the both of us tensed and ready for a brawl.

"Are you serious?" I almost laugh. "You're not gonna take the credit for this? Usually you're the first one to gloat about your dumbass schemes, Criston."

A grin slowly spreads across his face like he's the goddamn Joker, his fake silver tooth shining under the street lamps. Which would be unnerving here in a corner of a dark and mostly empty park if it wasn't Shelly Criston.

"You really don't get it? Shit, Lowell, I figured it out faster than you. Guess that makes me the superior intellectual after all—"

"What's going on, Criston?!" I shout, closing the rest of the distance between us until I'm directly in his face, using my few inches' advantage to tower over him. The teens lying around the playground are all dead silent, leaning forward and watching the two of us with bated breath.

Shelly's face snaps back to his pouting glower as he shoves his chest forward, knocking me back only a couple steps.

"I don't know, Lowell. Maybe it's got somethin' to do with my buddy Rooney seein' those rich goons nab Danny Macklin and stuff him into the trunk of their car earlier today? Or when I saw them roll up to your snobby little girlfriend and drive her out to Dover Road? Probably out to the field by the old Brighton farmhouse to do God knows what, don't ya think—"

My fist slams into his face, sending him to the ground. I leap on top of him before he can get up, grabbing him by the collar of his dinged-up leather jacket.

"What the fuck is this?!"

Shelly growls, swinging at my face, his fist colliding against the side of my head. I fall to the side and he jumps on top of me, something flashing in his hands. Something stings at my ribs as he drives his fist into my side. I grab him by the throat, trying to wrench him away, and an object clatters to the ground beside me. Shelly grabs my collar now, his lips turned into a growl as blood trickles from his mouth.

"You don't get to pull me into your rich boy bullshit, Lowell! If you and your buddies wanna mess around with Marcus Tanner's girlfriend, you fuckin' deal with the outcome without tryin' to pin any of this shit on me!"

It all makes sense. Suddenly, I feel like an idiot to have ever believed it was Shelly Criston behind any of this.

Marcus and his friends could have easily taken the gun from Nulty's house. Could have seen me walking through their neighborhood any night on my way to Addy's place.

Now they got me out of the way. So they could drag Danny and Addy out to the middle of nowhere. With a gun...

I knee Shelly between the legs, throwing him backward and sending him crashing down into the middle of the cement pathway before jumping on top of him again.

"You wanna have a go at me, Criston?" I growl, yanking him up. "Do your worst. Out in Brighton field. Bring any loser who'll follow you. Let's show these rich boys a real brawl."

I throw him back onto the ground, ignoring his hollered insults and the gaping stares of the teens now practically lunging over the metal playground in awe of the brief scuffle as I march down the pathway, back the way I had come.

He won't follow. He'll run to his lackeys now.

I can't remember a time that Greydon felt as big as it does right now. Impossibly big, with no one around for miles and miles. No way to reach Danny and Addy in time.

Something warm is spreading along my torso. A pain that pulses throughout my side like a second heartbeat that makes my stomach lurch and my footsteps flounder as I cross the street from Cropsy Park, toward Ward's unlit shop.

His car's gone. I'll have to run, then.

I stumble in after unlocking the door, touching a hand to my side as I make my way through the darkened liquor store, my free hand fumbling around for the phone against the wall behind the counter.

The phone picks up on the first ring.

"This is Ted."

"Teddy. It's Jackson."

"Jackson," Ted breathes on the other line. "Thank God. Where are you, they let you out?"

"I'm at Ward's place."

"Okay. Danny's been missin' all day. Benji said his boss told him he didn't show up for work today and no one can find—"

"I know where he is."

"Oh. God, okay... good."

Ted never cries. Not in front of people. Maybe not at all. But I can hear how close he is.

"Marcus and all them... they got him. Him and Addy. Took them both out to the field out on Dover road, by the old Brighton farm."

Fuck, it sounds like a goddamn horror movie.

I pull my hand away from my side, looking at the dark liquid coating my palm. "I'm gonna go."

"Jackson... are you alright? You don't sound good."

"Yeah, m'fine. I'm gonna go get 'em."

"... Jackson, what happened?"

"Nothin'... nothin', just got into it with Shelly. It wasn't him. It was Marcus and Deran and all them the whole time... tryin' to get back at us..."

"Jackson, wait there, alright? Benji and Jay and I will meet you—"

"I gotta go, Ted."

I have to... I have to get to them before...

"Jackson, please wait. Don't go on your own, okay?"

I press my hand to my side again. And my voice comes out shakier. A whisper, almost. With words only Ted will understand.

"I can't lose them too."

Ted doesn't answer me. I wouldn't hear anything if he did. I straighten up, sucking in a small but sharp breath, forcing my voice louder and firmer.

"Bring the cavalry."

I hang up before Ted can say anything else. And then I run.

Greydon has never felt so big.

Everything has always been so close, so stifling. Now every step feels like less than an inch, pulling me farther rather than closer to the back-road I'm desperate to reach. My ears rush with noise that I can't tell is from my own head or not. My side feels numb as I press my hand against it while I run.

I've gotten sliced with a blade before. Across my knee, a scuffle with one of Shelly's idiot cronies not long after I first got here. It healed. Tiny scar. It was fine. This will be fine.

Danny will be okay. Addy will be okay.

They'll both be fine. I'll stop it. I'll get there in time.

I'm gasping, my lungs aching for breath as I race across the empty streets, everything feeling empty and barren for miles and miles around me. Like I'm the only person in the world, running toward nothing.

My eyes sting. I blink away the tears that track down my face. I run harder as I keep pressure against the wound in my side.

She'll be okay... She'll be okay this time... She has to be...

Chapter 27
Addy

I can't remember the first thing Marcus said to me when we met. It was something that made me laugh. Not because it was funny, but because it made me blush. Because he was cute and sweet and I couldn't believe he would want to say something nice to me, of all people.

I want to believe something changed in him since then. Like something changed in me. But maybe this was there all along.

"Dude, Marcus," Eddie laughs nervously. Marcus swings around the gun in his hand casually, grinning as he watches everyone's reaction, our every flinch at his movements. "C'mon, quit messin' around."

"Yeah, man," Steven says from behind us. "This is dangerous."

He's been pacing nonstop since Marcus pulled out the gun, his hands running nervously through his hair. I don't know if I'm comforted that all the guys are as appalled by this as me, or if I'm more scared of wondering what Marcus's plan of bringing us out here has been all this time.

Deran is too drunk to even know what's going on.

"Hey, don't shoot me, dude," he laughs, raising his hands playfully before stumbling and slumping against the side of Marcus's car. At least without him holding me back, I'm free to begin moving slowly toward Danny.

Danny has pulled himself up against the tire of Eddie's car. He looks more awake now that he's registered Marcus standing above him with a gun.

"You're not so tough walkin' around with my girl now, are ya, you little freak?" Marcus taunts as he rounds on Danny.

"Marcus, I'm not your fucking girl."

Deran laughs as Marcus turns toward me. "Shit, you hear that? Never heard Marcus's girl with such a filthy mouth before."

"Somethin' else she picked up from her new trailer trash friends," Marcus mutters.

"Marcus."

Marcus whips back toward Danny, whose voice is small and hoarse, yet steady. He blinks up at the other boy, the same cautious, terrified look on his face that is on mine. I move closer once the attention is away from me again.

"Look, we can all just leave, alright?" Danny says. "Nobody has to get hurt or get into trouble. You guys can all drive off and we won't say anything, okay?"

Marcus laughs loudly, making me jump and freeze. Danny meets my eyes. He gestures ever so slightly with his head. Telling me to go. To run. As if I'd leave him alone here.

"Oh, is that right, Danny-Boy? You're gonna let me off the hook, huh?"

He steps back, raising the gun in front of him. Aiming it at Danny's face.

"Wait, stop!" I shriek, lunging forward.

Danny shouts something at me, but I don't hear it. He climbs against the car, heaving himself up onto his feet as I stand in front of him. Staring Marcus and the barrel of the gun down, my limbs shaking, but my feet holding me firmly against the ground.

I can see Marcus's face clearly for the first time tonight in the harsh glow of the car lights. Drunk. Angry. Gloating.

"What do you think, Addy? I think I could get away with shootin' him dead right now. Steven's dad already thinks that worthless delinquent Jackson Lowell is responsible for stealing this gun. They'll blame a murder on him too. No one's gonna care about two losers getting wiped off the face of the Earth, will they?"

"Marcus, this is crazy." My voice is shockingly steady as my eyes follow the gun he jerks carelessly in his hand. "I know you, you're not gonna kill someone."

But I don't know him. Not really. Not at all, I don't think.

He raises the gun again, this time straight at my eyes as he moves closer. But I still don't move. Even though every instinct is screaming to get out of range of the weapon aimed at my face.

"Whoa, Marcus," one of the guys speaks up, sounding miles away in my ears.

"Hey, man, stop wavin' that thing around!" Jeremy the football quarterback's deep voice thunders from somewhere. "It's gonna go off!"

"*Addy.*"

I feel a hand against my arm. Danny stands behind me, trying to push himself in front of me, but I keep myself firmly before him. I do reach down to grab his hand though.

Marcus glares at me, the harsh lights from the car looking like a fire in his glassy eyes. I glare right back.

He won't do it. I know he won't.

I'm only vaguely aware of the others all turning to look at something off in the darkness. I don't realize what it is—a figure barreling through the empty field—until we all hear a voice shouting loud enough to momentarily wrench our attention away from the gun.

"*I'm gonna kill you, you piece of shit!*"

The voice is amplified into a throaty growl, but I know who it is without having to look.

I'm surprised to feel a twinge of annoyance. Of course Jackson Lowell would charge straight toward someone with a loaded gun.

Marcus jerks toward Jackson, looking as if his body is trying to decide whether to run or steel himself for a fight...

And then the gun goes off.

I don't know if I yell or not as I dive toward the ground at the deafening crack. All I know is I'm curled in on myself beside Eddie's car, Danny gasping in pain behind me along with the sound of the tire behind us popping and hissing air.

My shaking hands lower from my face just in time to see Marcus standing, staring down at the gun in his hand. His expression is different. He looks at the gun as if it's a horrifying insect latched on to his hand. As if he hadn't expected it to go off. As if he didn't think it was even loaded.

He looks terrified.

Jackson slams into him, throwing them both to the ground.

I turn back to where Danny is crushed up against the car, his brows furrowed as he grips the side of his upper arm.

"Oh my God, Danny..."

"It's... it's fine," he stutters as I pull his hand away from the bleeding wound. "I think... I think it just... missed..."

He breathes heavily, staring between the small gash on his arm and the bullet hole in the tire behind him in disbelief. I feel sick.

The sound of a brawl whips my attention back to where Jackson and Marcus have become a blur of tumbling and punching. The other boys jump in, pouncing on Jackson and throwing him off of Marcus before raining down a series of kicks and punches themselves.

Steven stays off to the side, pulling his hand back and yanking his sleeve down over his palm before picking up the gun like it's a burning coal and bringing it back to the car.

"Stop! Stop it!"

My screams are useless against the noise of the fight as I scramble to my feet and race forward, only to stand helplessly outside the circle where Marcus and his friends practically pummel Jackson into the ground. I can't see him. I can only hear him growling and swearing and fighting.

My hands rip through my hair as I stand here, helpless. I can't do anything. I can't stop it. I can't help.

Then there is the sound of more voices, more footsteps running through the grass.

"Addy!"

I turn around to see three figures racing across the field now. Three figures... and a dog.

"Get 'em, killer!" Benji shouts after setting Skerritt free from his grip. The tiny dog lets loose a string of growls and yips as it scrambles across the field, not even stumbling on the grass. His legs are getting steadier.

Deran pitches back from the group, squinting into the array of car lights.

"What the—"

He yelps before he can finish, Skerritt the beagle launching a full-scale attack, leaping and barking and pushing with his now much stronger paws against Deran's legs so that he continues falling back away from the others.

"*Shit!* Guys, get this fuckin' dog off me!"

Benji dives into the mess, practically falling in the clash of bodies until he and Eddie emerge, each attempting to lock on to the other's neck.

"Addy," Ted repeats as he runs up beside me, Jay moving past us both to help Benji and Jackson. Ted holds my arms, staring at me with a look that makes my chest seize as I try my best to stop the spinning in my vision. "Are you alright? Where's..."

He follows my gaze down to where Danny has sunk along the side of the car again, watching the scene before him with horror.

"Danny!"

Ted runs to his side, quickly looking him over before bringing him up to standing again.

"Danny... are you okay? Shit, you're bleeding..."

Ted drags Danny away from the mess as yet another car rips across the field from the road, bathing us in more lights as it approaches. The tires squeal to a halt, followed by a barrage of slamming doors as a group of boys exit the vehicle.

"Alright, Jackson Lowell!" Shelly Criston's voice yowls into the night as he and his cronies march up to the mess. "Where the fuck are you?! Let's finish this!"

He has a blade in his hand. God, and the others have *chains.*

Everyone freezes, going completely silent, as if someone had pressed pause on the scene of the brawl. It's almost comical the way everyone stares at one another, petrified in a variety of stances.

Ted and the boys. Marcus and his friends. Shelly and his gang.

No one knows what's going on for a moment.

I move first.

I shove past whoever is in my way until I get to Jackson.

Jackson, who looks like he's been dragged across the entire field by his foot. Who still throws a perfectly aimed punch at Jeremy's face that sends him falling away from him, giving me a familiar cocky grin through the blood covering his mouth.

It doesn't hide the brief look that flashes through his eyes. A look that is unlike anything I've ever seen on him. A look of such intense relief that it makes him appear like a sob is going to tear through him.

Has he been crying?

I grab his hand as the sound of police sirens echo in the distance. Chaos breaks.

Some of Shelly's gang end up in a scuffle with the others. Jackson and I run deeper into the field, away from the headlights of the cars and the flashing blue and red lights that move in from the road.

Ted, Jay, and Danny head in the same direction. Benji tosses Eddie onto the ground before turning toward Deran.

"Let's roll, Skerritt!"

Skerritt yips back, leaps away from where he had been terrorizing Deran, who is currently cowering in a ball on the ground, and trots along after us.

A shout echoes behind us that the others don't hear as they run toward a dark structure that looks like some sort of barn in the darkness beyond the car lights.

Jackson and I turn around in time to see Marcus diving after us, tackling Jackson to the ground and sending me stumbling back onto the grass as well.

Jackson twists around to try to throw him off, but Marcus crushes his hands around his throat, slamming his head into the ground.

"Thought we took care of you, you son of a bitch," he grunts, struggling to keep his hold as Jackson hooks a hand onto the collar of his sweater and tries driving his palm into his nose with the other. Marcus moves his face out of the way just in time, keeping his hands locked around Jackson's neck while I crawl back up from the ground. "You think you can run around with my girlfriend too, huh? You think you can go around and take whatever you want, like you're better than me? You're *nothing*."

"Hey!"

Marcus looks up at my shout. My fist is already shooting toward his face.

It hurts. A crack of fire across my knuckles, throbbing pain that makes me cringe and shake out my hand after Marcus falls backward off of

Jackson, his eyes squinted shut in pain as he curses, his hands going to his nose.

"*Shit.*" Jackson laughs as he jumps to his feet. He grabs my hand again and we both follow the others toward the abandoned barn. "I knew I liked you, Moreno."

A laugh shakes through me as we run through the darkness, Skerritt's barks resounding somewhere ahead of us.

"Don't ever call me by my last name, Jackson Lowell."

***

Shelly Criston and his goons all get hauled away in handcuffs once Sheriff Nulty and the officers are able to separate everyone. Marcus, Eddie, and the others get escorted into the array of police cruisers that have appeared. Not cuffed, but not being led away as heroes either.

Steven Nulty is the only one who drives away by himself in Marcus's car after exchanging a few tense-looking words with his father.

We wait here, hiding in the rickety old barn. Peering through a dirty window. All six of us holding our breath. Seven if you count Skerritt, who has gone uncharacteristically silent. His tiny wet nose is pressed up against the smeared barn window next to us, as if he shares our tense fear as we wait for another cruiser to show up, officers to make their way to the barn and drag us out too.

But they don't.

We follow Ted back to his truck, which he parked crookedly along an empty road on the opposite side of the field from where the police cruisers had arrived. None of us say anything. We just get in and Ted drives to the hospital.

I know I should get back home. There's no reason for me to be here. The longer I stay, the more likely my mother is to realize where I am.

But I don't care. Maybe because I know I'm going to have to face her. Because I want to know that Danny will be alright. Or because I like the way Jackson is holding me and don't feel like moving.

Ted had managed to convince the hospital staff that Danny had fallen off the roof of his trailer helping him repair a broken satellite dish. I guess where the bullet grazed his arm didn't look too suspicious, because they seemed to have bought it. Or maybe they don't really care. About someone like Danny. I hope that's not the reason.

Jackson couldn't as eloquently cover up the stab wound in his side. Knife fight. The only explanation he'd give. They patched it up quickly enough. He lost a bit of blood, but it wasn't too deep. He has to stay here, and talk to the cops in the morning. And of course, he's already snuck out of his bed to come and sit with us.

It is morning, I think.

My head is lying against Jackson's shoulder. His arm is around me, his fingertips playing mindlessly with my sleeve.

We both stare at nothing, sitting in the hallway outside the room where they're treating Danny. The sound of beeping, wheels squeaking, footsteps passing all dull around us. Ted sits next to us, his hands clasped together anxiously, his eyes unable to keep from worriedly gazing at the door. Jay and Benji are in the chairs across from us, Jay with that same annoyed expression that seems to be permanently etched on his face as he leans his chin against his fist and stares at nothing, and Benji the most still and quiet I have ever seen him, Skerritt curled up on his lap, both of them dead asleep after all the excitement.

"Thank you."

It's the first words I've said in hours. My voice sounds strange.

I feel Jackson shift to look down at me. I try to smile.

"Thank you for rescuing us."

Tomorrow and the day after and everything that will happen now is not going to be easy for any of us. But now, I can lie here against my boyfriend with his arm around me and feel safe. The most normal and the most *me* I've felt in months, despite all that this horrible night has brought.

He relaxes against me again, pulling me closer.

"Any time, princess."

Chapter 28

Addy

I find out from Ellen the next day about everything that happened after I have crawled back home at five in the morning, getting only two hours of sleep before anxiously jumping out of bed and pacing throughout the entire house. My mother is home all day talking on the phone with her friends about the gossip ringing all across town. I want to listen in, but whenever I try to inconspicuously hang around the same room as her, she shoots me a look like she is starting to suspect I was somehow involved in the whole thing.

She must know. She is my mom after all.

Thankfully, Ellen takes pity on me and rushes over before lunch.

She nearly tackles me to the floor the second I open the door for her, crushing me in a hug that makes my ribs creak. "Are you alright?! God, when I heard—"

She pauses when she glances at my mother standing in the hallway, watching us with what should be a suspicious glare, but is more a resigned look of worry.

"Ah... I mean, I... I heard how sick you were!" Ellen tries to cover herself. "Are you okay?"

I don't think it works.

Once we're alone in my room, she tells me everything her parents learned from their friends and have been talking about nonstop all morning.

The official story is that Shelly Criston and his gang were meeting up in the field with Marcus and his friends for an all-out melee. It's a ridiculous idea, especially to Ellen and me, but what else could Marcus and the others do? Admit they stole the sheriff's gun and dragged an innocent boy into the field to terrorize him?

So it seems like they're going along with the story. The story Steven Nulty perpetuated because he ratted Marcus and the others out for being the ones who stole the gun and tried to blame it on Jackson Lowell to get back at him for the prank.

"But since that Shelly Criston guy's name was being thrown around, they're saying that's why his gang wanted to fight them," Ellen explains. "I don't know if Steven made up the story, or if the cops suggested it and the guys are going along with it, or what."

"Don't Shelly and his gang have anything to say about this?" I ask her.

She shrugs, leaning back on her hands against the bed, while I slump in a sad, caved-in C-shape. "Who knows? Whatever Marcus and Steven and all them say is going to hold more weight anyway. And all of those guys are in major trouble regardless of what happened. Most of them are over eighteen."

"Do you know what's gonna happen to Marcus and his friends?"

Ellen doesn't know. But we can guess that whatever it is, it won't be as extreme as whatever happens to Shelly Criston and his wannabe gang.

"I don't think he knew," I say after a moment where we both sit on the bed in silence. Ellen looks over at me questioningly. "Marcus. I don't think he knew the gun was loaded."

She says nothing. She doesn't have to. We both know. And I can be satisfied with that. Knowing that no, my ex-boyfriend is not a complete psychopath. Maybe just lost. Like Shelly Criston, to a certain degree. Like we all are.

My mother is in the living room when Ellen leaves. She's pretending to read whatever magazine she currently has grasped in her hands, but her eyes aren't moving and she's sitting stiff as a board on the couch.

"Mom?"

She looks up at me, still with that worried gleam in her eyes. Like she isn't sure what I'm going to say. Like she isn't sure what to say to me.

"My friend was hurt. My friend Danny, the one I told you about."

She doesn't look surprised at the statement or the implication. She knows by now, like everyone in town, what happened last night. She must suspect, like most, that there's more to the story.

But thankfully she doesn't look angry.

"Could I go see him in the hospital?"

I try not to hold my breath as I wait for her answer, thankful again that she isn't affronted at my request. Actually, she looks almost... sad?

"Just for a few minutes? If I'm not back within an hour, you can ground me for the next year and a half."

I expect her to say no. But there's something that feels different between us. Something that isn't spoken, but is there nonetheless. Something I don't really understand, but makes me feel as if, maybe, she understands me a bit more. More than she did that night when we argued, at least.

She stands up from the couch, tossing the magazine onto the coffee table with a sigh.

"Alright, then," she says, her voice sounding tired. "Let's go."

Lorry tags along with us, I guess because our mother doesn't want to leave her on her own either. I can't blame her after everything that's happened. She got hit with a tidal wave today learning that the boys she thought were such upstanding citizens stole a gun and were in a giant brawl with a group of small-time criminals.

Lorry doesn't seem to mind. And I'm just relieved my mother allowed me to do this.

Once we venture out into town, I can feel the stares glued to our backs from every person we pass just walking through the parking lot of the grocery store we stop at first.

The news has spread like wildfire by now. And the story has changed who knows how many times. But no one bothers to hide their whispers. People aren't ashamed to pause and stare, their heads glued to our movements like we're a pack of wild wolves that have wandered into the Greydon Market.

The quiet, nice young daughter of Jeanine Moreno who visits every summer from New York. Involved with Jackson Lowell, or Shelly Criston, or all of the unscrupulous boys who got into trouble last night for a fight that involved a stolen gun.

Lorry wouldn't pay any mind if the entire President's Cabinet was staring at her, but I know my mother feels the looks and harsh whispers the second we step out of the car. Her face is like solid stone as she leads us through the aisles, robotically scooping a box of oatmeal, a container of blueberries, pasta, sauce, and a can of mushrooms into the basket.

I don't particularly care anymore what the people in this town have to say or think about me. If they suspect I'm involved in getting their precious golden boys into trouble, I'd be happy to tell anyone the full story if I could be sure it wouldn't get Jackson and the others into trouble.

But my mother cares. Even if she won't say anything, I can see the pain and panic underneath her thin grimace as we walk through the store like the town pariahs.

My mother may have some ridiculous ideas about this place and what she hoped my future would be, but Greydon has always been her safe haven. Her escape for a brief time into the life she wishes she had at home. The life she once had when she was my age. Now I've ruined that for her.

Our trip to the store makes going to the hospital, where everyone will be far too involved in their own business to gawk at us, a relief for both myself and my mom.

She stays by the door with Lorry once the nurse signs us in and takes us to Danny's ward. I practically run the rest of the way to the bed he's currently sitting up in, grinning at me the moment I get through the door, as if he'd been expecting me.

He already looks a million times better than he did last night, the blood all gone from his face, a patch on the cut above his eye and a gauze wrap around his upper arm where the bullet had grazed him. The swelling has gone down from the other marks on his face, making him look beyond exhausted, but alive. Still *him*. Still his shy face, his bright blue eyes, his light brown hair that falls sloppily over his face.

I'm glad I decided to come. I know Danny has people, like Ted and Benji, who've surely been by his side all night and throughout the day. But he's my friend too. And God, I care about him so much.

We embrace for a long moment, the both of us laughing through the tears that want to fall. I let him sit back, worried that I had grabbed him too hard.

"Mild concussion," he says, shrugging as he leans casually back against the bed. "They gave me some pain meds. They're gonna discharge me sometime today."

"Thank God."

"Tell me about it."

We fall into silence, the sounds of the hospital ward whirring around us, the mumblings of the surrounding patients, the nurses running back and forth with supplies.

I start with the apologies. I have to. Even though I know none of this was really my fault, I'm still sure I did something or could have done something at one point so that he and I didn't end up in an abandoned field with my lunatic ex-boyfriend waving a gun at us.

"Stop," he orders me with a pointed look before I can get halfway through an apology. "I told you, Marcus and his friends have been on me for years. It's not your fault they found an excuse to act even more crazy."

"I know." I nod earnestly. "It's just... if anything worse had happened, I'd feel so—"

"It didn't." Danny leans forward to where I sit at the edge of his bed, placing his hand on top of mine. "Trust me, I started to go down that road too, but... nothing happened. We're all alright."

We are.

I glance over toward the door. My mother is standing still with her arms close to her chest, trying much too hard to pretend she's not watching us. Lorry of course is already deep in conversation with one of the patients in the bed closest to them.

"Are you leaving soon?"

"At the end of the week," I confirm. It doesn't feel as gut-wrenching as before. Maybe because I've had enough of Greydon to last me a long while, and because of the knowledge that I don't think I'll really lose anything once I leave. Not now.

"You think your mom will bring you back next summer?"

"I don't know," I laugh, though it's an honest statement. Something tells me my mother might rethink her choice in friends after she's had some time away. God knows what Marcus's, Deran's, and Eddie's moms sounded like trying to defend their sons this morning amid all of the phone gossip.

"I'm gonna miss you," I tell him. "All of you."

Danny turns away, his eyes searching around the room until he calls a nurse over. He asks her for a pen and paper and then jots something down while I watch curiously.

He looks up, handing me the scrap of white notepad paper that I see has a mailing address scribbled on it.

"Write to me." His mouth turns up into a warm, small smile as I take the paper from him before he gives a light shrug. "It'll give me a reason to be more consistent about getting the mail."

I hug him again. He holds me tightly, the both of us clinging to each other because we don't know when or if we'll see each other again.

"I will. I promise."

I'm not sure if I'll ever see him again. But we can at least have this. He can still be in my life. He'd better believe writing a letter to him is the first thing I'm going to do the moment I'm back home.

And if Danny Macklin insists on believing he'll never get out of this town in his life, maybe I'll find a way to start convincing him.

I didn't ask about Jackson. I knew Danny was waiting for me to, but it felt weird to bother him about it. I don't even know if he's here. Danny would have said something if he got arrested again or something bad happened. I knew he had to stay the night, but I have no idea what happened after.

I only see him once my mother, Lorry, and I step outside, heading down from the entrance of the hospital toward the parking lot. My eyes find him immediately, unintentionally searching for him.

He's leaning against the wall of the building across the lot. It looks like the designated smoking area, but for once, Jackson isn't pretending to enjoy a cigarette. He stands there, his arms crossed, in the same bloodstained clothes he'd been in last night, bags under his eyes that mix with the bruising from the fight. Looking at me.

As it has been many times before, my next instinct (after I have stopped to take him in, to enjoy the rush of fluttering in my stomach at seeing his messy golden-brown hair and his dark eyes pointed my way) is to keep walking. To turn away and act as if I'd never seen him.

I have to now. My mother is here. I can see from her expression as she glances back at me that she knows something is up.

So I keep walking. I rip my gaze from Jackson Lowell easily, moving behind my mother and my sister as if nothing is wrong.

But I can do it for only a few steps.

My mother screeches to a halt, gazing after me in shock, only calling out my name once, questioningly, as I run across the parking lot to the opposite medical building where my boyfriend is standing, waiting for me to walk away from him.

His expression is surprised, caught off guard only briefly, but he's quick to put on his cool, unbothered face by the time I slow down, moving until I am standing a foot or so before him.

"Hi."

"Hi."

My eyes sweep over him, lingering on his side where his shirt and jacket hide the bandaged wound at his ribs. "How are you?"

He shrugs, his arms uncrossing, one going to his hip, the other going to lean against the corner of the building. He winces only slightly at the movement, trying to cover it up. "Been better."

We're quiet. He glances over my shoulder where I imagine my mother is either looking at us in absolute horror or giving him an unbelievable death glare.

"You see Danny?"

I nod.

"He'll be alright. Teddy and Jay had to head off for work. Benji's been in and out all day."

"Running around trying to get the word, I imagine."

Jackson nods in confirmation. So they're all caught up on everything.

"Cops talked to me this morning. Would you believe it? Looks like I'm in the clear on this one."

I take a small breath of relief.

"Just had to tell 'em Shelly Criston and I got into it after I got out. Seemed to fit with their story. Moron's tryin' to blame the whole thing on me, according to Benji. Not goin' too well for him. Benji went and fessed up to the prank though."

I look downward as he tries to catch my gaze. I reach out to take his hand as he moves to reach for me.

"I'm leaving on Saturday."

Our fingers lock together and he pulls my hand toward him.

"I know."

"And I'm not allowed out of the house for the rest of the week."

"I know."

I look up at him. He stares at me with uncertainty until he sees the grin spreading mischievously on my face.

"But I was thinking... you could always stop by. My window's always open."

Jackson's eyes narrow. "You're gettin' much better at sneaking out. Word on the street, anyway."

"I hear there's a midnight showing of *Tourist Trap* this week. I'd hate to miss that."

Jackson nods thoughtfully. "Best thing about this town is the drive-in."

I smile again, dragging his hand toward my chest until my heart is beating beneath his palm. "So... I'll be expecting you, Jackson Lowell. If anything, I *will* be getting a second date out of this bizarre summer."

He grins back as he reluctantly lets go of my hand when I step back and tug it free. "I never miss a date with Addy Moreno."

I try not to look at my mother during the drive back. Neither of us says anything. The car is filled with a million unspoken words. I can tell Lorry really wants to say something, but even she knows now may not be the best time. Until we can decipher Mom's mood.

I follow her into the living room once we get back to the house. Lorry seems eager to be anywhere else.

We're both silent at first. My mother stands in front of the couch, looking as if she is considering sitting and pretending to go back to her magazine. But she stands still, her eyes on the ground, her teeth worrying her bottom lip as I move to stand in front of her on the other side of the coffee table.

"Danny, he seems..."

I startle at her words, my eyes going wide as I wait for her to decide how to finish.

"He seems like a nice boy."

My shoulders sag like I've finally released a breath I've been holding on to for hours. Like with those words, some sort of tension between us is broken.

"He is. He's a good friend."

She nods. I can tell she wants to say more. And I assume it's about Jackson.

She knows who he is by now. And I'm sure there was no mistaking what he means to me by the brief interaction she had seen today.

I can't imagine how it matters now. Not when we're leaving.

She finally sits down. I move to sit beside her, but end up staying where I am, standing at the end of the coffee table.

"Adrienne, I'm... I am proud of you. You've always been so kind-hearted. And you are smart. I know that." She looks up at me earnestly, with that same tragic look in her eyes, as if she thinks she's going to lose me to a life-ending illness. "But sometimes you don't think about what you're getting into before you jump into it."

Something in her look or the way she says the words makes me sense there is more than what she is letting on. I used to think she had always been speaking from her fearful, outrageously cautious and somewhat prejudiced mom standpoint.

Now it sounds as if she's speaking from experience. Because she knows something I don't. Because she's been where I am before.

"Just promise me you'll be careful? Please?"

Before I can answer or ask her what I'd like to, the phone rings, making us both jump.

She sighs, giving me one last forlorn look, before standing up and heading into the kitchen.

I follow behind her before moving down the hallway toward my bedroom. I catch Lorry's eye when I pass her room.

She holds a gigantic library book in front of her that she looks like she's at the end of, eyeing me over the edge of the cover showcasing images of Virginia Woolf, Mary Wollstonecraft, and Maya Angelou.

"Running off to your criminal boyfriend in front of Mom, huh? You're a lot cooler now than you used to be, by the way."

I smile at her, rolling my eyes as I head down the end of the hall to my room.

Chapter 29
Addy

The one day my mother lets me out of the house on my own is the day we're leaving. Maybe she figures I can't get into any real trouble when I have only an hour to run around town and say goodbye to everyone. Maybe she feels sorry for me.

Thankfully she didn't overhear Lorry goading me first thing this morning as we finished packing, telling me if I don't run off to give an epic, romantic farewell to my delinquent boyfriend before we're separated forever, I'll regret it for the rest of my miserable old life.

As I head to Ted's house, there is a more somber air to the place than most of the other times I've visited, aside from when Jackson was arrested, of course. But I'm shocked to see not only Ted sitting out on one of the picnic tables, but also Benji, Jay, Danny, and even Skerritt.

Skerritt runs up to me before I've crossed over the creek, barking and splashing through the water, hopping up and down like a spring toy until I'm close enough for him to try to paw his way up my legs.

"See, I told ya the guest of honor would arrive!" Benji calls as he jogs up to me. I give Skerritt a few scratches behind the ears until Benji calls him over and he shoots back like a rocket, where Benji catches him.

"You've got him pretty well trained up," I compliment as I follow him over to where the others are sitting. The smell of coffee wafts through the early, misty air from the steaming mugs Ted and Jay are nursing.

"I didn't get a chance to run down Cherub Road naked or learn those 'Johnny B. Goode' lyrics, but I did find the love of my life this summer!"

I cock my head at him until he holds up Skerritt triumphantly in one hand. The beagle lies flat on his belly in Benji's palm, his legs splaying out lazily, his tail beating back and forth.

"Behold, the greatest love/hate relationship this town has ever seen!"

Skerritt yips.

"Isn't that right, buddy?"

"What're you all doing up so early?" I ask, chuckling at Benji's dumb joke.

"It's your goodbye party," Jay mutters, his eyes hardly open and his face looking like this was one hundred percent not his idea.

"We knew ya couldn't take off without sneakin' off to say goodbye." Benji nudges me, shooting me a wink before letting Skerritt run free around the grass.

I laugh, feeling myself flush, and also keenly aware that Jackson is absent.

We've seen each other every day since the hospital. Every night, rather. We snuck out a few times, but mostly we sat out in the yard outside the rental cottage by the maple tree late at night when he came to my window. We never talked about me leaving. It seemed a waste of the time we had left. We'd rather talk about horror movies, or the insane songs my cousins used to come up with, or he would try to make me laugh with stories about the outrageous things he did when he was a child that only made me admonish him.

Or we wouldn't talk at all.

Now, I'm hit with the real possibility that last night, when I snuck back in at three a.m. after our night out watching *Tourist Trap* at the drive-in and walking aimlessly around the empty town afterward, Jackson leaning forward to kiss me on the lips then giving me his usual, somewhat sarcastic but somehow endearing "See ya" before walking off into the night (morning), might be the last time I see him in a long time.

Or ever.

"Well," Ted sighs as he stands from the table, sets his mug down, and moves to stand in front of me, "guess this is it, then."

I smile, surprised at the sudden tears burning behind my eyes.

"Thank you for everything, Ted." I look at him meaningfully.

He nods. "No problem, Addy. You keep your chin up and take care of yourself, alright?"

"I will."

"I know it."

I turn down to Jay, the both of us nodding at each other as he cradles his mug of coffee like a lifeline.

"See ya, Addy."

"Bye, Jay. Don't let Benji kidnap Skerritt."

"Huh," he huffs into his mug. "Let him try."

My eyes move to Danny, who's been quiet the whole time, sitting at the end of the picnic table. His face looks almost healed up. Only he looks as if he's trying to hold back a wave of emotion, like myself.

He stands up as I move toward him. I hear Ted and Jay step away from the table.

"I hope you've got the guitar down, because I'm not leaving mine here," I tell him with a raised brow. He meets it with a taunting smirk as he juts his chin out.

"I've been savin' up. Next time you see me, I'll be a pro with my own guitar."

We both move at the same time then, embracing each other firmly.

"I'm gonna miss you."

"Yeah," I whisper, holding back my tears just barely, letting only one trail down my face.

We don't let go of each other for a long while, the both of us in desperate need of the comfort after everything. With the unspoken fear that I might not come back next year.

When we pull apart, I decide not to let that line of thinking settle any more than the last time it had tried.

"We're gonna see each other again," I decide as I grip his elbows and he holds me back. We will. I know it. Even if it isn't next summer. "And we're gonna see the world."

He doesn't argue. He doesn't even look as hopeless as he did that night we talked. That's at least something I can live with.

"Looks like we're gonna have to break apart the band now," Benji sighs as I approach him next. He is casually trying to separate himself as far from the group as he can, watching Skerritt run tireless circles around the grass.

"Don't." I shake my head. "Danny's gonna need all the practice he can get."

"Ain't that the truth," Benji chides, and God am I thankful that he sounds like his usual self. That I can pretend we'll all see each other tomorrow and the day after.

Even the side hug he gives me feels brief and light-hearted as he jostles me against him, making me laugh.

"Now, you can't stay away too long, ya hear? You're part of the crew now. And we've benefitted from a female presence."

"Yeah," I laugh. "You almost got killed twice."

"Never. Not us, Addy."

I stay for only a few minutes longer before I anxiously turn back toward the creek. Jackson's absence feels more and more prominent. And my time is running out.

"I haven't seen him," Ted says, noticing my tension. "I looked in at Ward's this morning, but he wasn't there. I thought he might... I'm sure if you look around—"

"It's alright." I nod. "I'm sure I can find him."

I'm not sure, but I don't want to have a nervous breakdown in front of all of them about not getting to say goodbye to Jackson. So, I hug everyone one last time, turning back toward the creek and away from their shouted goodbyes before I can let my tears fall, waving behind me before I cross the creek and head back through the patch of trees into town.

I'll see them all again. I have to. Just like I'm gonna see Jackson one more time before I leave.

It feels like I look all over Greydon in the span of fifteen minutes. Feeling the time sinking further and further away. Feeling my panic grow.

I don't have time. I don't have time to look for him. He could be anywhere, all the places I don't have time to search through, like in the fields on the outside of town he likes to frequent, or somewhere in the clusters of brush, trying to trap me in another hidden pond. But I have to go.

Until something triggers in my memory. A place I had stood, away from the crash of noise and people, out in the cool air, with a view of the end of a sunset. The first real conversation we had. The first time I realized I was falling for him.

I make my way to Johnny-Jay's, walking around the side of the unlit building, listening to the early morning stirrings of the rest of the town becoming muted as I hop over a small chain-link gate until my feet are kicking through gravel and bits of trash.

Jackson leans against the back of the building, one foot kicked up against the brick wall, his hands in the pockets of his denim jacket. The sunrise glows around him as he turns to me. The side of his mouth quirks up in a grin.

"You weren't gonna leave without sayin' goodbye to your favorite boyfriend, were you?"

Chapter 30

Jackson

My smug-ass grin fades the moment I see the look on Addy's face as she forces a smile past the tears running down her cheeks. I push myself off the wall as she walks toward me. I open my mouth to say something. I don't know what. But we both decide better on it.

She runs into my arms before I can move, and I catch her the same way I did that night when I had found her wandering the streets past midnight after her mother had reamed her out. When she had looked like she so badly needed someone. When I had been relieved we somehow found our way to each other.

The tension seems to leave her as I hold her, and when she leans her head back, the smile on her face is a bit more genuine. I reach up to brush the tears away from her face as her hand traces up the back of my neck, curling through my hair before she pulls me closer to press her lips against mine.

Fuck. *Why does she have to leave?*

"Well, princess," I sigh after our lips have broken apart, doing a good job of sounding as normal and playfully unbothered as I intend to, "it's been a ride."

"Mm." Addy nods, her brows lifting, like she can see right through me. "The best summer romance I've ever had. Ten out of ten."

That draws a quick laugh out of me. Neither of us let go, as if we're a dramatic 1930s romance movie poster. Sunrise behind us and everything.

"It doesn't have to be just that."

She takes a step back, our arms still tangled around one another. "What do you mean?"

A strange sense of anxiety ripples through me before I continue. Before I admit to her what I've been thinking about in the back of my mind for some time now. What at first was a faraway, ridiculous idea that became more and more real every night this week when she snuck out to see me.

"I could come back to New York. It's not too crazy, right? I made my way here, I can make my way back."

I realize as the words leave my mouth what I had been nervous for. That her expression would slowly turn. That she would take a step back, thank me for the gesture, but admit she didn't want me to. That she always planned on whatever this is between us finishing up for good at the end of the summer. That this was supposed to be real for only a little while.

"Jackson, that's... that's crazy. You don't have to do that for me."

She doesn't sound disgusted. Or awkward. Just rightly pointing out what an insane idea it is. Okay. I can take that.

"What's crazy?" I insist, shrugging, thankful that she hasn't pulled away. "I've got other people down there too. Guys I haven't seen in ages. You're not the only woman who has my heart, Addy Moreno."

She rolls her eyes, shoving me lightly as I laugh. "You still sound like an idiot when you say my full name, Jackson Lowell."

But she isn't protesting. She isn't turning away. The look in her eyes isn't unsure or guilty. It's exactly how I feel, how I've felt as I've sat up all hours of the day and night the past week thinking about this. How we could see each other again.

Hopeful.

"Hey."

My hand turns her face back to me from where her gaze has sunk somewhere toward the ground beside us. I try to sound as serious as I can. Because I am serious about this. I can't think of much I've ever wanted to be serious about before. I guess that's why it's so difficult. But I also can't think of any other reason worth a damn to be serious about.

"I'm not done with this, Addy. I like talking with you. I like bein' around you. I'll be there."

It'll take some time. Damn it, it's gonna take a lot of time. I don't know where to begin dragging myself back to White Plains. Or what I'll find when I go back. There's a reason I ran away after all. A shit ton of trouble I'm not looking forward to having to face again.

But I'll find a way to deal.

Because there's no way this is it. If Addy's mom never brings her back here, there is no way this is the last time I'm gonna see her. I'll make sure of it.

"I've got one more bit of psychology for you to deduce from me, Doc."

"What's that?"

I take a short breath. I know I can tell her. I know I can talk about it now. Know that I have to share it with her before she leaves.

"I did have something like a sibling when I was little. This girl who lived on my street. Vera. We... well, it's like what you and I got. How we start talkin' about anything. Or we don't talk, but still feel at home?"

She nods without question.

"When my mom died, she was there. And it was like the world could still be normal. Like I knew I was gonna be alright. There was still us. Something that was good. Someone who wanted me there. Who cared."

There's an image that flashes behind my eyes. The vision of the two funerals five-year-old me had to attend within the same breath. The two flower-covered boxes I had stared at that had swallowed up what felt like the only good things about my life. The people I assumed would always be there. I hated those fucking boxes.

"But then I lost her too. And I had no one again."

Addy opens her mouth to say something. But she doesn't have to. She pauses, taking me in with her gorgeous soft brown eyes. Understanding.

"That's why. That's why I can't stand losing people. That's why I'm not gonna lose you."

I grin, my hands moving up toward her face, caressing her skin.

"Not while you still want me around."

She smiles at me, reaching up to grab my hands.

"Something tells me you'd stick around to bug me anyway."

"Hm, true. You're way too fun to bug."

She dives toward me again. I hold her even more tightly. We stay like that for a long time. Not long enough for me though.

"I have to go," her voice squeaks out, muffled against my shoulder.

"I know." I still don't let her go. "Hey, maybe I could sneak on the plane with you. Save us a lotta time."

She laughs against me. "Can you do that?"

"I can do anything, remember? Your words, not mine."

We finally pull apart. The tears are gone from her face. She looks at me as if she's just taken a breath of fresh air and feels more alive than ever. Which is more than I can say at the moment, but I can pretend.

"You can count on me, princess. I'll find a way."

"I'll count on you to stop calling me that when you get there."

"Deal."

She grasps my hands in hers, our fingertips touching until the last moment when she turns away. It's quiet as she walks away through the gravel, back toward the side of the building. My instinct to break the strange quiet kicks in.

"Just try not to miss me too much!"

She turns back, sticking her chin up.

"You're not the only thing that has my heart, Jackson Lowell. I'm in a new chapter of life."

She throws her arms out as she says it, smiling at herself before turning away again. I watch her go, keeping the carefree grin etched onto my face until she's gone. Until I'm sure she's not going to turn around again and run back.

I know what she means, I think. I feel it too.

A new chapter of life. It sounds so stupid, but that's what it must be. I can't think what else this feeling might mean. Not only more okay than I've felt in a long time. But also thinking about what's ahead. Thinking about it without dreading it.

Because there's so much life to live. There's way more crazy shit to do. And now I have Addy to do it with me. Or scold me about it. Either way's fine with me.

I stay behind Johnny-Jay's late into the afternoon. When the sun is turning a sharp gold in the sky. Watching different planes take off from the airport beyond the edge of town until they're small specks somewhere in the clouds.

Thank you for reading *Young and Lawless*! Reviews are always a fantastic way to support authors. If you enjoyed the book, **it would mean so much if you left a review!**

About the author

Emily Irving lives in her hometown of Petaluma, CA, and is obsessed with writing about love and romance that perseveres through any circumstance, in every genre. When she is not indulging in her conflicting tastes for both horror and Disney movies, she is reading epic Star Wars novels and fluffy romance stories, or making video edits that nobody but her sister will ever see.

Emily has a BA in Communications from Sonoma State University and planned on becoming a published author before she even learned to read. *Young and Lawless* is her second novel.

Learn more at:
www.emilyirvingauthor.com
Instagram @authoremilyirving
TikTok @authoremilyirving
Facebook.com/AuthorEmilyIrving

www.ingramcontent.com/pod-product-compliance
Lightning Source LLC
Chambersburg PA
CBHW031139160726
47991CB00004B/1484